BEYOND THE URALS

Reggie Gibbs

LifeRich
PUBLISHING®

LifeRich Publishing is a registered trademark of
The Reader's Digest Association, Inc.

LifeRich Publishing books may be ordered
through booksellers or by contacting:

LifeRich Publishing
1663 Liberty Drive
Bloomington, IN 47403
www.liferichpublishing.com
844-686-9607

Scripture taken from the King James Version of the Bible.

ISBN: 978-1-4897-3284-2 (sc)
ISBN: 978-1-4897-3285-9 (hc)
ISBN: 978-1-4897-3291-0 (e)

Library of Congress Control Number: 2020925780

Print information available on the last page.

LifeRich Publishing rev. date: 01/15/2021

For Sara

ACKNOWLEDGEMENTS

This is a work over ten years in the making, and once the second book is completed the entire project will have probably stretched close to one quarter of my life. But, much like the main character, I set out on this journey not always knowing for sure where I was going. It was due to a few rest-stops and fellow travelers I met along the way that I was able to complete this first part with - at least to me – a satisfactory conclusion, and in a manner I hope is compelling, or at a minimum mildly interesting.

First, the rest-stop. It was by chance that in early 2017, after completing the first draft of Beyond the Urals, I stumbled upon a call for manuscripts for a writing workshop sponsored by Taliesin Nexus (TalNex). Up until then, my success in publishing had only been through a few articles National Review graciously agreed to feature. I possessed no credentials in the creative writing world. Thankfully, TalNex identified potential in what I had written, invited me out to Los Angeles for a few days, and in the process introduced me to like-minded authors, while also providing a window into a world with which I was very unfamiliar. The novel in its current form grew from the chance investment TalNex made in me. To the organizers of that seminar, I am indebted.

Second, the fellow travelers, both of whom I had the pleasure of meeting while in Los Angeles three years ago.

Jared Buccholz, a fellow TalNex invitee, was the earliest to provide much needed encouragement. Before having even met in L.A., he emailed me unsolicited compliments from his home in South Carolina, suppling a bit of preliminary confidence in my story and its themes. While at the conference, we bonded over Tarkovsky, Endo, and Criterion, and after going our separate ways, remained in close contact. For the next year, we embarked on weekly calls where we reviewed each line of the novel, sentence-by-sentence. His support and expertise were invaluable, enabling me to complete what amounted to a full draft rewrite of the first narrative.

Last, but in no way least, Ann Bridges. If TalNex took a chance, Ann took a high-stakes gamble. Ann is distinguished, recognized, and a master in her craft – in short, everything I am not. Like TalNex, she saw potential in what I had written, but recognized early on there was much work to be done. I had no track record in this field, so Ann could have easily, and justifiably, passed on my request for assistance, but she did not. She believed there was a story here with important ideas to transmit, and put faith in me that I would work diligently to complete what I had started. Throughout our two years of working together, she balanced encouragement with tough critiquing, never shying away from telling me the things I needed to hear, no matter how much I may have wanted the opposite to be true. She was exactly what I, and the novel, needed. I am forever grateful for the time and effort she spent in helping to bring Beyond the Urals to publication.

TIMELINE

1917 Autumn: Bolsheviks seize power from Provisional Government; Russian Civil War, primarily waged in eastern Russia, begins.

1918-21: Arkady and Natasha are born in western Russia; David is born in eastern Siberia.

1922: The Soviet Union (U.S.S.R) is officially formed.

1923: Russian Civil War ends, Bolsheviks victorious.

1924: Vladimir I. Lenin dies; Josef Stalin consolidates power.

1930: Large scale population transfers begin east of the Ural Mountains.

1931: Jewish Autonomous Oblast "Birobidzhan" established.

1932: Famine begins.

1933: Metro construction begins; Natasha's father departs for Moscow.

1934: Famine subsides; Arkady's mother dies.

1935: First stations of Moscow Metro open.

1936: Kamenev/Zinoviev trial (first of the three "Moscow Show Trials" that lasted from 1936–38).

1937: People's Commissariat for Internal Affairs (i.e., NKVD, the predecessor of the KGB) Order No. 00447 issued; Natasha's father returns home & shortly dies.

1938: Natasha and Arkady meet.

1939: Natasha and Arkady are married.

1939: Soviet Union invades Poland, approximately two weeks after Germany; additional population transfers/deportations to areas east of the Ural Mountains initiated.

1941 (June): Germany invades the Soviet Union (Operation Barbarossa); GKO established.

1941 (August): Evacuation of heavy industry and factories begins from western Russia to areas east of the Ural Mountains.

1941 (September): Siege of Leningrad begins.

1942 (February): Arkady drafted into the Red Army; Natasha sent to factory town deep within Siberia shortly after.

1942 (August): Battle of Stalingrad begins.

1942 (late fall): Arkady separated from unit, begins search for Natasha; David arrives at Natasha's camp.

MAP

(Source: https://commons.wikimedia.org/wiki/File:Eurasec_Map.png)

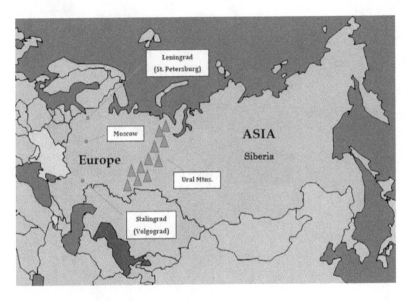

PROLOGUE

"What is happening? Today there is a great silence over the earth, a great silence, and stillness, a great silence because the King sleeps; the earth was in terror and was still, because God slept in the flesh and raised up those who were sleeping from the ages. God has died in the flesh, and the underworld has trembled.

Truly he goes to seek out our first parent like a lost sheep; he wishes to visit those who sit in darkness and in the shadow of death. He goes to free the prisoner Adam and his fellow-prisoner Eve from their pains, he who is God, and Adam's son.

The Lord goes in to them holding his victorious weapon, his cross. When Adam, the first created man, sees him, he strikes his breast in terror and calls out to all: 'My Lord be with you all.' And Christ in reply says to Adam: 'And with your spirit.' And grasping his hand he raises him up, saying: 'Awake, O sleeper, and arise from the dead, and Christ shall give you light.

'I am your God, who for your sake became your son, who for you and your descendants now speak and command with authority those in prison: Come forth, and those in darkness: Have light, and those who sleep: Rise.

'I command you: Awake, sleeper, I have not made you to be held a prisoner in the underworld. Arise from the dead; I am the life of the dead. Arise, O man, work of my hands, arise, you who were fashioned in my image. Rise, let us go hence; for you in me and I in you, together we are one undivided person.'"

"Harrowing of Hell" (Descensus Christi ad Inferos), stanzas 1-5, as composed by St. Melito of Sardis (d. 180).

PART I

Western Russia, late fall, 1942

CHAPTER 1

Snow drifted straight down on the eight young soldiers huddled on the frigid metal bench of the idling transport truck, thick flakes softly piling between the cracking leather of their boots. The lack of wind added to a quiet peace that, much like the icy white crystals themselves, had descended onto the decimated city just days before.

Bundled in a wool overcoat, Arkady held onto his rifle with just one hand and shivered in the night air. He peered upward, trying to spot a single star through the clouds. No luck. The snow fell faster, settling on his forehead and cheeks, the wetness eventually worming down beneath his clothes. He shook his head, wiped his eyes, and squinted at Sasha sitting beside him. Unlike Arkady, his friend gripped his rifle tight with both hands. Yet Sasha's shoulders were hunched, his attention focused intensely on the rusted truck bed, almost as if he were clutched in a trance.

"Hey. You still here?" Arkady nudged him.

Sasha stirred, and looked up at Arkady. "Sure, sure." He immediately reverted his gaze down again.

Arkady squirmed, feeling an ominous foreboding from Sasha's trepidations. Since their first night in Stalingrad over a month ago, when the two soldiers stood sentry in a shallow fighting hole dug out from the rubble of smashed buildings,

Arkady sensed his friend possessed preternatural insights into the unknown. Hailing from eastern Russia on the doorstep of Siberia, Sasha subtly reflected, at least in Arkady's eyes, the perceived mystical powers of that far-off land.

Arkady glanced again at his friend. This time Sasha's eyes were closed, his arm bent, his right hand slipped inside his overcoat, creating a bulge over his heart. It appeared Sasha held onto something.

"How much longer do you think until we move out?" Arkady asked, hoping once and for all to break his friend free from his thoughts and relieve both their tension.

Sasha eyes fluttered open and he shook his head. "Any minute now. I can't imagine it will be much longer. If they really want to find the other unit, we don't have much time to spare. The Germans could start shelling again at any moment."

"This is so pointless. We haven't heard from that missing patrol in over a week. If you're not inside this perimeter, the Germans already have you. The Germans or God."

"Yes, the Germans or God," Sasha said wistfully. His eyelids again drifted down.

Arkady pulled his collar closer against the bitter cold. There were so many aspects of soldiering he hated, but it was the small things, things he had never imagined in the comfort of his home, that chewed steadily away at his humanity: moisture on his scarf which would in-turn freeze to the rough stubble starting to take root on his face, reminded him constantly, through smell and taste, of the filth that surrounded him; a slight turn-of-the neck that caused his scarf and hood to displace, allowing melted snow to seep in and down his shirt; dried, frozen food lodged in his beard.

If only the trucks would start moving! Another overlooked torturous detail in war—waiting, sitting, wondering, imaginations left running wild as to what lay ahead, and deft, existential debates instigated by frightened youths drifting heavily into topics beyond their age. All at once, with death staring them in the face, young men became philosophers, historians, trying, with their limited knowledge of life, to make sense of everything, to include their nightmares from which it seemed they could not awake. Although never mentioned, Arkady felt confident he and Sasha shared the same horrid dreams. After all, they had experienced the same torments and subsisted in the same purgatories. Ones where human beings were abruptly cut to pieces in a shower of machine gun fire, silencing all at once young screams in a barrage of explosives. Ones where out of the sudden loss of a trusted comrade—those Arkady believed to be beyond the reach of the enemy—sprung the stark realization that nobody was safe, and that one's fate was left invariably to forces beyond one's control.

Minutes crept by, the transport trucks' engines still idling in the freezing night.

"I wonder what she's doing," Arkady finally said.

"Natasha?" asked Sasha.

"Of course," he replied, his voice dropping. His turn now to drift toward a trance.

"When was the last time you heard from her?"

Arkady tilted his head all the way back, the unrelenting snow descending faster but still vertically onto his wide-open eyes. He didn't know why he kept staring into the heavens. It seemed to provide some hope, a confirmation of sorts, that Natasha was okay. He could interpret a star's twinkle or faint shine however he wanted—a sign of her well-being, a signal, perhaps, that soon they would reunite. Anything to ease his mind. But still, he could see nothing. Just flakes falling from a sky crowded with clouds.

"I got a letter from her two days ago," Arkady answered. "I don't know how it made it through, or even how it found me." He paused, swallowing his worry. "It was dated three months ago. I hadn't even arrived here in Stalingrad yet."

"What did it say?"

"It's hard to describe. But it was a beautiful letter, more beautiful than anything I have ever written her." Regret flooded Arkady with this stark admission.

"Where is she?" Sasha's question was as pointed as his sentry's aim.

"She couldn't tell me exactly. You know they're strict with that kind of information. But I think she's somewhere far from here, somewhere east of the Ural Mountains."

"She's at a factory town," Sasha said matter-of-factly. "I'm sure of it. Anyone who lived along the railway lines, like you and she did, was transported from the west to the east in order to help assemble and operate them. With the western industrial sectors evacuated, whole cities have been reconstructed out of thin air in Siberia to support the war effort. They produce everything—munitions, tanks, guns, even aircraft. Smokestacks and machinery stretch from one end of Siberia to the other, far away from any advancing German army."[1]

"It sounded something like that in her letter. At least she's safe, right?" This time Arkady didn't bother hiding his nervousness.

"Sure." Sasha's reassuring smile and gentle nod seemed forced. "She's safe."

"Did you actually witness these cities being built, or have you just heard of them?"

"I saw the supply lines on hastily ploughed roads, and the trains, weighed down by machines, sometimes whole buildings,

---

[1]   See endnote 1.a.

it seemed, racing east, like arteries feeding the far reaches of the empire, reaches that had never been spoiled by industry." Sasha's gaze lingered on the eastern horizon as if his thoughts were heading home.

"What was it like, growing up out there, on the edge of Russia's frontier?" asked Arkady. "To us in the west it seems so out-of-place from the rest of the country. I remember my professors trying to capture exactly what Siberia was through literature, through stories. But they could never seem to explain it, never seem to justify why Russians were there. It's such an enigma. Even after the Revolution, it was the last place to surrender the past or—"

"Not likely that it's surrendered it even now," Sasha interrupted, sounding suddenly like a watchman, warning all would-be trespassers. "What was it like, you ask? Sometimes I got the feeling a dream was right on my doorstep. Step too far outside, and you had ventured into something unpredictable. Primitive, wild, but not foreign as many would like to believe. I always thought of Dostoyevsky."

Sasha's voice took on an eerie quality as he repeated the author's familiar words:

I felt something was drawing me away, and I kept fancying that if I walked straight on, far, far away and reached that line where the sky and earth meet, there I should find the key to the mystery, there I should see a new life a thousand times richer and more turbulent than ours.

"It's definitely part of Russia," Sasha said. "But it's our subconscious state, a space in our soul waiting to be occupied, filled, and discovered." He drew a deep breath and began speaking again, reciting a poem that seemed to roll without effort from his mouth, as if its presence was always manifest on the tip of his tongue.

> *In Siberia's wastes*
> *The ice-wind's breath*
> *Woundeth like the toothed steel;*
> *Lost Siberia doth reveal*
> *Only blight and death.*

> *Pain as in a dream,*
> *When years go by*
> *Funeral-paced, yet fugitive,*
> *When man lives, and doth not live.*
> *Doth not live—nor die.*

"*Doth not live—nor die,*" Arkady repeated. "What does that mean?"

"It's not something I can explain; only something I can feel." Sasha shrugged. "I know that sounds strange…especially since that poem wasn't even written by a Russian, but by an Irishman[2]. It took a Westerner to capture its essence." Sasha was no longer addressing Arkady, but rather speaking to the windless night. "The Buddhist natives of the steppes compare Siberia to the Bardo, the realm between death and rebirth. Some perceive that concept literally—a place where wrathful spirits dwell, condemned to plot, scour, and roam until they attain enough merit to re-enter the world of the living. To others, it is a reflection of our own fears and unholy desires—a haunted realm where our regrets wander in human form, where our grandest dreams confront us in a manner that strips them of any noble pretense, revealing, like a mirror, the grotesqueness of our ambitions."

"Whoa! Very dramatic!" Arkady said, impressed by Sasha's sudden eloquence, but wanting to disrupt his descent into another trance-like state. In the midst of their worry and

---

[2]   *Siberia* (1845), by James Clarence Mangan (b. 1803- d. 1849)

impatience, the two soldiers had inadvertently drifted into one of those dreaded, combat-ripened existential debates.

"To me...in fact to most of us in western Russia," Arkady countered, "...it's just a vast desert, which is why no Russian in his right mind voluntarily goes east of the Urals. There's nothing there. Think about it. From the Tsars to now, our country was defined by events and people on this side of the mountains. What has Siberia ever contributed to our literature, politics, or philosophy? Nothing meaningful that I know of. Even now, when Russia is under siege, the native conscripts from the steppes can't be counted on. It's widely known they don't fight; they flee as soon as they come under fire. They've all been relegated to positions in the rear. They desert in record numbers —"

"I suppose, Arkady," Sasha interrupted, growing visibly uncomfortable, "that one could view the natives—the non-ethnic Russians that is—as cowards. But I'm not so sure. They are of a different civilization from those of us in the west. Our world is not their world. Our wars are not necessarily theirs. But you're wrong to discount those of Siberia as separate, though. What is it Siberia contributes to Russia, you ask? This same question, this same debate you and I are having, has waged in our nation's history for a very long time. And yet here we are in Stalingrad. Why? Are we here simply because this is the namesake of Marshall Stalin, or because of the oil fields in the south? No. We defend this city because it is a gateway to the east, a portal to something else."

"And what is that something?" Arkady asked. "If we lose this city, if we lose Siberia, what have we lost? This seems all so pointless to me!"

"What do we lose?" Sasha echoed, his voice harsh and cold. "We lose our soul."

Arkady stared back at his friend. Sasha's trance had steadily transformed from wandering and lost into a fierce warrior's glare. Sasha seemed to have mutated into the embodiment of that which western Russians feared from the east, an unearthed, hidden energy that, when summoned, could be deadlier than anything they had yet faced in the onslaught of the Wehrmacht.[3]

In the charged silence Arkady recalled a series of lectures during which his professor had insisted that while Russia's greatest writers, thinkers, and philosophers had not come from the east, their life experiences had intertwined with and been informed by it. It was only after their encounters with that seemingly empty realm that these men had contributed their most important ideas and lasting works. Russia's philosophical lineage was littered with radical genius, revolutionary brilliance haunting the nation's pursuit of paradise and redemption, a still-fanatical pursuit not evidentially tempered by years of tumultuous uprisings and severe repression. Arkady had never considered this in depth before. But as he sat debating his friend, shivering in the cold, perhaps near to his own death, the chasm between what he thought he knew and what he actually did know grew deeper. He understood so little, and believed even less.

"You're foolish!" Arkady snapped, allowing his insecurity free rein. "There is nothing in Siberia except forests, frozen lakes, mosquitoes, and…and…superstitious primitives."

Sasha sighed. "In school we're all taught the Party line— the infallibility of science, rationalism, numbers, statistics," he answered in a gentle voice. "But, Arkady, I'm telling you, there is something else, something just like Siberia, within us. An empty, undiscovered, unconquered space. Something that can't be explained or proven through formulas. Mysteries which must

---

[3]   The unified armed forces of Nazi Germany from 1935 to 1945.

be explored by means other than that which the laboratory or classroom equips us. This realm is critically important to who we are. If not tamed, if occupied or conquered by something foreign, it can control us, even destroy us. Don't you see that? We must protect it at any cost, or we will cease to be what we are, condemned, and unrecognizable."

"Enough!" Arkady said. "Sasha, what you say...well, there's something in me that wishes you're right. I wish all of this had some higher, more noble purpose—the defense of our country's soul, and all that. But I can see that look in your eyes. You believe you're condemned to die. You need what you are saying to be true. You need your death to hold meaning!"

Arkady met Sasha's uncompromising gaze. He was neither wise enough nor worldly enough to combat Sasha in this type of argument, so he wielded his only weapon—the gravity of the moment against whatever uncertainties Sasha might still possess.

Pointing to Sasha's chest, Arkady continued. "I think I know what you have beneath your overcoat; what you've been cradling tonight, close to your heart, but still hidden away from anyone else to see. I know that you want to believe all this. You want to believe that there is more to what we're doing than just wasting our lives. Sasha, I've tried to justify this myself, amongst the blood, amongst the filth, disease, and death. But I just can't. Trust me, if the chance presented itself, I would leave. There is only one thing I've found that brings me any semblance of happiness and peace, and she is, as you said, somewhere far to the east, in Siberia, that wasteland you attribute so much mystery and spiritual power to."

Sasha took a deep breath. Removing his hand from inside his overcoat, he placed it back on his rifle. His mouth softened and curved into an understanding smile. His head dropped low, and he seemed content now to stare at the metal truck bed below his feet.

The roaring growl of the transport trucks revving their engines filled Arkady's ears. A grinding of gears, a lurch forward. Finally, they were leaving.

The unit headed east, beyond the boundaries of Stalingrad, racing to find the wayward unit that had been lost days ago.

CHAPTER 2

The transport trucks rumbled along under the cover of night and falling snow. Pot-holed and frozen, the broken roads were more like paths cut by livestock, their complexity contrasting against the simple, flat terrain into which they were cut. The heavy vehicles darted this way and that, around heaps of destroyed steel, metal scraps left over from skirmishes, burned-out buildings on the outskirts of the city, and any combination of fallen trees, poles, or upended concrete. It seemed everything was smoldering, a wasteland mowed down, cleared and occupied by an energy foreign to any life-sustaining pulse.

As the trucks sped farther and farther away from Stalingrad, the evening's calmness penetrated Arkady. Tilting his chin up, he looked again toward the stars. This time he spotted them as they appeared one by one, their shining lights representing a comforting order, organized with purposeful patterns. They painted pictures, spelled words, their place in the sky constant and predictable. They were the foil to the chaos of the battlefield, as well as the incertitude mysteries about which he and Sasha had argued just hours before. Away from the city and in the cold, night air, Arkady sensed freedom, renewal, sensations suppressed and inevident within the confines of bleak, urban cavities. Refreshed, naturally thoughts of Natasha seeped back into his mind. Slipping dreamlike into a zone that allowed him to expel momentarily all his misery, he looked once again for evidence of his wife in the sky above.

Her eyes, penetrating, seductive—there they are, in the stars.

A smile, as she turns to look at him, a divine joy overflowing into a laugh—there it is, in a celestial ripple, perhaps a shooting star.

Her bare skin, warm, pressed next to his, her breath moving over his face—he heard her in the wind, whispering past his ear, words from her letter...

> *O my dove, that art in the clefts of the rock,*
> *in the secret places of the stairs,*
> *let me see thy countenance,*
> *let me hear thy voice;*
> *for sweet is thy voice, and thy countenance is comely.*[4]

BOOM!

Arkady jolted awake from his dreams. The stars faded, taking refuge behind a cloud. Natasha's eyes closed, her smile relented, the softness of her skin grew callous, like the edge of the truck biting into Arkady's spine. Only emptiness, insecurity remained. Why was it that only Natasha seemed capable of providing something lasting and final, a peace saturating his whole being?

BOOM!

A second barrage of artillery shells landed far behind the convoy. Probably the Germans, cloaked in the desolate night, starting another advance. Arkady and his comrades, on bended knee, stared reverently, silently, as the sky lit up in flashes of red, orange, and yellow. The response from the Red Army, cloistered and trapped inside Stalingrad, ricocheted with

---

[4]   Song of Songs (of Solomon) 2:14 (King James)

rockets dispelling in every direction, as if the omnipresence of God himself were being targeted.

Arkady closed his eyes. Inhaling, exhaling. Shadows from the onslaught danced beneath his eyelids. Rational thoughts, now imprisoned within the putrid smells, nightmarish visions, and physical tortures of war, began failing him. Visions of his wife replaced by the rolling thunder of artillery, he subconsciously sought release another way. In his mind's eye, he stood up from his fighting position, purposely revealing himself in plain sight, throwing his rifle on the ground, spreading out his arms cross-like in a sacrificial gesture. He imagined that Germans slipped over barricades, into the compounds, through the trenches, advancing in wave after wave after wave. He refused to move to cover. Taunting the illusory enemy to take him down, in his dark fantasy he encouraged the bullets to ripple through his body, puncturing every vital organ with which he had been blessed to be born.

There is no god. There is nothing. Only pain.

Despair enveloped him. Hate shot through his limbs, erupting subtle spasms beneath his heavy coat. His soul was lost. Having been forced into this hopeless abyss against his will, it had become imprisoned in an underworld. He could not escape the bitterness and regret for a life interrupted by things he cared nothing about. A life before the war he had started to treasure.

A life starting with Natasha.

The truck braked. Arkady heard doors slam and the crunch of snow below. He peered over the edge. Shilov, the patrol leader, had halted the entire convoy. He too stared at the inferno kilometers behind them. Lighting a cigarette, the old Sergeant watched in somber advertence; his men were now cut off from the city. Arkady awaited an anxious few minutes while Shilov finished his smoke. Following five, contemplative puffs, Shilov signaled for the drivers to climb back up into their seats. Soon the vehicles resumed movement—heading in the same direction.

The mission, it seemed, would continue.

★

The convoy traveled deep into the night. Hours passed. Arkady, burrowed in his coat, ruminated on the assault. Many by now had been killed in this latest salvo; many more lives had been untenably altered. But had anything really changed? No matter who conquered what building, street, or bunker, would the fighting really end? Would orders to commence the next campaign not be waiting, inevitably, on the cold, unfeeling lips of his commanders?

The moon was high when the trucks finally again stopped. Repeating drills practiced countless times throughout months of patrols, the soldiers jumped from their seats and onto the ground, fanning out in a circular pattern, eventually falling onto their stomachs, their weapons pointed outward into emptiness. Arkady's eyes searched the night for anything out of the ordinary. But there was nothing except the low voices mumbling behind him, followed soon by the slushing sound of steps trudging through the snow.

"Arkady." Sasha's tones were brisk and serious. "Let's go. We're here." Arkady sensed nothing indicating that their earlier debate lingered in his friend's mind. He picked himself off the wet ground and followed.

"What have they found?" Arkady whispered.

"Just equipment; evidence that the lost patrol had been here for a while. But…no bodies, and no sign of a fight. It's like they just vanished."

Arkady noticed a few other soldiers, including Shilov, scrounging around the site.

"Alright, comrades," Shilov called, a fresh cigarette hanging from his lips. "This place has been deserted at least a couple of days. Scour it, take anything you find useful. If you uncover any ammunition or fuel, turn it over. We need it."

The soldiers went to work amidst the persistent snowfall. Clouds covered the moon now, but every so often its beams would peek through a break, allowing Arkady to glimpse more completely the site they were searching—a small tree grove sitting aside a larger forest. Light periodically reflected off the whiteness, but the darkness enveloping the forest resisted any penetration. The soldiers worked in quick silence, like planets circling in equilibrium around a black sun.

Arkady soon uncovered a few useful treasures: a long overcoat and warm hat that pulled down over his ears, both in better condition than what he was wearing; and a pair of leather boots, the soles firm, intact, the insides lined with dry cloth. And most importantly, he stumbled upon a map with coordinates scratched onto it, which he immediately turned over to Shilov.

"Good find, Vyshinsky" the patrol leader said with an approving nod at Arkady, who was standing at attention. Examining the worn and folded paper, the leathery Sergeant flipped it over, holding it up to the moonlight. "There's a few markings on it."

Shilov pivoted and faced east, apparently trying to match the map to the terrain far ahead. When his cigarette smoldered and the remaining ashes floated away on the wind, the Sergeant put the map into his side pouch. Eyes averted from Arkady, who was waiting expectantly, a grave expression painted his face. Hands on his hips, he sniffed the icy evening, his chin jutted, jaw clenched.

Arkady keenly sensed the drama building to Shilov's next command. The lost patrol was nowhere in the area. The map indicated they may have left for someplace, inexplicably, far to the east. Stalingrad itself was under assault. Reentering friendly lines right now was out of the question.

"Okay, five more minutes, comrades, then we're moving out," Shilov shouted. "The Germans have changed our plans. There's no possible way we're returning to the city tonight. We'll head further east, instead; try and visit these coordinates, see what we can find there or along the way. It will be long and cold. Be ready." Shilov turned and spoke to the lead driver, "How are we doing on fuel?"

"Okay, Sergeant. We have some in reserve, and we uncovered more cans here at the site. It seems they really left in a hurry," the driver responded.

Arkady donned his newly acquired clothing and stepped toward the trucks. The cloud cover starkly dispersed, illuminating in black and white shadows the area immediately around him. For some reason his eyes were drawn to the farthest side of the grove where, on the doorstep of the dark forest, Arkady spotted Sasha sitting with his back against a tree, his shoulders slumped, his gaze fixed downward yet again. Seeing his friend in this obvious posture of misery softened the callousness Arkady had felt earlier when the two had argued. His pride dissipated, remembering the first night he and Sasha met, when all around him seemed a void from which emptiness crept, seeping out into the world, infecting souls with the blank eeriness of desertion and spiritual isolation. From that horror, Sasha had appeared, an emissary of light, hope, security.

Quietly approaching his friend, Arkady knelt down on one knee next to him. Not staring vacantly at the ground as Arkady had supposed, Sasha was instead watching a bird hop around, its beak plunging frantically toward the earth followed by short stares at the man staring back. The light captured and outlined only the basic patterns coloring the creature. Although mostly black, a small region directly above its eye was white, the same color as its lower belly. Sasha silently motioned Arkady to take care not to scare it away.

"Do you know this bird?" Arkady whispered.

"Yes. It's a Siberian Thrush. I've never seen one this far to the west. Extraordinary. They're rare enough in the Ural Mountains, but to see one in these parts is truly amazing. We used to search for them as children. I was sitting here, and he just flew out of the forest." Sasha waved his hand. "The moonlight makes him appear black, but he's really a dark and beautiful shining blue. When his wings are stretched there's a streak of white underneath, too, like a lightning bolt."

Sasha's voice drifted off, and he thrust his right hand back inside his overcoat, appearing once again to slip into an otherworldly place.

"This bird is not of this face of Russia," Sasha mumbled. His somber words, rolling off his tongue with a fearful dread, seemed to electrify the emptiness of the forest upon whose edge they hovered. "It comes from beyond the boundaries of Europe, beyond the boundaries of order and reason. It comes from beyond the Urals, and it has not flown here to remain idle…"

Arkady's previous frustration with Sasha returned, now mixed with foreboding, as he felt powerless to help his friend. Convinced that Sasha was indeed slowly descending into a madness, one not uncommon amongst soldiers, amongst those who had experienced the worst war had to offer, the security and assuredness Sasha had once provided Arkady was gone, too.

Standing up to leave, Arkady watched as the bird took flight into the tree above. A strong grip suddenly wrapped around his bicep. Arkady jumped, and he turned. Sasha drew close to him. Intensity radiated from his eyes.

The two soldiers, standing amongst the wreckage of the deserted patrol base, stared at each other in the still night. Sasha's grip loosened and a tired, but relieved smile crawled over his face. His hand dropped from Arkady's arm and again slipped inside his jacket, tugging something from its folds. As he did so, an enigmatic moonbeam angled onto Sasha's palm as he opened his hand, spotlighting a brass icon in which was cast a crucifix. Worn down by time and veneration, it was clear the icon's past owners sought to contemplate the mysteries of the heavens through its lines, indentations, and edges. Upon it, the image of the Christ was barely visible, as He hung nailed to a three-tiered cross, looking down. Two saints, kneeling in sorrowful adoration beneath Him, stared upward. Two smaller crosses were pictured in the distance on either side, while a barely discernable dove hung in flight above the main figure, beams of light shooting from it in every direction.

Laying it into Arkady's hand, Sasha held his friend close, and gently kissed him on the cheek. He stepped back, the pained smile still painted on his weary face, and walked toward the trucks, the soft grinding of the snow growing ever fainter as the distance between the two men increased.

Arkady had never seen such vexing torment in his friend's eyes. What to make of Sasha's gesture?

...*the kiss*, a sign of friendship and love, or something else?

...*the smile*, the right word to describe it somehow escaped him.

...*the small icon*, the greatest mystery of all, weighed heavily in his hand.

Disturbed, lost, Arkady stood motionless. In the distance the trucks' engines revved into a rumble, and he mechanically headed in their direction. Stepping fully out from under cover of the trees, a sudden and intense fluttering noise directly above made him duck his head. Swooping around in the thick flakes of snow, the Siberian Thrush darted up and down, its flight pattern as chaotic as the stars above. Seeing the mysterious bird, so far from its home in the Ural Mountains, did not assuage Arkady's fears. Foreboding overtook him. Tucking the precious relic inside his thick coat, he ran toward his comrades, away from the black forest, fears similar to a frightened child building within him.

By the time Arkady made it back to the truck, all of the seats but the one on the very end were taken. He hopped quickly up.

"Took you long enough, Vyshinsky," Shilov belted out. Arkady acknowledged the Sergeant with a sheepish nod and sat down. He was just happy to be back, sitting on that familiar hard, cold metal, surrounded by known comrades, away from the deserted patrol base, and the forest.

The trucks pulled away. Looking down the row of seated soldiers, he saw Sasha near the front. As before, Sasha had both hands on his rifle, but this time, instead of looking down, Arkady's friend gazed straight ahead, eyes fixed on the empty plain spreading out in the darkness before them.

★

As the sun's resplendent rays peeked over the horizon they heated the earth, igniting slumbering molecules in a dance that resulted in a precipitous temperature drop. The soldiers clutched their jackets close to their bodies, except for Arkady who, as watch, crumpled his as a cushion between his forward-leaning chest and the side of the truck's bed. For three hours, Arkady remained in this position, peering blankly out into the distance. Many images danced through his mind. Home. A warm meal. Natasha. But as much as he tried, he couldn't push the scene with Sasha and the Thrush in the grove from his mind. It stayed with him, its meaning unclear and muddled, a strange tale seemingly still in the making.

The convoy lumbered east, sometimes slow to avoid moonlike craters piercing the tired road, and sometimes quickly when the snow and ice had effectively re-paved it. Soon Arkady felt a tapping on his shoulder— his relief signaling to him that it was Arkady's turn to sleep, at least for a few hours, until he again took watch closer to sundown.

Arkady was thankful for the break. The brightness of the sun's beams reflecting harshly against the snow up into his face had caused Arkady's eyes to grow heavy. And the land through which they traversed…well, there was nothing, not even a small village. It was a desert, flat, unending, and unforgiving. Every so often a patch of trees appeared. Periodically a small animal emerged from beneath the snow, curiously observing the passing formation. But nothing else really broke through in the icy wilderness. The lost patrol…what were they searching for? What led them into this desolate land? Arkady turned himself inward, facing his comrades huddled together in the back of the truck. He fell into a restless sleep.

The midday sun eventually passed, and soon it took on the bright orange glow of dusk. Arkady again found himself on watch as the convoy slowly came to a halt. Engines idling in a low, warm rumble, he witnessed the lead vehicle's cabin door open. Arkady observed Shilov dismount. The Sergeant hit the ground and stood looking into the distance, map in hand, studying it against the roads and the terrain surrounding them. The convoy's lead driver soon joined him. Arkady leaned closer to listen.

"We're at a three-way fork. I think I've found it here on the map," Shilov said, pointing. "We'll need to keep on the road to the far right, the one here that goes directly east."

"This one? That goes straight into the mountains?" the driver responded, also looking at the map.

"Yeah," Shilov replied matter-of-factly. "I think we have about six more hours, give or take. We should arrive around midnight. The closer we get, the more we need to be on guard. If the patrol is anywhere in the vicinity, they'll be looking for enemy vehicles. Friendly fire is just as deadly as the other kind."

With that stark reminder he folded up the map and returned to the truck. The driver scurried back behind the steering wheel. Arkady heard the slow crank of the released brake, a pressed clutch, then the gear shift down. The trucks started off, turning directly east. Arkady saw in the distance terrestrial aberrations piercing the endless flat plains of their journey so far. Off near the horizon, small rolling hills took shape, perhaps forerunners to larger peaks still hidden in the clouds.

A bird swooped down in front of him, shiny blue reflecting off the sun's fading rays, interfering with his study of the far-off realm. Arkady noted the white streaks beneath its fully stretched wings, matching Sasha's haunting description of lightning bolts. Ready to strike unsuspecting travelers?

★

Arkady awoke. The truck slowed to a grinding halt. It was dark; night had fallen as he slept, exhausted from the travel of the past two days. He heard whispers next to him in the shadows.

"We're still far...at least an hour..."

"That smell...I've smelled it before..."

"Burning...charred flesh..."

"...and oil...petrol..."

"Did you hear it?"

"Hear what?"

"Screams. Low screams..."

"No, but there is an orange glow ahead of us..."

"Where's my rifle?"

"...I'm freezing..."

"Dismount!"

This last voice was familiar—Shilov.

The Russian soldiers tumbled over the sides of the trucks. Arkady's boots struck the freezing ground; his legs, stiff from hours of sitting, felt like they would break. His eyes strained, trying to glimpse what lay ahead. He could see very little through the omnipresent curtain of snow, but noticed the familiar dance of red flames, slowly simmering, the dying embers of a once-raging fire.

At least twenty meters ahead, directly in his path, Arkady saw something sway. Low to the ground, black, a shadow, it moved gently to one side and then the other, gyrating in delirious motion back-and-forth, back-and-forth. Arkady stopped. His pulse raced, his breathing quickened. He gripped the cold metal of his rifle. He squinted, trying hard to make out what it was. The snow seemed to fall faster and harder. Arkady wiped the wetness away from his eyes.

"Oh no! Oh no!" he cried, rushing forward. He fell to his knees, arms outstretched. The clouds thinned and light from the full moon revealed a young soldier, no more than sixteen years old, prostrate in the snow. A streaked trail of red stretched behind him, proof he had clawed himself away from the burning wreckage, certainly the remains of the lost patrol which now lay smoldering in the path of Arkady's rescue convoy.

Carefully, urgently, Arkady tipped the youth onto his side and angled his own face inches from the soldier's. Though his eyes were open, they were dulled, vacant. Arkady watched them roll slowly, searching, confused. Eventually they settled their focus on Arkady himself. He felt the young man's warm breath gently brush away the night's cold air, as if his life, on the verge of extinction, was itself rushing past Arkady's face.

Tears rolled down Arkady's cheeks, helpless. The teenager— the horror and confusion of what had happened still evident in his face —fought to turn his entire body into the full embrace of the man caressing him. In doing so, Arkady noticed that one of the young man's arms had been cut to pieces by gunfire. His other arm reached upward into the sky, grasping at the stars, as if trying to grab hold of the twinkling lights, those cryptic patterns that had overcome the clouds and conquered the darkness.

"Shilov! Sasha!" Arkady cried out. But his cry for help was cut short by a violent spurt of machine gun fire racing through their position. Arkady threw himself over the wounded man and smacked his head on something sharp. A rock buried in the snow perhaps, or another piece of wreckage. Disoriented, Arkady sat up and put his hands to his throbbing forehead. Blood covered the entire front of his coat. Gunfire splashed everywhere in the snow. Soldiers returned fire in all directions. From where the ambush came, Arkady had no idea. An explosion. Then shrapnel flying past Arkady. The force of the blast threw him back on the ground. In a daze, the world slowed.

Reality succumbed to the nightmarish visions he imagined earlier while watching the bombardment of Stalingrad from afar. Believing he was back in the condemned city...

...he stood up from his fighting position, purposely revealing himself in plain sight, throwing his rifle on the ground, spreading out his arms cross-like in a sacrificial gesture.

...Germans slipped over barricades, into the compounds, through the trenches, advancing in wave after wave after wave. He refused to move to cover...

A voice from another realm broke through the delirium.

"Get down! Get down!"

A shadowy figure ran frantically toward him, dodging machine gunfire, stumbling and slipping as it made its way exposed across the open field.

Just as Arkady lost all remaining sense of reality, just as he fell further and further into the surrounding emptiness, the figure collided on top of him, tackling him, burying him in the snow, away from the racing bullets, away from the explosions, away from the chaos.

"Forgive me!" a voice cried.

It was the last thing Arkady heard as he slipped fully under, into an abode as chaotic and infinite as where the stars dwelled.

CHAPTER 3

Arkady was lost, somewhere in a dream. Unconscious, his mind had seemingly reached the eye of a vast storm swirling intensely with memories. They rushed through him like a powerful wind, cold gusts piercing his soul with a thousand daggers tinged with regret, fear, and bitter thoughts.

There is no god. There is nothing. Only pain.

The horrors and tragedies he had experienced since being carried off to war whipped through his mind: nights in Stalingrad, huddled and freezing with Sasha, barrages of artillery raining down upon them; exhaustion, dysentery, frostbite, rats, insects, disease, death...

Death. The act of life departing the body, causing to grow limp and cold the physical vessel whose sole purpose was to house and give form to the spirit—that indefinable essence containing all of the intangible worth of human existence. Death terrified Arkady, but it wasn't just the unfathomable mystery of what lay beyond life that haunted him. It was the immediate power held sway by death's emptiness, somehow rendering all else vacant and pointless. Sasha had tried to argue for meaning in existence, even meaning in mystery, but Arkady could not comprehend such purpose.

There is no god. There is nothing. Only pain.

His first encounter with death had not been in war. Rather, it had been in a place where peace was meant to reign, where, especially in youth, the harsh realities of life were not to be revealed nor experienced.

"There is nothing left we can do," Arkady remembered the doctor saying, as his mother lay suffering in the next room. In that sentence spun a spiraling, hopeless abyss to which there was no end.

By witnessing death at home, as well as at war, the barrier between the two had been shattered. Life had become primitive, peace and safety forever elusive, the whole world a battlefield.

Where did the soul scatter, after it had been set loose by the ravages of time, sickness, or violence? Arkady did not know. Above, perhaps, to those very stars upon which he incessantly pondered. Or maybe these spirits never left the earth. Like Sasha had implied, maybe they lingered, wandering condemned throughout the in-between, searching, hunting for the redemption that would finally give them the satisfaction they had longed for in life.

Contemplating this in suspended quiescence, the violent storm of emotions still raging around him, Arkady sensed something wholly new. Like a foreign disturbance sending ripples skimming through the ocean, he felt unnatural movement in the haze around him. He looked up into the mist.

Fluttering.

Wings flapping.

Out of the dark grey terrain of these nightmarish visions flew the Siberian Thrush. It swooped down, and, as if performing a ritual of anointment, touched his cheek with its feathers. Arkady recalled Sasha's kiss in the forest, except with this tender brush, the tragic visions, pain and bitterness, regret and sadness, all disappeared. In their place he heard a voice from the past: a sweet, beautiful sound immediately immersing his tortured soul in tranquility, far away from the violence, filth, and uncertainty that had come to define his life.

"You will come back to me, won't you?" It was the voice of Natasha.

With all the strength he had left Arkady focused on the Thrush, winging toward a light emerging in the distance. Perhaps following it would bring him back to his wife. Perhaps joining his soul to this mysterious creature would deliver the peace he so desperately wanted.

The faraway light shone brighter and brighter, subsuming the Thrush into a shadowy image immersed within its glow. As Arkady sensed himself draw nearer, he became aware again of his hands, his fingers, and then his toes. Suddenly, an immense cold enveloped him. Physical pain shot through the far reaches of his body. The bird disintegrated, and he walked through the light.

★

Arkady lay face-down in the snow. He lifted his head. He could breathe, but a heaviness made it difficult. Wearily, he glanced around; the gentle whiteness of his surroundings, intermixed with dark, smoldering heaps, started to spin. Everything shifted in and out of focus, soft shimmers on golden rays; night had passed. The charred smell hanging in the air, however, had grown more pungent and severe, while the cold was devouring his body, inch by inch. He observed his deadened fingers. They stretched out before him, still attached

27

to his hands, which were still attached to his arms. He bent his elbow slightly. Relief swept through him.

And my legs?

Turning to inspect them, he instead saw a lifeless arm draped over his back. Arkady's heart jumped, and he jerked— legs moving upward violently toward his chest—desperate to crawl out from under the dead body pinning him down.

At last wiggling free, he sat akimbo in the snow next to the motionless figure. Face down as well, its arms stretched open in a protecting sprawl, like the Christ depicted on the figurine Sasha had given him; wrists pierced, not by nails, but by bullets.

Arkady rolled the corpse over and flinched, staring. Sasha's eyes looked past him, up into the sky, inanimate, but still retaining the same unfathomable look Arkady saw the evening before in the grove, reflecting an indescribable emotion. Red-tinted snow dripped out of his friend's mouth.

"Oh, Sasha."

Tears formed as he touched the familiar face, closing the lifeless eyelids.

Out from under Sasha's protective embrace, Arkady could breathe deeply once again. Gradually, his surroundings came into clearer focus. Behind him, wrecked trucks smoldered, and uniformed bodies littered the ground in various unnatural poses, stretching from one end of the convoy to the next. He recalled Sasha running toward him as he had drifted into unconsciousness, dodging machine-gun fire that splintered across the frozen landscape. Arkady must have been standing up in full view, acting out the suicidal fantasy he had imagined earlier, because he remembered being thrown to the ground, shielded, and then hearing Sasha's final words.

"Forgive me."

As wind whisked the surrounding snow into small, harmless funnels, Arkady sensed he was all alone. Had the entire convoy been wiped out except him?

Moving his arms to his side, shoving his frozen fingers into the snow up to his wrist, Arkady hoisted himself first to his knees, and then fully upright.

Dizziness.

Legs wobbling, he fell down, defeated.

Blood trickled slowly from his forehead—the wound from the previous night.

Once again, now. Hands on the snow, toes digging in, knees braced, palms on thighs. Straighten...

This time, steady.

With a concentrated effort, Arkady focused on the wreckage surrounding him. He counted eight of his comrades, faces buried in the snow, bullets in their backs, the snowy ground spotted red with their blood.

"And the others?" he asked himself.

There they were, in various pieces, cut down in the deadly crossfire, their remains scattered next to the vehicles.

"Can I walk?"

Arkady tried to move his legs, to make his way toward one of the nearby bodies, the one he suspected was the young soldier who first caught his attention, the one whose eyes reflected a torrent of confusion, bewilderment, the very opposite of what Arkady thought he had detected in Sasha's stare.

"One foot forward, now the other."

Every time he moved, the world around him spun.

Arkady finally reached the body. In death, the soldier appeared even younger. When Arkady had first encountered him, an inkling of life remained, the last flicker of a candle as its flame struggled against the shortening wick, the melting wax.

But now, it too was gone, another soul released to the stars, or left to haunt the world.

The young soldier's face pointed skyward, frozen in a state of disbelief, shocked at life's cruelties. Here, sprawled on a battlefield, was a boy who had not yet fully grasped the complexities of existence, had not the opportunity to plunge into life's mysteries, and ask himself if, despite its hardships, living had any meaning beyond the pain now exhibited in his empty stare, his final testament. Lying beside him was his rifle, useless, unable to answer any of the questions so evident in his expression.

Bitterness resurfaced and bit Arkady's tired soul. The tears, inspired by the sight of Sasha's body, dried up. Hate remained. He dropped heavily to his knees, exhausted, and yanked upward on the teenager's jacket, covering the cold gaze.

Feeling dizzy again, Arkady sat on the wet snow. The wound on his forehead had stopped bleeding, but he could feel the depth of its cut. It was sharp, a thin but ragged blade.

"Ignore it. Concentrate. The sun is going down. I will freeze. The enemy will come back. I cannot stay here. What to do?"

From where he sat, he could see billows of grey and black smoke rising from decimated metal hulks.

"What to do?"

No vehicles, no companions. He was isolated in the dead of Russia's harsh winter, perhaps as much as five hundred kilometers to the northeast of Stalingrad.

"What to do?"

Return to Stalingrad: Out of the question. Hopeless.

Retrace the highway west, try and find help: There was nothing along the way. No villages. No life.

His hand, like his thoughts while observing from afar the German assault on Stalingrad, crept out on its own, somehow landing upon the icy metal of the young soldier's rifle lying in the snow. Perhaps this weapon did, after all, contain an answer? In one moment—a moment Arkady would not remember, nor even feel—all of the pain would disappear, all of the mysteries would be solved.

Death: Was he ready to face that which he so passionately feared?

A wind blew from the east against his back, gently wisping past his ears, over his head, and around his body. Its calmness momentarily soothed Arkady's mind. He turned around and there, far away, were the rough outlines of the Ural Mountains. The low foothills he had seen earlier punctuated the flatness of the terrain near the horizon. There they gradually became larger, more rotund, until their defining smoothness gave way to rough edges, ridges, and peaks shooting high into the heavens. It was the first time Arkady had laid eyes on the physical barrier between Europe and Asia, the boundary beyond which lay Siberia—the Janus face of Russia, the vulnerable, empty abode about which Sasha spoke so cryptically, yet so passionately.

The image of Sasha at the grove splashed into Arkady's mind...

...the kiss

...the brass crucifix

...the smile.

Arkady shuddered. His friend lay on the ground behind him. Still. Unflinching. Slowly, inevitably, Sasha was being buried by falling snowflakes, disappearing into the earth.

He stared at the mountains for long minutes. Every so often an errant drop of blood dripped from Arkady's forehead, staining dark crimson the elegant, cloud-like texture covering the ground.

Behind him the setting sun threw shadows from his hands, moving in concert with the sun's position, until out of nowhere a dark flickering deformed their outline on the ground. Arkady peered up, seeking the cause of the interruption. Swooping in loops above his head was the Siberian Thrush. Like a needle threading a complex quilt, the bird would dip behind a wrecked vehicle before emerging unscathed next to another one nearby. After making three or four laps around the whole of the site, it came to rest near Arkady. They studied each other, the only living creatures within sound or sight. He had last seen the bird in his delirious dream, when it had touched him with its wings, blessing him with a reprieve from his pain, when he heard the voice of Natasha succinctly reminding him...

"You will come back to me, won't you?"

Another option now entered Arkady's mind.

Natasha, somewhere on the other side of those mountains.

Her letter she had last written him...

Where was it?

Arkady frantically searched his pockets.

Empty. In the chaos, he had lost it. There was nothing now to remind him of his wife, except the stars in the skies, and the last lines from her letter, which he had memorized.

> *O my dove, that art in the clefts of the rock,*
> *in the secret places of the stairs,*
> *let me see thy countenance,*
> *let me hear thy voice;*
> *for sweet is thy voice, and thy countenance is comely.*

A verse this beautiful, a love this full, deserved a response, a response other than a deliberate bullet to his head, a bullet which would bring him suddenly face-to-face with answers to mysteries not yet fully explored, and into secret places that usually take lifetimes to uncover. There was more to learn, more to understand. Arkady was not ready to invite death. For now, it seemed the answer lay in only one place, with one person.

"I may never make it. Even if my journey over the mountains is successful, what then? I have only the vaguest idea of where Natasha is. But is she not the only thing in which I find fulfillment, peace?"

Arkady's breathing evened out, his pulse slowed. A calm descended over him, the type of calm that arrives when one is, at last, upon the threshold of a decision. He stared harder at the bird, examining it, contemplating it.

O my dove, that art in the clefts of the rock...

At last Arkady nodded, and as he did the bird floated gently up into the sky. Whisked away by its wings, a rolling wind came suddenly from the west, expelling the creature from the plains more quickly than it could logically fly.

Arkady collected his rifle, his pack, and pulled his coat around him as tight as he could. Following the Thrush, he headed away from the setting sun, toward the mountains in the distant east.

CHAPTER 4

*I felt something was drawing me away, and I kept fancying
that if I walked straight on, far, far away and reached that
line where the sky and earth meet, there I should find the
key to the mystery...*

*I felt something was drawing me away, and I kept fancying
that if I walked straight on, far, far away and reached that
line where the sky and earth meet, there I should find the
key to the mystery...*

Over and over the passage from *The Idiot* spun around
Arkady's mind. He had not read the novel in years,
but Sasha's voice recounting the words lodged in
his thoughts, an apt parallel to his own dark, Dostoyevskian
torment.

Trudging along the rough, snow-covered road had already
taken a physical toll on his weary body. The clouds from the
night before were gone and the moon shone in full splendor,
its subdued light illuminating the slippery white terrain. Even
without the sureties of food, water, and a fellow-soldier to
watch his back, for the time being he embraced his solitude.
At the very least, he was moving, making forward progress,
toward something. Within his dreams the Thrush had calmed
his fears, bringing to his ears the voice of Natasha out of the

darkness. The decision to follow a dumb bird was irrational, but then again, what was rational? This war? Leaving one's family, home, safety, to fight for a city, a people for which Arkady felt no responsibility? Is sanity not doing the exact opposite of what is considered insanity?

Arkady moved stealthily along the brittle road, his breath clearly visible. Once again, the overlooked tortures of war made their appearance: the rough face stubble, scarred skin, stinking breath from rotting teeth, details reminding him in sum of every weight bearing down upon his body, working in tandem to debase his existence, pounding his soul into the earth until it became singular in spirit with the diseases thrust upon the world from Adam's first transgression.

I felt something was drawing me away, and I kept fancying that if I walked straight on, far, far away and reached that line where the sky and earth meet, there I should find the key to the mystery...

Having debated Sasha on Siberia's significance just days before, proclaiming emphatically that the region meant nothing to him, the irony was not lost on him that now it seemed to mean everything. As Arkady struggled along the road, the leather of his boots stiffening with each passing step, he began to recall all that he knew or had been taught about this enigmatic land in school, a realm which his professors could not themselves ultimately make sense.

Stretching from the Ural Mountains to the Pacific Ocean, Siberia had been called many things: the soft underbelly of Russia, the Sleeping Land, the Steppe Frontier. Only from this remote region had the tribes of the Far East ever exercised any kind of authority over Europe. The Golden Horde, descended from Genghis Khan, forced the Princes of ancient Rus into 13th century vassals. For 250 years, west served east until Ivan III

"The Great," "The Gatherer of the Russian Lands," overthrew their rule, proceeding to establish his own independent kingdom with Moscow as its capital. The roles then reversed. East now served west, and the two regions—European Russia and Asian Siberia—proceeded to exist in perpetual but uneasy symbiosis. Spinning upon the north-south axis that were the Ural Mountains, these two faces were forever attempting to stare the other down into spiritual and physical submission. Existing in separate dimensions, victory for either was always elusive.

Arkady considered his debate with Sasha: his friend adamantly convinced of the existential importance of the vast and untamed east, Arkady staking out that nothing of any importance had sprung from it. But deep in his heart, Arkady knew better. Russia's most noted philosophers, artists, novelists, and revolutionaries were all born and educated in the west, just like him. But their supreme contributions occurred after they experienced the east, as if their development, their mere existences, were not fully formed until they stepped into the Ural Mountains and beyond; as if their sleeping souls, crouching hidden beneath the formal rationalism and equations of their western educations, were suddenly awakened, infused with the obscure and cryptic passion that, as was once posited, enslaves reason.[5] He recalled lessons from his school days, recounting the brief biographies of many of the famous men whose lives entangled with Siberia...

Fyodor Dostoyevsky—After being convicted of revolutionary activities and sentenced to death by firing squad, the novelist's punishment was, at the final second before the

---

[5] Hume, David. Treatise of Human Nature (1739-40) "Reason is, and ought only to be the slave of the passions."

shots were fired, commuted. Instead of death, he spent four years of hard labor in a Siberian prison near Omsk, followed by compulsory military service further east of the Ural Mountains. During his time in Siberia he became devoutly religious. His greatest works appeared thereafter, exploring the dark philosophical complexities of mankind's soul.

Alexander Herzen—The so-called "Father of Russian Socialism" spent two years in a Siberian prison near Vyatka, wherefore after being released he became a writer, an activist, and a revolutionary. His politics influenced socialist movements all throughout Europe and were credited with helping to set the stage for the emancipation of Russian serfs in 1861.

Mikhail Bakunin—The founder of collectivist anarchism spent four years in political exile in the far eastern cities of Tomsk and Irkutsk. A revolutionary violently pitted against both the state and God from his youth, by the time he escaped his exile in Siberia he had suffered under deplorable conditions and attempted suicide. His experience radicalized him even further as he traveled throughout Europe participating in various burgeoning revolutionary movements, to include Italy where he first developed his anarchist ideas.

Nikolay Chernyshevsky—The revolutionary and socialist philosopher spent eight years in political exile in Vilyuysk, where he died. While waiting to be exiled to Siberia—understanding all that that entailed—he wrote the pivotal political novel *What Is to Be Done?*, credited by many as more seminal in pushing Russia toward revolution then any of Karl Marx's works. Dostoyevsky's *Notes from the Underground* were written as a critical reaction to the novel's radicalizing influence.

...and others—like the great novelist and pacifist, Lyev Tolstoy; the leader of the "liberal" Decembrist movement, Pavel Pastel; the novelist and proponent of Russian Realism, Ivan Turgenev; and the Westernizer, Peter Chaadayev— wrote about Siberia, debated it, were inspired by its perceived primitiveness, or struggled to reconcile its "backwardness" with, in their minds, the more enlightened and rational west. To them Siberia mattered. To them it was all at once a prison, a graveyard, and Russia's "other," a means to both national downfall as well as salvation.

Arkady marched on. Hours passed, and so did the kilometers. He no longer found his view to the horizon unobstructed. Instead, hills leapt overland in the distance. Shortly, he too felt the gradual incline, his legs heavier from carrying his weight upward.

It wasn't long before he stopped to catch his breath and turned around. There, western Russia stretched out before him. It did not speak, it did not call him back.

I felt something was drawing me away...

He carried on east, the steady ascent growing coarser, as the road upon which he traveled became more ancient, less defined.

... there I should find the key to the mystery...

A familiar feeling shot through his tired legs: frozen boots pounding relentlessly against the rock-hard ground, feet growing more scarred with each passing step of climb. And even as Arkady's torso grew warm under the thick overcoat, his extremities numbed. Hands and fingers, previously in pain from gripping the cold metal of his rifle, now felt limp. Each minute the temperature plunged further, as if the deeper he marched into the mountains the more surreal his environment became. He looked up. No clouds. Instead the night was clear, the stars shining, the moon hanging gently above him. His breath moved in rhythm with his steps—in and out, in and out. Vapors emanated faster and more forcefully as the numbness previously confined to his limbs slowly devoured the rest of his body.

He jerked, once, unable to command his body to move. Arkady's breathing intensified, his heart pounding, pounding, pounding. His legs gave way. He tried to resist the collapse, tried to step forward. But he had lost all control. He fell to his knees. The Siberian Thrush came into view, fluttering passionately above him. He spat at it.

"Damn you!"

The words barely escaped his lips. His eyes rolled up, the earth spun, the blood from the wound on his forehead dripped down his face, and he folded, broken, onto the earth.

"I've found it," he muttered. "The line where the sky and the earth meet. Whatever mystery lies beyond, I will soon know what it is. God have mercy on my soul."

CHAPTER 5

Arkady's back pressed against the hard-packed snow, his eyes stared blankly into the vast, dark sky. The night swirled in whirlpool-like form above him, white flakes falling down upon his face, his clothes, his equipment. Either the heavens were rushing further away, escaping to safer spaces, or the more the snow blanketed him, the more it seemed as if the ground devoured him. A similar light to what he had seen after the ambush, in his dream, appeared. Desperate to save himself, he called out to it. No sound emerged from his mouth. Instead a comforting Voice soothed him, one which he had never heard.

"There is no sound in dreams," it said gently.

"But what about movement?" he asked silently.

"Movement in dreams, but none in death."

"Who are you?"

The peaceful Voice faded, departing as quickly as it arrived. In its stead the light shone, bright and steadfast.

Arkady moved his arms, reaching out to let know whatever was behind the glow that he needed help. He again remembered his conversation with Sasha.

"I'm in the in-between," he realized. "I'm in the Bardo."

The Thrush entered his view, fluttering past him. Now clear that it was a creature of the spiritual, itself existing somewhere between the living and dead, Arkady beckoned the bird onto his outstretched arm. As it touched down, Arkady felt as if he himself were lifting off the ground, experiencing a sense of liberation and vitality he had not sensed in so long. He stood up. He could walk. And so he walked toward the light, and then through its radiance.

Once on the other side Arkady found himself on a dirt road cutting through a field, breezy and familiar. But even though he saw things around him—grass, farm animals, people walking past him toward a small market in the distance—he could not feel anything beneath him, or the crowds brushing past him. His body was gone. The physical had diminished to the point of inconsequence, and along with it the logic, the reason, the rational, everything he had argued for, evaporated. He was an apparition, an intangible entity lacking substance or form. But, nevertheless, he felt her. *She* was nearby.

He closed his eyes; the soul, now acting in the place of his body, knelt to the ground. In this strange world of the in-between, his physical exhaustion still somehow affected his spiritual condition. He felt a surge of hope, of his energy aligning with another, and opened his eyes. *She* had passed through him, walking on the road upon which he knelt, strands of her golden hair auspiciously swaying beneath her peasant's headscarf in rhythm with her delicately balanced stride. With two baskets in her hand, she walked along with other villagers in the direction of the market. Arkady stood and followed her. He knew what would happen next. He had been here before. The scene was of their first meeting, and from afar, as if bathing in a pool of precious and sensuous memories, he watched the act unfold before him…

The great famine's[6] psychological and economic affects, although four years in the distance, still reverberated throughout the countryside of the upper Volga region. Those spared carried on somberly, picking up the pieces of their shattered lives. Arkady looked back bitterly on this period. His mother had died, a casualty of the inexplicably cruel and callous. Already weak from years of bad health, she had finally succumbed to her ailments during this time of unceasing pain, hunger, and confusion, a confusion wrought by those supposedly in charge, wrought by those now responsible—in Arkady's mind—for the war. His father had barely been able to carry on, blaming himself for his wife's death. Yet Arkady had somehow managed to summon the will to help him tolerate his sorrows, and survive. Today, market day, they were both headed into town. Even though the famine's peak had come and gone long ago, he still caught himself staring wide-eyed at the fruit, vegetables, wheat, animals, tea, and other items at the various stalls. While surveying these wonders yet again, he first spotted her.

She stood alone behind a wood counter, arms hanging loosely, hands clasped gently together at the waist of her simple, brown dress. She looked at nothing and no one in particular; every so often she would pick up one of the bright red tomatoes laid out in front of her, examine it, brush it down with her apron, and then lay it back in its resting place. Someone would stop by, she would smile shyly, maybe say a word or two, before the potential customer moved on. Her demeanor, and the way no one went out of their way to say "hello" or attempt conversation, struck Arkady as cruel. Why this separation? Why this wall? To him she was beautiful, the most beautiful thing he had seen in years, perhaps ever, but not just physically beautiful. Even from a distance, he could tell there was something behind

6   See endnote 5.a.

her eyes, deeper in her soul, a pull toward an unseen reality that held the satisfaction of desires he had yet to fully explore. The hardships Arkady and his family had endured during the famine had suppressed any feelings, any drive toward romance. But now with the sun shining, people walking and joking about him, and the sight of this seemingly alone and vulnerable young woman, that drive, that desire, kindled. Without even thinking about it, Arkady stepped in her direction. But before he could get too far, he felt a strong hand grab his shoulder. He turned around; the stern visage of his father faced him.

"Son, I know where you're headed, and you need to be careful."

"What do you mean?" Arkady asked, surprised.

"She and her family, they're...well...different. I worked with her father before he died last year. To me, he was a good man, one of the finest carpenters and craftsmen our region ever produced; he even worked on the Moscow metro stations as one of its chief sculptors. But some around here wouldn't agree. There's a reason not many people are visiting her stall."

Arkady looked questioningly at his father before realizing to what he was alluding. "I see," he said. "But you know none of that means anything to me. I don't care. She looks lonely. I think I know how she feels—at least I sense that she needs to talk to someone, someone other than a customer."

His father smiled slightly. "Okay, son. I just wanted to make you aware. It's your life." He walked away, leaving Arkady standing isolated in his thoughts.

"This is the problem with religion. It builds only barriers. And God—He provides no answers, none that really matter," Arkady muttered to himself.

He turned again toward the young woman. Drawing closer, he grew nervous. He hadn't considered what to say. In fact, he had no experience in matters like this at all. He slowed his walk, giving himself time to think.

"I'm too deliberate, coming over here like this. She'll know I was watching her."

He steered himself to the right and landed at a table of another seller, directly to the left of the young woman. Fumbling items in his hands, he eventually found his way to her table, poking and prodding fruits and vegetables, frantically going through his mind different ways to start the conversation. But in the end it was she, perhaps more stoic and daring than Arkady had originally believed, who was to set their love in motion. It was she who spoke first.

"Hello," the young woman said. "Is there something here you think you'd like?"

Arkady looked up. The noise around him seemed to fade into the background, and a feeling of warmth, of home, overtook him. Arkady smiled at her. She was more beautiful than he had originally thought, her eyes more piercing than he had imagined from afar. Still off-guard and unsettled, he nevertheless felt a weight lifted, a weight he didn't even realize had been pressing upon his chest, shoulders, and mind. It was as if, after a long night into which the famine had plunged his family, the sun had at last broken through.

"I'm just in town from the countryside," he stuttered. "I'm not really sure what I'm looking for. My father is over there."

He pointed behind him, and they both observed Arkady's father for a moment, bargaining with another man over wheat bushels.

"That's your father?" she asked.

"Yes." The two men's conversation grew more heated, easily heard even at their distance. "Prickly bastard, isn't he?" Arkady joked. The woman smiled, but said nothing. Arkady continued to look at the items, but the selection was too small, and soon there was nothing left to pretend to care about. He anxiously searched for what to say next. Speechless, Arkady looked up.

"Thank you," he said quickly, before moving along to another vendor.

"You're welcome," she replied, flashing a quick smile searching for the next customer. There wasn't one. Arkady walked away, but her image hung in his mind, filtered into his psyche, until her voice, her smile, and her eyes infected his whole being. He had to return, this time under no false pretenses, but rather with an action stating, "I'm here only for you. Nothing else matters." Isn't that what love is, after all? A denial of self, an act of sacrifice, the moment where an innate longing to protect, shelter, and comfort takes the form of something more defined, more personal, more tangible? These emotions, full of passion and insight, all ran through Arkady's mind at once, destroying each moment of layered bitterness built upon another ever since the death of his mother. This young woman represented things he longed for...hope, peace.

"You're back," she said enthusiastically, as Arkady suddenly found himself standing again in front of her. "Are you sure there isn't anything you are interested in?"

Arkady smiled shyly, "Actually, there is. I would like to take you for tea this evening if you'd like."

She blushed. Enthusiasm seemed to swell in her eyes, on her lips, and in her cheeks. She appeared poised to answer, but then drew back, as if the wall Arkady had previously noticed suddenly came crashing down between them. She looked at him directly, those piercing eyes growing both serious and apprehensive.

"Are you Jewish?" she asked meekly. Did she truly want to know? Or was this a first act of love, of sacrifice, a warning that to be with her was to be different, to be suspected without cause, and perhaps later to be convicted unjustly, then crucified.

"No," Arkady said. He wasn't expecting this question. "I'm nothing, and believe nothing." The young woman's eyes continued to study him. Arkady stared back, attempting to use his gaze to assure her of his genuineness, trying to confide that despite their differences, they were the same. In her look, he realized he had perhaps lied just now. He did believe in something, after all—her. He could take care of her, could comfort her, would always be there for her.

"Okay," she said. "The market closes at eight this evening. You can meet me here, if that's fine?"

"That would be fine," he answered with a demure smile. "I'm Arkady, by the way."

The apprehension behind her eyes receded. The wall now collapsed between the two of them, she responded, "I'm Natasha."

CHAPTER 6

The memory dissipated, but the comfort and peace of those first moments with Natasha remained.

"Can one cry in death?" Arkady asked the Voice who had spoken to him from the void, hoping for a response.

"No, to cry is an act reserved for the living to mourn a loss, to mourn past deeds."

"Then I am not dead. Can one cry in the in-between?"

"Did you enter via the path of the living or the path of the dead?"

"The path of the living."

"Then cry. Let it be known that you are still alive, that you still breathe, that you still have hope! The bitterness, the regret, the suffering inhabiting these realms can never fully devour you. There is still time, if you awake."

"Who are you?"

Silence.

The enigmatic Voice faded away once more, as did the solace carried with it.

Tears rolled down Arkady's face. The image of Natasha had disappeared, and again he was shivering, lying faceup, staring at the swirling night sky, at the falling snow, each flake sharper and colder than the one preceding it. He tried to shift his arms and legs. He could move neither; were they even there? His shivering gradually slowed and stopped.

"Hypothermia," he said exhaustedly, horror shooting into his veins. "That which I fear the most is near. This time I really will die. But if death is to spend eternity reliving my short life with Natasha, then it is an end I welcome."

He closed his eyes, coping with the inevitable by convincing himself he would be returned to the market where he met his wife, allowed to feel her presence, to see her smile, and experience the warmth of the peace she brought to his condemned soul. Then, perhaps in an endless cycle of birth, death, rebirth, he could partake in what came next, the days they spent alone together, exploring the mysteries of laughter, passion, peace the other offered. He wanted so desperately to devour at last the joy of being alive, of life while being in love.

But as he lay suffering in the snow, he did not see the light he expected. He did not see the Thrush flying above him leading him to safety, nor sense the ground of the market beneath his unformed feet. Instead he heard voices, deep, concerned, and penetrating. Like the war itself—the tragedy that had thrust itself between him and the life he had always hoped for—now these voices too interjected themselves into the eternal peaceful dreams which Arkady sought.

Disappointed, disoriented, he blinked and stared above him. The sky's blackness retreated into the background, relinquishing its empty dominance to a glistening orange fade. The color emanated from somewhere near Arkady's left, and, to his pleasant surprise, also delivered a soft warmth. He struggled to turn. He had to verify, in this land of the inexplicable, if what he saw and felt were real. The mysteries continued to build. Something had led him into these mountains. Something had shown him visions of his past. Something would not let him die, at least not yet. He would not be allowed to pass into the blissful realm where he would feel nothing but the serenity and satisfaction of being with Natasha. He squirmed, but like an insect pinned for observation, baited by visions of the life for which he longed, he stayed firmly in place, a fixture of helplessness on the frozen, rocky ground. What was needed from him to escape? Maybe these voices could provide answers, or at least a clue.

The voices grew louder, reflecting tones of deep anxiety. Arkady took a deep breath, summoning his remaining strength to turn his body toward the orange glow, as if his fate somehow hinged on the outcome of the conversation in progress behind him. He screamed in agony. No sound came from his lips— *there is no sound in dreams*—but there was, at last, movement. The force of his will triumphed. His weight shifted, not dramatically, but enough. His torso rotated to the left, and a slight turn of his head allowed him to view the scene unfolding just a few meters away. Panting, exhausted from the effort, he nevertheless lay still, confounded and confused by what he saw. Huddled around a fire, perched slightly higher on the foothill upon which Arkady was trapped, sat eight men.

To Arkady it appeared as if they were lined up on a dark stage, performers at a cabaret for the dead, the curtain just lifted, as a low light slowly emerged in the background, unveiling the actors of a surrealistic drama—the plot long in the making, the pivotal characters now at last revealed. Arkady squinted in an effort to see. Their profiles were worn and old. Backs hunched, clothes from centuries past hanging from sagging flesh. Folded wrinkles, scars, and ragged beards all outlined the contours of their rough faces. But the pitched intensity of their voices indicated they were not tired. To the contrary, they were absorbed in serious debate. And the insight Arkady gleaned from the determination in their tones revealed that while their bodies might be broken, their spirits were subtlety engaged with their surroundings, as if despite their age, they very much wanted to be heard, to be understood. To matter.

Arkady studied them one-by-one. He recognized them from history books, posters, and newspapers. In fact, they'd been his memory's unwitting companions this very night. As he had marched across the plain and trudged up into the foothills of the Ural Mountains, he had recounted their interactions with this land—Tolstoy, Dostoyevsky, Herzen, Bakunin, Chernyshevsky, Pastel, Turgenev, Chaadayev. Was their unexpected appearance now a creation of his delirious mind, an emanation of his own musings manifesting itself in his near-death state? Or had they, through the fiendish bird and a series of bizarre circumstances, been the ones to bring him to Siberia, a place where unformed spirits could take the shape of the personal and commune with the living? Terrified at these thoughts, he tried to force a scream past his lips.

Suddenly the Voice of peace reverberated in the empty night.

"There is no sound in dreams," it reminded him.

"But I can hear them!"

"No, you cannot. You can only feel them. You must awake! The choice is yours."

"Who are you? Why won't you answer me?"

But the Voice drifted into the background, and again Arkady was left alone, vulnerable, as the words of the eight men began to flow freely from their lips into his soul...

"Well, here we are. Again. All of us. No closer to a solution than a few months ago. And to make matters worse that tyrant in the Kremlin continues to rule. His Generals—the very ones he tried to purge from the army's ranks over the last two years[7]—had a chance to dispose of him after the Germans

---

[7]   See endnote 6.a.

invaded, but they let him live! I've heard that he lay quivering in his dacha for more than three months after the onslaught. A coward, and a stunted fool. After the last war, who in their right mind would have actually trusted Berlin?"

"True, true, Peter Yakovlevich.[8] In normal times everyone would see what a few of us recognized when he first showed up twenty-five years ago. He is stupid, uncouth, and brutal. Yes, a tyrant, and a naïve one at that. Even now the purges, the ones he initiated after he took power, could ironically end up destroying him. Those left leading our military cannot match the Germans' skill and intelligence. The enemy is better led and better equipped. But if the army can withstand the sieges in St. Petersburg and Tsaritsyn[9], we might have a chance; with victories in those cities we could still ultimately prevail. But at what cost? The human toll will be unimaginable. It will set us back a generation," said another.

"This war, and the decisions made by Iosif Vissarionovich[10], will set it back two generations, Fyodor Mikhaylovich[11]," answered Peter Chaadayev, the one who had spoken first. "This madman, just by himself, even before the war, had already set it back one generation. We were making steady progress for a time—tossing away the old, embracing the future, embracing Europe! But now our situation is the most precarious in our history. And I don't believe the leadership exists in Moscow to either win this war or, if by some miracle it is won, set Russia on a path to any kind of lasting recovery. I continue to wonder, where will our national salvation come from?"

---

[8]   Peter Yakovlevich Chaadayev (b.1794 – d.1856)
[9]   Russian Imperial name for Stalingrad, present-day Volgograd
[10]   Iosif Vissarionovich (aka Stalin) (b.1878 – d.1953)
[11]   Fyodor Mikhalovich Dostoyevsky (b.1821 – d.1881)

"That is why all of us have again gathered here, to search for that answer," Fyodor Dostoyevsky replied. "We all realized long ago Russia's salvation would not come from the places we had theorized it might. It will not come from the peasantry, which has been forcibly collectivized, nor the merchants or landowners, which have all been repressed beyond recognition. As we just discussed, the most experienced and thoughtful of our military leaders have all been killed or banished, those remaining reduced to mere servants of incompetent political masters. How about the Church, the vessel of Holy Russia, the torch bearer of the 'Third Rome'? Discredited and marginalized, regretfully—its ancient cathedrals burnt to the ground, boarded up, or turned into 'People's Museums'. Our country has been stripped of its soul. We have nothing left. This is why we must act on its behalf. We are what is left of its spiritual essence."

"Yes, Fyodor Mikhalovich. But I would add caution," said a third. "Iosif Vissarionovich is not as stupid as we all are led to believe. Behind his broken speech and deformed body is a cunning and cynical mind."

"Please expand, Ivan Sergeyevich[12]," Chaadayev injected.

"Indeed, this is a situation unlike any we have ever seen," Ivan Turgenev continued. "The circumstances are so dire, in fact, that even Iosif Vissarionovich seems willing, at least for the time being, to bow to reality. For instance, he recently authorized the parading of religious icons to our men on the front lines. Our Church has suddenly become fashionable again. So, we should be careful as we plot, as we seek to foment a challenge to him, out here in this place, where we believe he cannot see us. He is as much aware of the importance of Siberia to Russia as the rest of us, although perhaps for different reasons."

---

[12]   Ivan Sergeyevich Turgenev (b.1818 – d.1883)

"Of course, of course," Dostoyevsky replied. "My frustration for a moment got the better of me. He is certainly more clever than we give him credit for. We have to be careful, unlike those priests now suddenly in the good graces of the Kremlin. If I were them, I'd be covering my face as I paraded around; that's not a gamble I would be willing to make. They're taking names, believe me. The police under the Bolsheviks differ from their Tsarist predecessors only in the fact that they're more competent, more cruel. Isn't that ironic? Russia at last experiences a genuine revolution, however the results conclude in only greater efficiency for the most detestable aspects of the former regime. All of our centuries of debate, imprisonment, underground activity...this is what we get."

Chaadayev answered again, "Yes, yes. The Okrhana[13] was nothing compared to the new secret police. And their prisons! I've heard there is no escaping from those tombs. I had hoped, at one point, that Russia's social and political backwardness might actually save her from the purgatory that engulfed Europe after their revolutions. But we ended up worse!"

A man sitting immediately to Chaadayev's left snapped, "I'm tired of these words! I'm tired of these debates, especially coming from those of you who advocated for our last plan! After that failure we are here again, as one, to decide the next course of action. Let's focus on that, on what is to be done now. Besides," the man added, "You, Peter Yakovlevich, are as much to blame as those who came after you. In fact, perhaps even more so."

"Please, go on Aleksander Ivanovich[14]." With a crooked smile, Chaadayev answered in a tone that implied he expected, indeed welcomed, this attack; as if he wanted to again revisit the

---

[13] Name for the Tsarist-era Secret Police
[14] Aleksander Ivanovich Herzen (b.1812 – d.1870)

arguments of old, the never-ending discussions about Russia's ills and remedies, her place in history and the world.

Aleksander Herzen huffed; perhaps he knew he had been successfully baited, but the invitation proved irresistible. "I agree with you generally about the natural state of man. It is one of dependence, one of subservience. But where I diverge is in your belief that this is preferable! You genuinely believe the individual is nothing without society. This, comrade, is not a state-of-being to be embraced. It is one to struggle against. What you preach is essentially the virtues of slavery. You're too Russian after all! Your religiosity clouded your perception of what is preferable and what is not. These ideas—as articulate as you might have made them—only served to warp later debates about the nature of our country. They had the effect of convincing others that Russians were most comfortable in a state of subservience. They played very effectively into this emerging horror."

"My arguments, as to the natural state of man, were directed as much toward the rest of Europe as they were toward Russians, and this became particularly true following the revolution in France,"[15] Chaadayev replied. "Society, in whatever form it takes, seems to me heroic—it is a vehicle by which man moves forward, in sync, toward something greater than himself. These are not indictments against us. On the contrary, I hoped the Russian experience would uniquely serve to help our country avoid the tumultuous results of the European revolutions. I thought we could find our own way, a way to progress, a way to proceed toward our historical destiny without changing everything in order to get there. Your accusations, Aleksander

---

[15] Reference to the French Revolution of 1848 that led to the French Second Republic

Ivanovich, are unfounded. I love my country as Peter the Great taught me to love it."[16]

"The revolution of Peter the Great replaced the obsolete squirearchy of Russia with a European bureaucracy; everything that could be copied from the Swedish and German codes, everything that could be taken over from the free municipalities of Holland into our half-communal, half-absolutist country, was taken over; but the unwritten, the moral check on power, the instinctive recognition of the rights of man, of the rights of thought, of truth, could not be and were not imported. [17] In short, your Tsar was a tyrant. His reforms were not real," Herzen scowled back.

"What Peter Yakovlevich portends regarding 'historical destiny'—is there any such thing as historical logic, or just an evolutionary form dictating the stages of how societies advance?" interrupted another man who had not yet spoken but seemed anxious to move the debate forward.

"Interesting. Describe such form, Nikolay Gavrilovich," [18] answered Herzen, awaking from his disgust with Chaadayev.

"Well, as I have written elsewhere, history is fond of her grandchildren, for it offers them the marrows of the bones, which the previous generation had hurt its hands in breaking,[19]" stated Nikolay Chernyshevsky. "Is history not, then, ultimately

---

[16]   "I love my country as Peter the Great taught me to love it." Chaadayev, Peter. The Philosophical Letters, p. 173.

[17]   "The revolution of Peter the Great replaced...could not be and were not imported." Herzen, Aleksander, From the Other Shore, Author's Introduction: Human Dignity and Free Speech,1855

[18]   Nikolay Gavrilovich Chernyshevsky (b.1828 – d.1889)

[19]   "History is fond of her grandchildren, for it offers them the marrows of the bones, which the previous generation had hurt its hands in breaking." Chernyshevsky, Nikolay. Kritika filosofskikh predubezhdenii protiv obshchinnogo vladeniya (1858), C v 387.

driven by paradoxical revolutions? One overcoming the other, each redefining but also seeking to perfect the deficiencies of its predecessor, the grandchildren finding meaning in the aims of their grandparents, aims which the parents had perhaps cynically discarded? Are the romantic ideals of one age, reconciled with reality in the next, over and over again? If true, then when we speak of the Russian experience as a driver of history, we speak of something utterly non-existent and unattainable, something which makes sense in the abstract, but in reality suffers unrecognizable mutations as each historical stage is overthrown by the next. So, as far as form is concerned, the highest stage of development everywhere represents a return to the first stage which—at an intermediate stage—was replaced by its opposite."[20]

"Yes, I generally concur. The future is a variation improvised on a theme of the past,[21] as I have previously argued to Turgenev," replied Herzen.

Sitting across from the others was an old man. Adorned with a white beard and dressed in peasant's clothing, he spoke, skepticism lacing his voice. "Stages imply there is, ultimately, a historical end, no? So what does the end stage—the end of history—look like? And where are we then, as Russians, in the course of your historical stages, Nikolay Gavrilovich?"

"I suppose that is the question we've all been asking for decades, and given how the current regime assumed power, this is even more urgent. The Romanov autocracy was abolished by, yes, the liberals. But the liberals were weak. The Bolsheviks

---

[20]   "the highest stage of development everywhere represents a return to the first stage which – at an intermediate state – was replaced by its opposite." Chernyshevsky, Nikolay. Izbrannye filosofskie sochineniia (L. 1950-51, vol. 2, p. 484)

[21]   "The future is a variation improvised on a theme of the past". Alexander Herzen in personal correspondence to Ivan Turgenev.

took power almost immediately. Hence, the grandchildren of the autocrats gave the intermediate stage—the liberals— no opportunity to rule. What was to be achieved through social evolution, was instead achieved through force. This is an aberration, and brings so much into question. But it must be admitted that the Bolsheviks, whatever your opinion is of them, have made impressive advances since they assumed power in 1917. So, perhaps we are approaching the final stage. Or perhaps we were, that is, before the war, and before Iosif Vissarionovich, the man they refer to as Stalin. With his State, and with these leaders…well, I fear we may have arrived prematurely, after all."

"*Prematurely* is one view of Russia's current predicament, but a severely mistaken one, I think," the white-bearded man replied, plucking at his peasant tunic. "Prematurely can mean, for example, when referring to a child, that he was born in a place he was meant to be, albeit at a time when he was not meant to be there. Consider a child who is delivered to his parents, yet arrives four months before the intended time. He will, under those circumstances, die. Death, not life, therefore, is his destiny. Is this Russia's fate under this regime you label as merely ambitious? I don't know. But one thing is certain, events cannot be allowed to continue in this fashion. The cost is too high. If this does not all end in death, it ends in a crippling social and cultural deformity. Make no mistake, what was emerging in Russia prior to the war under Stalin was an unnatural order. Forces carefully cultivated throughout our past, tamed and harnessed into traditions reflecting Russia and all that she is, have been maliciously and violently thrown to the side for the sake of building an ideal, an earthly heaven, one might say."

He shot a hard look at Chernyshevsky, and then continued. "But our traditions, though they may be reshaped or suppressed, cannot be discarded, despite the best efforts of those now in charge. They will always be present, because, as Peter Yakovlevich pointed out, they are a part of our national soul. They are an inseparable part of our experience. However, now they are being unleashed in more primitive forms, rearing their heads in unrecognizable ways, each working in tandem with new and perhaps unnatural ideological partners. No, what was materializing was not Russia's natural historical destiny, but rather a grotesque and authoritarian shadow of the true Russia, one which will forever haunt the world if it is allowed to continue. That is why we are here. At this opportune time, when Stalin's eyes are fixed on the Germans, we can put things right. But we must act quickly."

"But what forces are you referring to specifically, Lyev Nikolayevich[22]? What has been tamed by the Russian experience that is now being distorted in unnatural ways?" challenged Chernyshevsky in an argumentative tone.

"Nationalism, religion, the spirit of the collective, even capitalism, for example," Lyev Tolstoy answered pointedly.

Another of the group, who had until now remained quiet, peering solemnly into the fire, spoke. "Such a shame, such a shame," he said.

"What is the shame, Pavel Ivanovich[23]? That these have been suppressed?" asked Dostoyevsky.

"No. The shame is that missing from Lyev Nikolayevich's list of national traditions is democracy. Our few attempts at political reform in the tradition of Western Europe and the United States have always resulted in disaster. I know, of course, from first-hand experience," Pavel Pestel answered dourly.

---

[22] Lyev Nikolayevich Tolstoy (b.1828 – d.1910)
[23] Pavel Ivanovich Pestel (b.1793 – d.1826)

Chernyshevsky interjected, "Liberal democracy, yes. Our uneducated peasants wouldn't know what to do with a ballot even it was already marked for them. They would immediately take it to the collective and debate about it for hours before finally deciding to vote as a commune. There is very little individualism in Russia with which to work. There is no sense of self. This is why the liberals, during their short time in power, failed so miserably. So perhaps the current political arrangement more closely resembles our traditions. Bourgeois democracy assumes all votes—all humanity!—are equal. The current system, however, takes into account the fact that a man's class can play a disproportionate role in how influential he is. So-called democracy in the West is a sham. It makes a mockery of the idea of true equality."

"This is an old debate, Nikolay Gavrilovich. Your concerns are legitimate, but only in a state whose legal culture allows for such inequalities to flourish. A proper distribution of power throughout a government, backed by strong laws, checks, and balances, can tip the scales toward the individual despite his class, despite everything! Russia's past attempts to implement such a culture have always ended in crisis, though; its bureaucracies too weak, its society too uneducated. The latest attempt occurred, as you noted, immediately following the Tsar's abdication, but the government that replaced Tsar Nicholas Alexandrovich[24] was ineffective. It was only a matter of time before the Bolsheviks took over. We had a real chance then, but the liberals, in the end, did not truly want the opportunity. They did not want power," retorted Pestel.

A man sitting slightly to the rear of the rest of the group, bundled in a dark cloak and slowly smoking a pipe, cleared

---

[24] Tsar Nicholas Alexandrovich Romanov (b.1868 – d.1918), the last Tsar of Russia; ruled from 1894 – 1917

his throat. At the mention of the word "power," his eyes grew wider and his back straightened. Flames from the fire burned brighter, highlighting in sharp form the peaks from the nearby mountains. They seemed to hover over him, ready to leap, ready to devour. Although last to speak, the others respectfully fell silent as he began.

"All of you argue interminably about theory, about institutions, about which laws need implementing, or about what conditions must be present in order to achieve your goals—your own earthly heavens." The man shot an ironic glare toward Tolstoy, and added, "I'm afraid you severely underestimate what this is truly about."

"How so, Mikhail Alexandrovich[25]?" asked Chernyshevsky.

"The war will be won by Russia," Mikhail Bakunin said. "With great human cost, yes. But it *will* be won. In fact, the war itself is the antidote to Iosif's fears and the key to his security. As Ivan Sergeyevich stated earlier, Stalin is indeed more clever than we realize. He may not yet understand all of the opportunities the war affords him, but he will. Why? Deep in his heart, before he died, Vladimir Ilyich[26] must himself have understood the nature of the regime he birthed. After all, one does not create utopia by welcoming dissent, or by celebrating for long the virtues of independent thought. To believe in a heaven-on-earth is to accept the infallibility and perfection of man, to believe, essentially, that man is god. Vladimir Ilyich must also have understood that only someone with this surety, this confidence, this ruthlessness, was capable of utilizing that which was necessary to move his Revolution forward, to move history forward. Though he may not have trusted him, though he may have warned against him, and perhaps even loathed

---

[25]   Mikhail Alexandrovich Bakunin (b.1814 – d.1876)
[26]   Vladimir Illyich Ulyanov (aka Lenin) (b.1870 – d.1924)

him, in his heart Lenin knew there was no one else who could sustain the current regime but Stalin himself."

Chaadayev insisted, "Mikhail Alexandrovich, western Russia is under occupation, and its major cities assaulted in the north, south, and central regions. At first the regime refused even to acknowledge this was the case! And if I hear you correctly, you are saying that not only will Russia be victorious, but Stalin will actually *improve* his situation politically and ideologically? Who in Russia will support him and the regime after this debacle?"

"The Russian people, of course. Slaves have no other recourse. Don't you understand? A war does not destroy a system such as our current one. On the contrary, it fuels it. Our debates are accomplishing nothing. To continue to pretend otherwise is naïve and futile. Despite all of our best efforts, look where we have ended up! Comrades, have you ever considered that the centuries of arguing, debating, and fighting have never truly been about ideas at all? Have you ever considered that perhaps our dreams, our political and social aspirations have been illusions, false fronts for something more primal, more base, more depraved? The truth is laid bare before us in what we are witnessing. Indeed, Pavel Ivanovich stumbled upon it just now. This has always been about power—raw, brutal power. Those who wanted power the most have succeeded in obtaining it. And now, like the gods they believe themselves to be, they will wield it without fear of retribution, without fear of error. Because, are they not infallible, after all? Are they not the ones ordained to usher in a new age, to usher in the final stage, the end of history itself?"

Bakunin paused. The other members of the circle stayed silent, considering his words, as if contemplating the ramifications for their plans if what he spoke was the truth.

"I'm afraid all of us are complicit in this." Bakunin bowed his head low, speaking in a deep, grave voice. "While we roamed amongst the living, although our means and methods may have been different, we were united in our efforts for one thing: revolution. And revolution to what end? Ask yourselves that question."

"I have to disagree, Mikhail Alexandrovich," answered Dostoyevsky. "Not all of us here wanted what you and your comrades did. Not all of us are complicit in this tragedy. Many of us wanted to work within the system. It was worth saving. Russia was worth saving. But the worst impulses of our country grew too strong. You, and those like you, wanted something fundamentally different. You wanted chaos, violence, destruction. And somehow, arising from the ashes, a perfect order was to arrive?"

As he stared threateningly at Dostoyevsky, Bakunin's eyes flickered in the light of the fire. He drew his cloak closer around him. "It's not that we wanted chaos. It's that we wanted something real, something new, something the world had never even imagined possible. The will to destroy is also a creative will.[27] No existing political structure—certainly not one created by a Tsar, King, or some Parliament—could have resulted in that. It all had to be torn down, and we were all vain enough to believe we could do so."

"We are called upon to execute institutions, destroy beliefs...holding nothing sacred, making no concessions, showing no mercy...," Herzen interjected, quoting from his past, when he walked the earth, as if recalling the very call-to-arms that gave credence to Bakunin's argument now.

---

[27] "The will to destroy is also a creative will." Bakunin, Mikhail, *The Reaction in Germany*, 1842.

"Were our naked ambitions any different from the tyrant we are now plotting against?" Bakunin continued, seemingly confident that Herzen was on his side. "Can we cloak ourselves in innocence when our words, our theories, brought Russia to this point?"

"Modern man, a mournful pontifex maximus, merely builds the bridge. The unknown man of the future will cross it...Do not stay on the old shore!"[28] Herzen again interjected, speaking into the night's chill air.

Bakunin dipped his head toward Herzen, taking his cue. "Not one of us truly expected this, this *nightmare*. At least I clearly recognize now our situation, unlike the rest of you. Comrades, we must match power with power, brutality with brutality. You—Lyev, Fyodor, and Ivan—you three had your chance with the last boy. Now it is my turn, and I have chosen this one."

A chill shot up Arkady's spine. The sound of "nightmare" echoed through his bones. The horror inspired by this word ricocheted within his soul. And like the ocean reacting to a large ship cutting through treacherous water, he felt his tortured emotions roll in violent waves toward the old men, hitting them simultaneously with a ferocity that caused each to straighten and finally look at Arkady. The young soldier stared back. As his eyes met theirs, he felt faint. How much longer he could retain consciousness he did not know, but already their faces blurred, and the "sounds" emanating from their mouths no longer made sense. Once more Arkady tried to scream, to yell for help, but nothing left his lips, nothing except a choked

---

[28] "Modern man, a mournful pontifex maximus, merely builds the bridge. The unknown man of the future will cross it...Do not stay on the old shore!" Herzen, Aleksander. *From the Other Shore, Author's Introduction: To My Son Alexander,* 1855.

gasp. He remained pinned in place, disoriented, in a state of septic-like shock. But still, their message continued to flow through his soul.

"What drew you to this poor, innocent boy, delivered to us by his friend from this land with a kiss, and anointed by the Thrush; the one who represents our next attempt to, as you say Aleksander Ivanovich, build the bridge and reach the other shore? Why are you sure he is the one?" asked Tolstoy looking down toward Arkady. "After all, we were certain of the last one too. And now he sits rotting, destined to die in prison, caught somewhere between the past and the future, in a village itself sitting on the edge of history's abyss."

"Because, Lyev Nikolayevich," Bakunin said quietly. "He has no love for life, as he currently understands it, or as he has experienced it. A bitterness exudes from him that derives from the hardship of losing those you love, one after another, and finding no reprieve from the emotional anguish burrowing into one's being as a result. He believes that to live is to suffer. This is the only truth he recognizes. And aren't those who believe only in regret, sorrow, and pain, are they not the most susceptible to causes such as ours? We must only give them a glimmer of our paradise, a taste of the hope and peace they so desperately desire, before they are ours, before we convince them that any action, any word, even any death is righteous for the cause of their happiness."

"And you have tempted him already with this paradise, haven't you Mikhail Alexandrovich?" Tolstoy asked.

"Using the Thrush, I have." The fire crackled brightly, exposing Bakunin's unapologetic expression.

Tolstoy and Dostoyevsky exchanged looks of apprehension.

"I fear we are missing something, a critical element, a variable that we, in all of our discussions and debates, have not taken into consideration or defined," Tolstoy said. "And I fear that as we did in life, so now in death we are again merely setting in motion the wheels of something we will not be able to control, an unnatural aberration and eventual tragedy culminating in immeasurable pain. Mikhail Alexandrovich is right. We sit here in arrogant judgment, vanities spewing forth on behalf of those who never appointed us their saviors. Have we not realized the irony? We ourselves are trapped, condemned. If we were not gods in life, we are not gods now. Who will save us, we, the so-called saviors?" The old man sighed. "But I have nothing left to say. I have nothing left to object to. The last plan failed, the one I advocated for. The forces of history proved too much for the man I chose. I do not mourn him, but I take responsibility for his fate. As agreed, the one Mikhail Alexandrovich has chosen is our next option. Perhaps through his success, we ourselves can be redeemed. Perhaps through him we will find our own salvation, leave this place at last, and reach the opposite shore."

"I confess I am in favor of a more humane policy, but as all are on the other side, I go along with the rest," Dostoyevsky spoke wistfully and submissively into the fire following Tolstoy, quoting from his novel *Demons*.[29]

Arkady jolted from his delirium, released like a catapult from the force jamming him into the ground. He gasped for air as if oxygen had long been withheld from him. Breathing deeply, cold air shot back into his lungs and rushed out. He rolled completely over, burying his face in the snow, seeking relief from the sudden sharp pain, as if the powerful unchaining from the supernatural caused the wound from the ambush to once again break open. Wriggling to orient his body fully

---

[29] Dostoyevsky, Fyodor, *Demons* (or *The Possessed*), Part II, Chapter VII, "A Meeting".

in the direction of the old men, he lifted his head, blinking away blood trickling down his forehead and into his eyes. Convulsive shivers wracked him. Blackness threatened. He watched helplessly as the old philosophers and revolutionaries approached, staring down at him with concerned and worried looks. With the last of his strength Arkady managed to glare back. Their collective spirits merged into one, and the Siberian Thrush arrived to perch curiously on a singular, unified shoulder. A wrinkled hand stretched out, touched Arkady's face, and closed his eyes.

He felt nothing more.

PART II

Somewhere east of the Ural Mountains, late fall, 1942

CHAPTER 7

N atasha's living quarters were sparse, clean, and cold. A low tin ceiling, propped up by hastily assembled wooden-beamed walls, the cracks filled with baked mud from the local earth, sheltered two long rows of bunk beds running neatly along the sides. Stoves at both ends attempted to keep the hut warm, but their ability to permeate heat throughout was usually in vain when faced against the harsh Siberian climate. Smoke from those stoves, joined often by the sound of dry, hacking coughs, saturated the air.

Natasha was approaching her seventh full month living in this isolated locus. Mobilization orders issued in early 1942, emanating from the hastily established but seemingly all powerful GKO [30], had resulted in her being scuttled onto a train from her village in western Russia, transported across the Ural Mountains, eventually arriving onto what appeared to be an outlying planet whose terrain, while scarred, cratered, and ancient, seemed still to be slumbering in an uneasy sleep, undisturbed by modernity's most recent descent into an existential inferno. There, a factory, that had itself been reinforced by other factories carried piece by piece from the Ukraine just weeks earlier, was rapidly enlarged. Like Natasha upon her arrival, it had been transformed into something useful

---

[30]   State Defense Committee. See endnote 7a.

for the war, and put immediately to work producing ferrous metals, which in turn were transported to other factories, located elsewhere in the recently populated Siberian universe, to be shaped and molded into vehicles, tanks, artillery, and other munitions.

Those same mobilization orders not only sent millions of women into centers of industrial production for the first times in their lives, they also established regimes that closely resembled in-miniature the military their husbands, brothers, and sons were drafted into en masse. The length of their workday, the rations each worker received, and the laws governing how labor troupes were organized, led, and disciplined, had all been articulated through edicts of the distant GKO. Days started early and lasted until quotas were met. Food, clothes, and other goods were issued in accordance with a strict hierarchy based on one's job and its perceived importance to the war effort. Thankfully for Natasha, factory workers were at the top, while the elderly and disabled, along with children, were at the bottom. Justice was no longer administered through the People's Courts, but rather through military tribunals trained to act swiftly and severely. In the span of less than a year, Natasha's life with Arkady was a distant memory, a dream cast in a glow that, were it to belong to a less passionate woman, would quickly dull, fading into the dreary grey paint that now peeled in metallic flakes from the factory's walls.

Following their shifts, Natasha and the thirty-five other women who inhabited her living quarters would attempt activities intended to keep them connected to their former lives. They would socialize with each other, and write letters to loved ones serving on the front lines. Exhaustion from hard work was rarely a factor driving them to despair. On the contrary, as weary as it was, they welcomed the labor, the distraction propelling the clocks' hands faster around the numbers.

Without their assigned tasks keeping them busy, their imaginations would inevitably stray, transforming into baneful but inquisitive spirits, whose questions could lead to unpleasant answers. Would the lives they had built prior to the war still be waiting for them when it was all over? Would their loved ones even be alive?

These spirits would have free and unobstructed reign on the desolate Siberian landscape were it not for this industrial outpost in which they now all dwelt. This was another consequence of the massive mobilization: the GKO having remained in Moscow, the factories emerged all-encompassing, all-powerful. They were the suns, the workers their stars. Attached to the machines by law and circumstance, these disparate emigres were fed by the factory's kitchens and farms, sheltered by its barracks, and medically cared for by its hospitals. To Natasha and the others forced to inhabit these steppes, the crude steel edifices were their fortress and refuge, an island of twisted iron and belching steam, but the dry ground of civilization nevertheless. Although still under construction, the exoskeleton of the factory city rose above the frozen desert, a symbol of Soviet man's victory over the barren, worthless, and primitive, a statement of resilience and defiance against the Nazi onslaught ravaging the west. Fixated as Moscow was on the German threat, the Soviet government left this oasis of industry, and many others like it, to itself; those in charge ran the lives of thousands as they saw fit away from the scrutinizing eye of the GKO. One of the war effort's multiple lifelines, this small but powerful collective exercised an outsized influence in an empire teetering on the brink of collapse.

Another day had ended. Natasha had not returned to her bunk before night had fallen; there would be no visible rays of sunshine for her today. Hungry, cold, she sat on her top bunk staring wistfully into the thick, unfiltered gloom. The lights had been extinguished for the evening, although one at the end of the short passageway leading to the latrines remained dimly lit. Already having survived the end of one winter, and the incessantly hot summer that followed, fall was once again upon her. The inevitability of the approaching winter heightened the melancholic mood already settled in Natasha's barracks, creating a stillness which disturbed the triumphalism sought by the mostly old and decrepit leaders assigned as the burgeoning city's overlords. In the forms of victorious banners, slogans, and speeches, their propaganda made it nearly impossible to discern between what was real and fabricated. And for those who had someone far away, someone suffering, bleeding, yet still alive, the lies and exaggerations were the most enticing, the most potent. Every report spewed forth spoke of military progress, as if total victory was but one more battle away.

Then the "postings"—as the workers referred to them— would arrive, a list of loved ones killed at the front, periodically published by the Soviet High Command. And the faint hope somehow clinging on in a seemingly hopeless time would dissipate, crashing hard and deep into the cold earth. For those who had only lost one, but not all, the process would begin again as new words and new declarations dripped from the lips of the authorities. Eagerly they would seek to rebuild mangled expectations, expectations that the war might now, finally, at last, be over. But for those that *had* lost all, there was little left to cling to. The strong would somehow find a way to carry on, yet the weak were devoured into the burgeoning smokestacks and bellowing machinery. For them, a new reality would dawn, one devoid of promise, of soul, but abundant in regret, and even more so in fear.

Brushing her flowing blonde hair over her shoulders, Natasha laid down and shut her eyes, content to sigh into the cold empty night, "What I'm doing is real. Matters. It will bring my husband back to me." She relied on the reserved self-assuredness Arkady had told her he noticed and admired when they met in the market—when it was she, not he, who had spoken first. As of yet, the war had not chased away her confidence. She still clung to hope, much as she had during the famine, much as she had when her village turned against her, and when her father died. But deep beneath her poised, quiet exterior, a swell of uncertainty was incrementally taking shape, the first gusts of torment whisking through a slowly weakening frame. She had not heard from or about Arkady since she had left their home earlier in March. She knew nothing regarding his whereabouts, and, as much as she tried otherwise, could only imagine the worst. Tonight, as she did every night in the absence of his physical embrace, she sought the comfort of his memory by clasping a single, small photo close to her heart, and repeating words that her father had spoken to her in reassurance as a child—spiritual, but passionate words imbued with the mystery of a deep and abiding love, one that would never cease even in the face of separation and loss.

> *O my dove, that art in the clefts of the rock,*
> *in the secret places of the stairs,*
> *let me see thy countenance,*
> *let me hear thy voice;*
> *for sweet is thy voice, and thy countenance is comely.*

She never let the photograph go, not even in her sleep. In parallel with the verse, Natasha had memorized every line of her husband's profile, the creases in his face, and the hair that heavily swooshed down the side of his forehead, as if he was waiting for her to brush it back away from his eyes. She would fall asleep with these images in her mind. But adding to her distress, the photo was beginning to fade. Similarly, the image of Arkady in her dreams had grown cloudy, distant, never fully forming into the recognizable figure of the man she had fallen in love with.

★

Natasha awoke as usual to the sound of screeching megaphones outside her hut. The 'Internationale' played loudly, meant to spur on the workers to yet another day, another inspiring moment to serve their Soviet motherland. The blaring music was a constant reminder that although they were, nominally at least, free citizens, the country was engulfed in total war. Every city faced potential risk. And, if one believed their superiors, potential saboteurs and anti-Soviet collaborators lurked everywhere in the vast expanse, outside the camp. This siege mentality accentuated the military-like atmosphere already imbued within the city's genetic composition. Although, at least for now, the settlement was safe from an invading army, from time to time Natasha gazed beyond its borders, pondering the empty expanse and those ghosts who inhabited it, hidden in the forests and behind the low hills sparsely dotting the ever-expanding terrain. In these moments, Natasha would feel completely exposed.

At the first notes of the music, Natasha sat up and pivoted her hips until she sat on the edge of the bunk. She hesitated, bracing for what would happen next. Already grimacing, she hopped down. The cold, roughly hued concrete floor sent an icy shock through her bare feet and up her body. Once standing she wasted little time donning her work clothes: long woolen socks first, followed by a drab, cotton frock hanging down just below her knees. Over the front of the dress she draped a white apron, and tied her distinctive elegant bow in the back, her fingers nimble despite the frigid air. She pulled on leather boots that went half-way up her calves, and tugged a fading light blue scarf over her head to keep her long hair out of sight. Natasha's name would be called during her troupe's roll call in a mere fifteen minutes. She joined the others in her living quarters pushing toward the wooden door in a makeshift column, scrambling to exit on time. Silently and quickly they walked, some still slipping on jackets, gloves, and caps, as they scurried along. Others, like Natasha, just stared ahead, deep in thought and memory, seeking the psychological equilibrium that allowed their minds to peacefully co-exist with the physical demands soon to be thrust upon them.

The troupe followed the broken, gravel path leading to the outpost's massive central courtyard where every day began, every announcement and exaggerated claim of progress declared. Here, absent any barriers, shelter, color, or warmth, the wind swept violently, delivering the piercing cold ferociously onto the faces of the assembled. At times the wind became so strong it seemed Russia's eastern nature was attempting to sweep these western invaders from its domain. The routine never changed. The feeling of insignificance never abated.

Upon exiting the gravel path, the sound of crunching footsteps turned into a hollow echo on the pavement, and the women formed quickly and mechanically into platoon-like formations.

"Lara!" the Assistant Troupe leader shouted.

"Here!"

"Rachel!"

"Here!"

"Natasha!"

"Here!"

There were very few men in the unit. Those present standing in the ranks were physically unable to serve at the front. The others held senior positions: factory inspectors responsible for delivering or procuring supplies needed for production and shipment; and various managers overseeing the vast logistical functions of the city itself, accounting for the needs of its many workers, including housing, food, clothing, sanitation, and medical care.

Leading the units directly, however, was an elite position. These Troupe Leaders coordinated every activity, enforced all decisions. They were directly accountable for human beings, responsible for that which fueled the city's growth and gave it influence. And every day, as the war dragged on and hundreds more lives were lost, the value of each worker increased, and consequently the prestige of the men who were their masters. Like their counterparts on the front lines, these workers did not question, they did not protest. They occupied their own battlefield, one just as lonely and, in its own way, as perilous. The Troupe Leaders were their appointed commanders, the ones who would see them safely through it all. The workers had only to trust, and all would be fine.

Unapproachable as these men typically were, however, the man overseeing Natasha's troupe was even more so. Unlike the others who were advanced in age, David Zaslavsky was young, probably no older than twenty-five. In the rare instances in which Natasha caught a glimpse of him, he did not seem especially dynamic, charismatic, or otherwise confident in the way she expected a man in his position to be. On the contrary, when he had deemed it necessary to appear at their morning formations, Natasha had detected reservation, pensiveness, perhaps even an inkling of fear. Standing well away from the mass of people at his command, he never smiled nor spoke. He merely observed, his hands clenched tightly behind his back, his eyes examining his charges as they stood stiffly in the cold. According to rumors, their new leader had arrived only two weeks ago from even farther east. But no one knew for sure, and no one had the ability—or courage—to inquire further.

Ten more minutes passed and at last the roll call finished. Soon everyone standing in the square would be free. As the season moved deeper and deeper into autumn, the cold became increasingly difficult to tolerate. The women sought nothing more than to be dismissed to begin the day's work, to bustle to the warmth and distraction of the factory.

Natasha glanced up and down the ranks seeking the whereabouts of her friends, Rachel and Lara. Their companionship was a critical source of solace for her. Every morning, following the roll call, Natasha would look forward to walking with them among the crowded rush, on their way to work. Not living in the same huts, their stroll gave them the chance to ask about each other's evenings, what letters from home they had received, camp gossip, or unsanctioned news from the front that had slipped through the censors. This morning, as luck would have it, both of Natasha's friends stood in formation two rows behind her. There would be no need to push or shove to get close to them once the formation broke up, no surreptitious loitering near the factory exit in the cold morning awaiting their appearance.

As the Assistant Troupe Leader finished calling out the names, Natasha turned her head slightly to the right peering discreetly back toward her friends. They stood, looking straight ahead, until her eyes caught theirs. Lara and Rachel broke half-smiles in a good-morning greeting, a sign that all was okay, that the normality of the world would remain as such, at least for another day. Natasha grinned back. The warm feelings and comfort she felt from their simple acknowledgements launched a kaleidoscope of memories and impressions from the first moments she had met them...

The long ride, seven days and nights bracing herself against the wooden benches of the railway car as the locomotive rumbled over the rough tracks. Stops, both scheduled and unscheduled, every so often breaking up the monotonous passage. Hours after the sun set for the third time upon lands Natasha had never seen, swirling fear and apprehension transmogrified again, as they had every night since she was corralled onto the rusting carriage, into the unholy spirits asking pointed questions not only about the future, but about the past. The sudden departure from her home, the one she at last had begun to create with Arkady, jolted her violently from the peace finally settling within her soul. Each night on the train, she could not help but recall the hurried and stoic goodbye of her husband as he, reacting to the sound of the Sergeant's voice outside, grabbed his hat and jacket off the bed and strode toward the door, swiftly pulling it closed behind him. The man she had come to trust and rely on, now departed, his presence disappearing into the chaotic sounds of engines roaring, people yelling farewells, and children crying far below their flat. Why, after everything, could Arkady not look into her eyes one last time? Why could he not release the same tears onto his face that flowed so freely down hers? Alone, surrounded by women she did not know, racing toward an outpost located deep within a region she had never dreamed of traveling, these questions tormented her.

As it had many times already on the journey east, the train suddenly began to slow. Natasha pressed her nose against the window, eager for distraction from the tedium. Outlined by four dim lamps blinking erratically, the small station's platform was covered with sleeping bodies and luggage arranged in disorganized patterns. The train's whistle blew as it crept into the station, causing the bodies to stir then stand. Officials donned in military attire barked orders. The previously slumbering bodies now quickly collected their things, then formed into groups, all while trying to decipher their superiors' orders through the pitch-black night and freezing temperatures.

The train jerked to a halt. Its attendants swung open each car's wooden doors, one at the front, one at the back. Natasha watched as chaos ensued on the platform outside. What was supposed to be an orderly embark onto the train quickly turned into a lively, if not quite dangerous, contest. Those in front trying to board were quickly shoved aside by others right behind. Belligerent warnings rang out as elbows jabbed in aggressive bids for the limited seats in the dusty interiors. Cries of frustrated despair filled the air by the losers of any tiny space claimed in the crowded compartment. Natasha examined the newcomers closely. Most possessed dazed, erratic expressions, as if they had been wrongly assigned, as if all of this was just one big mistake.

Amongst the faces, all different, yet all the same, one woman caught Natasha's attention. Nearly the last to board, and about Natasha's age, the woman had brown hair and thick glasses. She appeared bookish, cerebral even, her eyes scanning with hopeless incredulity the scene on the train, as if it reflected not merely the survival-of-the-fittest mentality that had descended on the present situation, but said something larger about the general havoc recently heaped upon mankind by the war. She entered the carriage cautiously through the rear door, carrying only two bags in comparison to the allotted three by the rest of the women. She too began searching for space, a place where she could sit and sleep, a place where she could temporarily exist while hoping for something better at the end of the tracks. But unable to find a seat, and with the train picking up speed, the woman sat, settling amongst the mess of hurriedly loaded baggage piled in the back of the car. Natasha studied this woman, sitting eerily still among a sea of tears, disheveled voices, and harrowed faces. She appeared a secluded island to herself. Leaning lightly against her bag, crossing her arms close against her chest, she stared into the distance, seemingly now immune to the surrounding chaos. Her eyes eventually shut, yet even in her sleep Natasha detected in the woman's expression a tired and exhausted uneasiness— perhaps experiencing unsettling nightmares, similar to those which tortured Natasha.

In the frigid dark carriage, rattling harder as it gained speed, Natasha rose from her carved-out space, pushed through the others to where the woman slept, and sat down on the floor beside her. Leaning against her, Natasha drew a blanket around them both. The woman shuddered, but her uneasiness seemed to dissipate. And, for the first time since Arkady had left, Natasha slept without dreams, without the visions of the door closing behind her husband, without mixing up the sound of the train for the sound of the transports that carried him far away from her.

The next morning, the woman was already awake when Natasha opened her eyes, motionless despite the weight of Natasha's head on her shoulder. As Natasha approached consciousness, she suddenly remembered the events of the previous night and lifted her head, embarrassed.

"I'm so sorry!" she said, sitting upright. "It's just you looked so cold sitting here on the floor last night."

"No, no. Thank you. I appreciate it," the woman replied shyly, plucking at the blanket covering their laps. She quickly put her glasses on and pushed her thick brown hair off her shoulders. She looked the other way, as if expecting silence to ensue, marking the end of the brief gesture of goodwill.

"I'm Natasha, by the way."

The woman's eyes lit up. A reserved smile appeared on her face. "And I'm Rachel."

She spoke softly, but Natasha felt a new aura of warmth emanating from Rachel, one not of the physical variety which they had shared the night before, but of a deeper form, a kind kindled then further strengthened by the tinder of hardship, trials, loneliness, or loss. And when the two women arrived at the bleak outpost four days later, even though they were assigned to different living quarters, they never sought the intimate friendship from others they had established between each other.

That is, until a few months later when, from beyond the western horizon, a new train arrived, offering up to the factory fresh looks of confusion, salted eyes from dried tears, and minds lately haunted by dark spirits taking form in the wake of shock.

"I need volunteers for a special detail this afternoon," the Assistant Troupe leader announced, walking briskly onto the factory floor one afternoon without warning. "We were just informed that a train will be arriving in one hour. It will be carrying around three hundred of our comrades. We require assistance organizing them at the station, carrying their bags, and then showing them to their living quarters. You'll be excused from the floor for the remainder of the day."

He stopped and waited for any show of hands. Rachel and Natasha both looked at each other. For months trains had arrived from all corners of western Russia, and at all hours. Some carried in their wagons only supplies, machines, tools, equipment. But most bore upon their wheels passengers, more workers whose hands would soon dive into the dull but monotonous arts of metallurgic craftsmanship. Yet over the past few weeks, train arrivals slowed to mere trickles, sporadically appearing with an increasingly inadequate inventory, perhaps reflecting shortages experienced by the rest of the Soviet Union in nearly every sector. The teams which had been dedicated full time to meeting the trains were disbanded, sent back to the factories or other workshops. Thus, hastily organized platoons were formed whenever a train was announced to be approaching.

Natasha was anxious for a change of pace, and she knew Rachel was, too. Activity away from the noisy machines, grating smells, and the incessant standing hurting their feet and stiffening their legs, would lighten their spirits. Besides, both were curious about the new, state-of-the-art train station. Finally complete, it was lauded by their leaders as a marvel of unmatched accomplishment, mimicking Moscow's metro stations.

These stations, in particular, held a personal interest to Natasha. Her father had been among the earliest artisans to assist in crafting the elaborate edifices that made up their interiors. Before he returned home suddenly from Moscow in 1937—a return still inexplicable to Natasha—his numerous and improbable artistic feats shaping stone, wood, and marble ensembles deep underground had resulted in a reputation that, amongst his peers, was without equal. On his surface, he was a simple man, with sensibilities and tastes imbued by practical experience, not a formal education. However, Natasha always sensed something deeper, a driving, incorporeal force inspiring a genius to his creations. Perhaps it was for this reason that his work was often looked on with suspicion by the authorities. Natasha understood her father. She knew that the forces influencing his style did not originate from the ideological precepts of the Party. Although he adhered to the guidelines set forth by the metro's architects, his work was not mechanical or mundane. On the contrary, when she had heard others consider his work, they described it as spiritual, sublime craftsmanship, the type that could only be fashioned by one who acknowledged the existence of the divine. His tools were those of the carpenter, the sculptor, but the true blades that sawed wood and chiseled stone were metaphysical, unseen.

Since first stepping off the train, touching her feet upon Siberia's soil, Natasha had felt her father near her, the arid cold seemingly acting as a conduit between her, the living, and his wandering spirit. In moments of solitude she would scan the horizon, observing how the buildings of the factory city stood out gargantuanly against the flatness of the surrounding terrain. In the process of observing these monstrous structures, Natasha's father would appear on the wind, his voice speaking in his usual, sometimes brusque tone, telling her exactly what he thought of the edifice standing before her. His presence, at times, had become so animate, that Natasha had even once mentioned it to Rachel, knowing her friend had studied the region before arriving. What was it that made this inhospitable land so spiritually penetrating? Why did it seem to reach into the depths of her soul, pulling out from its farthest and most inaccessible reaches feelings, thoughts, emotions? Rachel, without more than a quick glance into Natasha's eyes, had merely replied with a poem:

In Siberia's wastes
The ice-wind's breath
Woundeth like the toothed steel;
Lost Siberia doth reveal
Only blight and death.

Pain as in a dream,
When years go by
Funeral-paced, yet fugitive,
When man lives, and doth not live.
Doth not live—nor die.

The two women had discussed nothing more about the phenomenon since.

The pervasive metro stations—spread like hives throughout Moscow—had just been finished before the war. Their massive granite statues, depicting the glories of the working class, the wall-to-wall marble floors and pillars, and the glass chandeliers hanging elegantly from the underground ceilings, had been the talk of the country. The stations were hailed as authentic Soviet achievements, not only in the architectural, but also ideological, sense. At last the luxuries reserved for the aristocracy had been transported from beyond gated courtyards and palaces, delivered directly to where the common man dwelt—in the agricultural communes, the factories, at the train stations. These were the new castles, the palaces of the proletariat, and what had been done in Moscow was replicated throughout other cities—and now here, deep in Siberia, even in the midst of war.

The Assistant Troupe Leader, dour, scowling, waited for his volunteers. He would not wait much longer. Natasha and Rachel stole a quick glance at each other, and smiled, nodding. Enthusiastically, they raised their hands, and were soon joining a large formation filing quickly beyond the gates of the city.

Since their arrival, neither had stepped beyond the confines of their urban sanctuary. Now, departing through the fence, they both witnessed the stark exposure of the vast Siberian plain.

As she marched with the others along the broad, recently dug gravel road, Natasha spied a blue-tinged building about a kilometer away.

"It's small," she heard a whisper in her ear, as she hurriedly approached the station's facade. It was her father, appearing out of the aridness sweeping past her face. "But just as striking on the outside as the anecdotes suggested."

The train had not yet arrived, so along with many others, Natasha took a few minutes to duck inside the station's grand hall to take in all that she could.

Gilded with gold paint and the ceilings dripping with glass and brass chandeliers, the elaborate ornamentation injected into this construction stood in stark relief to the grey and drab urban encampment a short distance away. Pillars supporting the hall's heavy ceiling protruded triumphantly up from a polished stone floor, as paintings stretched above in Sistine-like form celebrated four scenes: first, Lenin's April 1917 return from revolutionary exile to St. Petersburg concealed in a train car; second, his famous speech from the balcony of Kshesinskaya Palace urging the Russian proletariat to unite, rebel, and overthrow the liberal government; third, the storming of the Tsar's winter palace by the Bolsheviks, formally ending all other governments but their own; and at last a scene depicting the building of the Communist ideal, the worker's earthly heaven, a project still in motion but powered by advanced factories, plentiful fields, and smiling faces. Above these series of paintings, looking confident and assured, approving of all occurring below them, were three massive profiles of Karl Marx, Lenin, and Stalin. The philosophical lineage, which this portrayal of the Communist Trinity sought to establish, could not be clearer. Natasha stood in wonder.

"It is indeed beautiful," she heard her father say. Natasha never saw him, but felt his presence in the glittering of crystal, and in the sparkling reflection of shiny stones and smooth marble. "But this is typical of our architects. As intended, whoever arrives here will be led to believe this is a portal to something grand, something much bigger than what it actually is."

Natasha heeded what sounded like a warning from her father, prompting her to reflect on the city itself: its expansion, growth, the new construction projects beginning every day, doing so, even somehow, with a severe lack of supplies and manpower. Maybe it would one day live up to the aspirations of this architectural masterpiece. Maybe, one day, the city would reflect accurately the ambitions of its creators whose images sprawled across the ceiling, those revered and holy men imbued by the station's artists with insight, wisdom, and an understanding of an eternal truth concerning the arc of history and destiny of mankind.

"But it would take a miracle to build something so incredible out here, Father. It would take thousands more workers than what we have now. And," Natasha whispered in her mind, invisible shudders running along her spine, "someone with a will more ruthless than I would care to know."

"This way! Out onto the platform! The train is only two minutes away!" Natasha's father faded away into the chandeliers and paintings, while the volunteers all scurried outside at the sound of the command.

In the distance, the locomotive's steam plume appeared. On the flat desert, devoid of anything but the mountains on the horizon, multiple red flags sporting the yellow hammer and sickle fluttered along the sides of the train, a bright contrast against the surrounding greys. As the locomotive pulled in, the colors seemed to meld perfectly with the elaborate new station itself. The final piece of the puzzle had arrived.

Natasha stood on the platform, peering into each train window as it slowly passed. Finally halted, staring back at her were expressions she recognized—worried, frightened, vacant. But no matter which face, which person, all were exhausted. One by one the new arrivals disembarked, bags in hand, eyes searching, trying to quickly gather as much information of their surroundings as possible, struggling to put their minds at ease, convincing themselves that their situations were not as horrible as they could have been.

"And these women are seeing the best their new home has to offer," she thought with a sense of irony. The lavish station was far from emblematic of the factory itself, to say nothing of where they would eat, wash, and sleep.

Loud voices sounding like a heated argument interrupted her scrutiny. She nudged Rachel and the two of them hurried to the end of the platform to investigate.

"Please, I'm not a factory worker!" The high-pitched wail bordered on a shriek.

"I'm sorry, but this is how everyone is initially assigned." This voice carried overtones of years of tried patience stretched thin. "You'll be screened later for any special skills, and you can make your case then."

Natasha and Rachel pushed through the last of the crowd blocking their view. No more than twenty years old, a young woman with blond hair and an attractive figure glared at one of the senior women responsible for organizing new arrivals into their assigned troupes. The older woman waved them over, as if jumping at the opportunity to immediately unload this troublesome girl onto someone else entirely.

"Natasha, this is Lara. She'll be assigned to your troupe. Help her with her things and let her know where to go." The lady marched away toward another group of women wandering aimlessly around. Lara stared at her back, looking despondent. Her argument, whatever it was, had failed. She threw a crestfallen glance at Natasha, who smiled at her gently.

"Here, let me take that for you," Natasha said, taking hold of Lara's suitcase. Rachel grabbed a second suitcase, and Lara clutched her handbag to her waist. Without saying a word, the three traversed the platform and re-entered the grand hall.

"Just wait here," Natasha told Lara. "We have to go help others, but this is where our group will be assembling." Lara nodded her head compliantly, and Natasha followed Rachel again pushing into the noisy crowd.

Another two weeks passed before Natasha and Rachel again came into direct contact with Lara. Every morning at roll call, every afternoon at lunch, and every evening at dinner, they would see the beautiful, young girl from afar. She was always by herself, but not because she repelled others away from her, nor because she was unpleasant to be around. On the contrary, she was radiant, and her youthfulness should have been a welcome and contagious attribute to the dreariness saturating the camp. But those things that should have worked in her favor seemed to work against her, particularly with the women. Lara's beauty inspired disdain, jealousy. The way that the few men in the camp paid her attention incited unwarranted gossip, especially considering the strict regulations in place governing the interactions between the sexes. So Lara kept to herself.

Natasha had also learned the source of the argument that captured her attention on the day Lara arrived. Prior to the war, the young woman's intentions were to become a nurse. But the lack of any formal training had resulted in her simply getting swept up with everyone else, pushed onto the train, and sent east. Despite that, her determination had not faltered. Each and every day she petitioned to be sent to the medical ward, intent that the war not interrupt her life as it had interrupted countless others. This relentlessness of purpose also contributed to the suspicions surrounding her. In an environment already ripe with incertitude, Natasha often overheard speculative mutterings about exactly what Lara was capable of doing to achieve her goals.

But as the days had worn on, growing colder and greyer, Natasha noticed Lara's demeanor changing in much the same way. There was still a fire burning in her eyes, a desire to get out of the factory and realize her passions. But her beauty was fading, her outward characteristics fleeting. The ferocity and independence underlying her drive softened. To Natasha it was if she was witnessing Lara the young, Lara the kind, Lara the optimistic, die. Shortly all that would be left would be the Lara others already shunned. She would have nothing left of her humanity, nothing left of her warmth. The camp, the factory, this land, would have defeated her. It would capture her soul, another victim to the hopeless spirits stalking the night, infiltrating their moments of stillness and solitude. So Natasha befriended her. First through small steps—a simple hello in the morning, an invitation to eat together, finding her before and after formations.

Soon Rachel followed Natasha's lead, and very naturally the three women blended together, each complementing the others in ways they had not imagined, yet often talked about, as friends tend to do once absolute trust is established. After all, they posited during their frequent discussions, are human beings ever truly aware of the myriad spiritual and emotional gaps unknowingly plaguing souls, souls dimensionally infinite? Are human beings ever fully cognizant of what can be discovered and learned about themselves until they have discovered friendship, partnership, love? The three women, in hardship, admitted that to be left alone was to die. Without the embrace of others, without embracing others, their demise would be assured. Here, amidst the loneliness and harsh Siberian landscape, that demise would be made all the quicker and more pronounced. Each possessed attributes the others spiritually and emotionally fed upon.

Rachel was intelligent, curious, but also quiet and restrained. Upon learning she would be sent deep within Siberia, Rachel had read every book about the region she could find, eventually assembling her own small library she had thrown into her couple of bags before she departed. She studied its geography, languages, native tribes, and became familiar with Russia's multiple excursions in attempts to tame it. Yet for all her knowledge, Rachel remained insecure. Awkward and restrained around other people—especially men—she was at times in a world unto herself.

Lara, so beautiful and charismatic, so daring! She was the opposite of Rachel in many respects. Opinionated, but not rash. Lively and humorous, but not ignorant. Her intelligence was evident in the questions she asked and the keen observations she made regarding human feeling and emotion. But still veiled in youth and inexperience, her intelligence had not yet matured into wisdom.

And Natasha viewed herself as the steady one; a stable anchor planted firmly against an ocean of raging and sometimes violent change. To Rachel and Lara, Natasha made sure she exhibited a stoic exterior in which nothing seemed to affect her; she used her fierce gaze to pierce into another's soul. Positioned on either side of Natasha, Rachel and Lara respected her as an otherworldly being who was a sure ally in this other-worldly place...

Pulling herself away from her musings, Natasha's memories receded into the morning clouds, pushed by an unusual sight taking place before her on the platform. Instead of the typical dismissal following the roll call, the Assistant Troupe Leader remained at the podium, his hand raised in the familiar motion for silence. Natasha caught her breath. Was he about to announce another round of the casualty postings? Her heart hammered. How could this day, when everything seemed to be going so right, now go so wrong? Imagining the worst, nausea swept over her. Her hands trembled so hard she gripped the sides of her workpants to quell the tremors.

Out of the corner of her eye she saw movement along the far side of the troupe. Turning her head slightly to the left, she caught a glimpse of David, their young commander, making his way towards the front. She followed his path with her gaze as he strode forward. David appeared nervous, as if consciously trying to contain his apprehension by walking straighter than normal, which left his arms swaying awkwardly and out of natural step with his legs. His attention stayed fixed on the small stage ahead, the one that he had to mount, the one from which he would be forced to look out over his charges and tell them whatever the camp's regime required he tell them in person this morning. Would he exude confidence, an honesty that would be infectious to everyone, giving them hope that now, at last, victory might be at hand? Or would his voice quiver? Would his eyes betray a sense of guilt saying things he knew to be exaggerated or untrue?

"A few words now from Comrade David before we begin the day's work," the Assistant Troupe Leader stated matter-of-factly, and he looked to his right. David climbed the stairs, a small sheet of notes in his fingers. There was nothing in his movements that signaled any emotion whatsoever—no fear, but no confidence either. His movements were robotic, lifeless...dead. He stepped to the center of the platform without even acknowledging his Assistant. Natasha subtly glanced back to Rachel and Lara. They were both looking straight ahead; curiosity and anticipation laced their faces. Their eyes met Natasha's, and their brows peaked upward as if to say "let's wait and see." Natasha tipped her chin down in brief acknowledgement, relieved that the threat of possibly learning the fate of Arkady, at least for now, had passed.

"Comrades," David began, glancing down at his notes then raising his scrutiny in deliberate fashion at the crowd. Natasha thought she saw his hands slightly tremble as he took in the vast expanse of the courtyard and the workers in front of him, a sort of disquiet that he was fighting to overcome.

He continued. "This is an important day for our Army, and our cause. I am pleased to report that our brave citizens and soldiers of Marshall Stalin's namesake city have turned the tide on the enemy. They have successfully occupied new forward positions in Stalingrad after much sacrifice, pushing the enemy to the brink of retreat into the southern Caucasus. Additionally..." David paused as if he was catching his breath from just accomplishing something momentous, something that took every ounce of his courage to complete.

"Additionally!" David exclaimed with a forced sense of the urgency. "Our comrades-in-arms in Leningrad are making daily progress against the vicious siege of our motherland! I...I have been authorized to tell you that Comrade Stalin himself has proclaimed that the tide of the war has turned, and...and any day now we will expel the fascists from our homeland, and chase them with a vengeance all the way to Berlin."

A robotic "hoorah!" broke out from the crowd, apparently unconvinced of his sincerity. Natasha and her fellow workers had heard variations of this multiple times before: hazy details about progress in the urban sieges, general proclamations about unspecified heroic deeds, and aspirational statements about "expelling" Germans from the Soviet Union. There was nothing new here. Soon they would all be ordered to the factory, just like every morning. The cycle would begin again.

"He's failing," Natasha thought. She watched as David scanned the crowd, searching, perhaps, for a sign that he was breaking-through. But there was only dutiful quiet. Plainly, the workers were eager to be dismissed, ready to get on with the day understanding that nothing had changed. The future still remained cloudy and unforeseeable, the spirits busily planting doubts in minds would continue to roam freely.

Patiently waiting for the predictable final—and usually rousing—call to arms and subsequent dismissal, Natasha surreptitiously rubbed her hands to warm them. She would soon be talking with her friends, the warmth of the factory and its machines foremost in their minds. But just as quickly as David had opened his mouth, he snapped it shut. His gaze had settled on something, something in Natasha's vicinity. She ceased her movements and stared obediently ahead, wondering just for an instant if his eyes were fixated on her. Still staring in her direction, he shoved the paper inside his coat in a smooth movement and withdrew steady hands, fingers now unclenched. His whole demeanor had altered. He relaxed into the pose she expected from someone of his height, looks, and position. Confidence seemed to wash over him, the seedling of a leader taking root before her eyes.

"Comrades," David said, his voice soaring unrestrained and certain. "The success of our brave soldiers on the front lines is truly significant. It is difficult to overstate just how much progress has been made. Everything you are doing here has contributed in countless ways. I—we—the leadership, are very proud of everything you have done. Together we surely are winning this war. And since this is such a cause for celebration, we have been authorized this evening additional rations and time off. I have informed your officers that our troupe will cease activity three hours early and together, as a single unit on the verge of victory, celebrate our collective accomplishment!"

Throughout his short but assured announcement, David had cast his eyes over the entire crowd before him. But as he shouted out his last sentence, as he let it be known that this evening they would all have true cause to be happy, his focus seemed to settle on Natasha again. She blushed.

The crowd cheered, this time enthusiastically. She too smiled in her gentle, but radiant way, and relaxed. The tension that had been building within her ever since she thought there was to be another round of the postings dissipated, and her spirit soared. Along with her co-workers, this time she felt assured that the truth had been spoken, and that their hopes would not again be dashed. At last, something new; someone in which to believe.

David walked smartly off the platform. The Assistant Troupe Leader finally yelled, "Everything for the front! Everything for victory![31] Dismissed!"

A single tear rolled down Natasha's cheek.

---

[31] "Everything for the front! Everything for victory!" (Все для фронта! Все для победы!) Most common call-to-arms for Soviet factory workers during World War II, utilized on posters, banners, and following speeches and important announcements.

CHAPTER 8

"Awake!"
"Awake!"
"Awake!"

The words throbbed and pounded on Arkady's consciousness, bringing him back into the world of the living. The Voice of soothing and comfort had returned, waking him once more from some ethereal maze, rapping on an incorporeal door, requesting entrance. But this time Arkady did not ask who it was, or what it wanted. He was content to let it knock, allowing it to revive his soul from the unbodied chasm into which it had been cast.

Arkady opened his mouth. Cold air coated his tongue, tickled his gums, irritated his teeth. He gasped for air and its life-affirming oxygen, coughed, spit up, and rolled over to one side. Blood trickled lightly down his forehead, sprinkling red dots onto the pristine snow encircling him in sparkling shades of coral from the dawn's rays.

As Arkady's awareness became more acute, vague impressions of what transpired the night before sharpened into distinct, and appalling focus. He remembered being pinned to the frozen ground. He remembered the old men, debating, arguing, looking him in the eyes as he felt their spirits enter the deepest recesses of his soul, searching for an abode they could inhabit, perhaps allowing them to cease their wandering. He remembered the Thrush sitting on the shoulder of their collective body.

His head was pounding, his breath heavy. Not only his body suffered, however. His entire being felt ripped open by what he had just experienced: a shock to the reality he had come to understand, an inexplicable and fantastic vision laying siege to every argument he had ever made against the unknowable. That look in Sasha's eyes, the cryptic way he had spoken of the Thrush, and of Siberia, as if it were a place beyond man's physical and material experiences. But what of its nature—good or evil? Why did Sasha not speak of that? The stars...circling in patterns, or in chaos?

Arkady groaned and struggled to sit up. Finally, he managed. Torso erect, arms bent, hands holding his thighs in an effort to steady himself and calm his dizziness. How did he get here? He recalled being restrained, the pressure on his chest, his legs halted, unable to move forward, until at last he had collapsed onto the ground. Then the old men had appeared. The seriousness in which they debated, and the haunting essence of their dialogue, came rushing back in full. Their words he could not hear, but nevertheless they had pierced his soul, and he had understood them.

He looked ahead, right, and left, remembering he was somewhere on the slopes of the Ural Mountains. But where exactly? How far had he come? In front of his extended legs the ground gradually ascended. If the mountains' peaks were in that direction, they were still lost in the early morning cloud cover. He could not tell how far he would have to go to finish crossing them. He was hungry, thirsty, his hands scarred from struggling, and his feet numb from inactivity in the freezing uplands. A horizontal sunbeam broke through a gap in the fortress-like granite to the east. Dotted by awnings of ice, the cliffs were periodically broken up by dead trees, their limbs hanging loosely like the flesh of the old men in his vision.

Suddenly a wind blasted down the slopes of the mountain with a ferociousness that seemed intentional. Hitting him in the face, the powerful gusts pushed him off balance. He tumbled backward like a ball farther down the slope, slamming against a rotting mangle of trees a few meters away. A new breeze gently wisped over his broken body. It seemed to be a stark message reminding Arkady that nature had dealt him another blow, crushing his will. Daring him to move.

Lying in agony, behind closed eyelids, Arkady catalogued his injuries once more, wondering if this time the cold would declare victory and the falling snow bury him for good. He heard a flutter, a flutter signifying life. He opened his eyes, squinting into the vastness angled above.

"The Thrush!" he exclaimed. But the enthusiasm of seeing another living creature was fleeting. After all, this was no ordinary bird. *"It has not flown here to remain idle…,"* Sasha had said.

"…the choice is yours," Arkady remembered the Voice saying.

"No, I'm done following you," he called out to the bird. "If I manage to get up, I will go my own way. I will make my own decisions. I am a free man! Free from this war! Free from God! Free from whatever it was that brought me here! Go away!"

Arkady's forehead twinged. Blood from the wound flowed freely across his nose and angled down his cheeks toward his jaw. The earth spun, and he vomited.

Raising his fist defiantly, he yelled, "Go away!"

The emotion was too much. He collapsed into the snow, and sunk once again into unconsciousness.

★

"Awake!"
"Awake!"
"Awake!"

"Who are you?"

Silence.

The sun beat bright on his face. Radiant light pierced his eyelids. Arkady blinked until he could open them fully. The snow had ceased falling while he had been out. Arkady welcomed the clear skies, along with the sunlight shining high overhead. This would give him an opportunity to progress, to move forward. How long had he been unconscious? As he looked around, still lying half-vertically in a glistening white hue, he found himself staring again directly into the eyes of the Thrush.

Anger raged through Arkady at the sight of the bird and electrified his limbs. "Unless you deliver me straight to my wife, even through death, leave me alone." He jerked his body into an upright position and jumped up.

"Go away!" he yelled.

The bird flew off. Arkady teetered, watching as it disappeared into the bushes below him.

"Hmmm." His heart sank, taken aback by the ease with which he scared it away. The bird's sudden flight seemed to Arkady to say, *"Okay. Have it your way…for now."*

A cold gust blew down from the faraway slopes. Arkady, his legs planted firmly in the snow, looked off in the distance, toward the west. The sky grew dark, darker than any winter storm he had ever seen. All hope-giving sunshine choked out of existence by swiftly gathering clouds. He could not wait any longer. Once again his only path was east, up, up, up into the peaks.

With a premonition of futility, Arkady scanned the ground nearby. His pack remained on his back, but his rifle had long since disappeared. A sense of vulnerability enveloped him—no protection, no shelter, his will and the freedom to make choices seemed not even his own. He had arrived here, on the edge of the Ural Mountains, through circumstances designed by another dimension, and now he was completely exposed, helpless.

Yet...

...could he still not choose left or right? Backward or forward?

"These are simple movements, simple decisions, but still mine," he said to himself.

If he were allowed these freedoms, as basic as they were, then did he not still possess a will of his own? *"...the choice is yours,"* he remembered again the Voice of comfort proclaiming.

Arkady headed to the slope, retracing his chaotic path of stumbles and falls. Perhaps he would find his rifle, maybe shelter, wait out the storm, and then the answer would be clearer about what to do, where to go.

He hurried back up the mountain, racing against the accelerating storm gathering pace behind him. The edge of the blizzard soon engulfed him, wind gusts wrapping around him in circular, tornado-like fashion. He persisted putting one step in front of the other as fast as his mangled body allowed.

There! In one of the overhanging cliffs above, he spotted a cave. He stumbled as he ascended, slipping on the ice, falling onto sharp rocks. The sky grew dark with a ferocity Arkady had never before seen. He struggled to right himself and crawled on all four limbs up the side of the mountain, chased by powerful forces as if he were an animal being corralled, rounded up for eventual slaughter.

Despite losing sight of the cave in the swirling storm, Arkady continued his forward march undeterred, like the trained soldier he had become, led only by faith that his eyes had not deceived him. Deep pockets of snow felt like lead shackles around his legs, the drifts threatening to imprison him forever. He struggled free step after step, using his hands like shovels.

The cliff! The cave! At last! A shelter, a refuge from everything harnessing in concert against him. Arkady crawled forward with renewed vigor. He clung to the rocks jutting out around the opening, searching for footing, testing their strength. Although sharp, dangerous, and foreboding, to him they were saviors.

Arkady collapsed under the overhang, still facing the storm but away from its icy reach. He breathed heavily. Thirsty, starving, but relieved to be safe, free from the blistering storm's torture, free from succumbing to the will of the old men, even free from the Thrush. With a silent thrill, he applauded this small, but important victory.

He rolled over and peered into the cave's darkness. As his eyes adjusted, he could see it did not run deep. Black and grey rock walls sprang up around him in gothic form, as if he had stumbled into a cathedral still under construction, one not occupied by the Divine, an empty soul not yet adorned with the vibrant images of Saints, nor depictions of their kind acts and good deeds. Instead of climaxing into beautiful stained glass, the cave's ceiling descended gradually toward the rear, where it fully melded into the mountain's bulk. Water, collecting above, dripped down knife-like stalactites, forming icy puddles on the stony ground. But compared to what was raging outside, this dark, damp, and cold cell was paradise.

Arkady lifted himself onto his aching knees. Removing his pack, he laid it beside him. As the burden was lifted, he felt an object poke into his chest. His hands, shaking, felt inside his coat and touched the small icon of the crucifixion Sasha had given him. For the first time since departing the site of the ambush, he took it out. Memories of his friend lying outstretched in the blood-spotted snow bombarding him, he peered through the gloom at the figure stretched out on the cross. Christ stared, not at the heavens, but on the mourners below.

As Arkady contemplated the ancient figurine, visions of the old philosophers rushed back. Those decrepit men had also looked downward. Gazing at Arkady, the spirits had pierced his soul, grabbing hold of him, forcing him to remain locked into the frozen ground while they debated the currents of history, plotting their next move, rationalizing their interference, and their use of him—an innocent soldier—in their schemes. Did these mourners, staring up at Christ below his bleeding feet, feel the same sense of spiritual penetration as Arkady had beneath those who represented Russia's thought, tragic past, soul? And if they did, was the feeling one of foreboding, or was it relief, perhaps even freedom? After all, the old men peered down at Arkady from lofty positions of strength. Christ, on the other hand, looked down upon those mourning Him as one who was dying, bleeding on a cross. Crucified by the powerful.

He knew the stories behind this personage. Arkady's mother, despite everything, had remained devoted to her faith. Swept away by the famine, a force of unimaginable decimation birthed by the same forces responsible for driving her beliefs underground, she had never relented. The wooden church she had attended as a young girl was eventually turned into a barn. Like so many other places of worship and veneration, it became, under the Soviet government, disused, desecrated by filthy, starving animals, its original purpose lost to a long-ago age. An age forgotten, dead, similar to many of those who refused to renounce their religious beliefs.

Arkady recalled the story behind the scene depicted on the icon. Backed by an empire, high priests, convinced they possessed a truth that only they had the authority to enforce, condemned Christ to death. Their vanity cloaked in the language of righteousness, these men were intent on not allowing anything—not even a humble carpenter—to penetrate the powerful dominion they had created on behalf of themselves. In any conventional sense, nailed to the cross, Christ, just like Arkady's mother, had been defeated. What good, then, was this ancient symbol? If Christ could not save himself, if he could not save Arkady's mother despite her fervent devotion, what was the point of believing in Him?

Gripping the crucifix tighter, Arkady lumbered to his feet. He stretched his arm out behind him, fully prepared to cast it away, convincing himself that by doing so it would lighten his load, and even the tiniest alleviation would help him traverse the mountains. After all, it was just another worthless relic that, in the face of horrific events, had proved its fallacy.

He hesitated.

True, Christ may have been defeated. His mother may have been naïve, even devastatingly wrong. The crucifix may have meant nothing. But had Christ not fought the very forces against which he was now struggling? To throw this symbol away seemed in this moment to acquiesce yet again to the Thrush and all that was behind it.

He dropped his arm.

If nothing more, keeping the icon would spite those whom he now so despised. He tucked the figurine back inside his overcoat and again lay on the frigid, stone surface. Weariness, exhaustion overcame him, and he was soon asleep.

★

"Awake!"
"Awake!"
"Awake!"

Arkady sat up with a start at the familiar, formless pounding still with him.

"Who are you?"

Silence.

Beckoning stars shone brightly through the cave entrance—a reassuring indication that the storm had passed. Precipitation dripped from the ceiling in faster cadence and collected into deep puddles. He scooped water into his mouth, quenching a thirst that had steadily grown into a tortuous burn. Yet a gnawing hunger now took over. With stark awareness he soon would become too weak to escape the mountains, he picked up his pack and walked out into the night, the icon of the crucifixion snug and secure in his coat.

Once outside the cave, the wind blew gently from above. Arkady started climbing the slope. Step by step, stone by stone, he made his way higher and higher.

A group of trees blocked his path, and he picked his way around them.

A rock cliff unexpectedly appeared in front of him; he felt his way for a safe route to the other side.

For five hours in the dead of night he attempted to traverse this granite labyrinth. At times he felt he had found a path. But then, to his disappointment, the path would dead-end at a junction blocked by fallen rocks, or another would invite to him to fall into a deep abyss, and he would have to reverse his steps. No matter which direction he turned, he always seemed to be going opposite of where he wanted.

The sun rose, finally shedding bright light on his predicament, and he again spotted possible shelter in the distance. His feet, scarred and numb from constant pounding against the frozen earth, carried him swiftly toward the overhang. But when he arrived at its entrance, his heart sank.

"The same cave!"

The same drab and ragged grey walls, meeting unceremoniously in a shallow roof near the back; the same puddle he had drank from earlier, still slowly deepening from the water dripping above. He sighed and sank onto his hips.

"First the storm, now a maze of rocks, cliffs, and forests."

Arkady decided to rest only an hour. He would try again when the sun was at its peak, when no shadows could confuse him. Perhaps this time he would find a sure path, one that would lead him safely through the mountains. He slept restlessly, images of the past few days mixing into his dreams.

A light thumping stirred him awake. He opened his eyes and there the Thrush stood in front of him, its head jerking in curious fashion, but his gaze fixated nonetheless on Arkady.

"Have you had enough?" Arkady imagined it saying. *"Are you ready to follow my lead? There is no way out for you. There is no path to victory. You are a lost ship in a raging and stormy sea, a fallen leaf carried by the wind."*

"No," Arkady answered out loud. "I have not had enough!"

Propelling himself off the ground, he grabbed his pack, threw it around his shoulder, and ferociously started ascending. This time when he saw an outcropping, he immediately found a way around it. This time when the way seemed too steep, too sheer, he ran to the next available path. Every so often he would look behind him, expecting to see the Thrush following, taunting him every time he turned his head. But he never saw the shadow from its wings, nor its frantic profile against the horizon.

After another few hours, Arkady looked up. The peaks appeared no closer. He had still not passed the timber line, the altitude where the mightiest and strongest trees are unable to survive. In fact, if he were to be honest with himself, it seemed he had accomplished nothing but sideways movement, perhaps even descending a few meters in the process. Incessant hunger swelled within him. The cold bit at his hands, fingers, ears, legs, and feet. He looked off to the west. Once again clouds were gathering ominously. Another storm on the way.

Arkady sighed. There was no way out, no way around.

"Maybe if I follow the Thrush at least I will avoid permanent suffering; pain of the kind that will affect whatever life I might eventually have with Natasha."

The storm grew closer.

"I relent!" he cried out.

At least by submitting he would preserve himself. And was not preservation a form of resistance in itself? Wasn't survival a form a victory?

As if sensing his thoughts, the wind slammed against his face, and out of the blackness of the approaching storm appeared the Thrush. It flew directly overhead, not even stopping to look him straight in the eyes, to taunt him in his defeat.

Arkady gripped his pack straps, holding them tightly around his shoulders. Staring at the bird floating away into the distance, a clear path momentarily opened before him, zigzagging first to a cave—a new cave—for shelter from the coming storm, before finally winding headlong up into the peaks of the Ural Mountains.

No longer surprised by anything he saw or experienced, Arkady trudged as quickly as he could to the shelter, and fell into a deep sleep. He rested easily, certain that upon waking, his uncommon journey would begin once more.

He had lost this battle, but more were sure to come before the Thrush, or the old men, could declare a definitive victory.

CHAPTER 9

The hand-delivered message arrived shortly following morning formation. After reading the distinct cursive, David sat motionless. He stared at a worn, tired photograph in an old frame atop the small, wood stove standing in the corner of his room, deep in thought. His meager living space was one of ten located in the large hut reserved for the Troupe Leaders, the hut itself having been purposefully isolated from the living spaces of the workers. The Troupe Leaders' quarters were meant to inspire a relaxed atmosphere, an environment that encouraged socialization amongst the leadership, where informal debates on everything ranging from prospects for a victorious conclusion to the war, plans for the camp's rapid expansion, and strategies for increased production, were to occur, resulting, ideally, in coordination and collaboration. According to the camp Commandant, the arrangement was intended to foster unity, a spirit of collective responsibility, and mutual accountability.

David had noticed nothing of the sort after his arrival only two weeks ago. At first, he thought he was being shunned because he was new, an outsider. But as time went on, as his attempts to engage his peers in conversation, to speak with them, to eat with them, were rebutted, he observed that this was not a phenomenon restricted to relations having solely to do with him. On the contrary, in the long, smoky hut, all the doors to the private rooms typically remained shut, the main hall always quiet, except when the various Assistant Troupe Leaders and other trusted senior cadre members would make their way to their respective leaders' rooms. Only between these men did David notice true comradery, and only within this group was real work accomplished, each crafting plans of their own handiwork regardless of what the other Troupes were doing. When a conflict arose, it was not resolved between the Troupe Leaders on a personal basis. It was resolved by Koslov, one of two Commandants charged with overseeing every aspect of the camp's functions, production, and growth.

Since arriving at this outpost David had not spied Koslov, let alone been summoned to meet him. This meant David had not been asked formally about his background, about how, at such a young age, he had achieved the lofty appointment, nor asked about his ambitions following the war. However, this came as no surprise to David; he did not wonder about why he had been ignored by the Commandant. To him the reason was obvious, written in large letters across his face, his back, and in others' expressions. Everywhere he went inspired looks from others that spoke loudly back: *"You do not belong here. You do not deserve your position."* And in his heart, David too acknowledged that truth. He was nobody, at least in his own right. At this point in his life, he had grown used to these attitudes, yet he still deeply resented them. They were attitudes that many in his situation faced, a struggle which only those born privileged could relate. It was a struggle that he had so far failed to win. His natural timidity, his reluctance to step outside the protective shadow under which he had dwelt for so long, time and again prevented him from doing anything of real consequence, playing into the disparaging and suspicious eyes that cast those silent judgments into stark relief against his own false sense of importance. Humiliating, but unavoidably true.

During this morning's formation, though, he had felt a new sensation. Standing before his workers, looking into their cold, wind-scrubbed faces, eager to hear a fresh pronouncement— perhaps that a life-altering event had occurred, that the Red Army was truly making real progress against the Germans— something ignited within his otherwise timorous soul. For the first time in his life David had felt powerful, as if he was finally in a position to do something really important, something for his country; and emerge out from behind his father, whose reputation followed him wherever he went.

While standing on the stage he desired to be eloquent above all else, to be the inspirational leader rallying those in his command. But at the critical moment, just when he had thought he had at last found the courage he always wanted, he couldn't think of what to say! Stumbling in his mind, he started to panic, believing the words would not materialize on his lips. Once again, he would be laughed at behind his back! Scorned as the spoiled, untalented son of a towering figure who had made history in the Soviet Far East. But as this fear came rushing over him, his eyes met hers.

Those deep-set eyes were piercing, open doors. They were inviting entryways into an enticing and limitless soul. A desire for the opportunity to explore them further came rushing over him. In these few seconds, his longing for rejuvenation and belief, the longing for truth that he had felt collectively emanating from his troupe, became embodied completely within her gaze. Barely realizing what was happening, he had put his notes away and words slipped easily from his mouth. He transformed suddenly into what he had always wanted to be—an orator, a leader, a man. The sight of her became a divine spark igniting a passion, a drive, for something better than what he had known thus far in his life.

And how clever he had been! As the words rolled off his tongue, as they formed a parade of utterances so convincing and victorious that a surge of smiles emerged like a wave amongst the faces gazing in adoration, he crafted the perfect opportunity to meet her, the perfect opportunity to see if, face to face, she would inspire the same feelings in close proximity as the very sight of her had inspired in spirit.

David smiled nostalgically at the photograph in front of him. In it were two people: a man, and a fourteen-year-old boy. They stood erect facing the photographer, awkwardly together, yet seemingly far apart. Neither smiled. Their faces were as drab as the surroundings in which they stood, a backdrop of half-built buildings in a swampy and wooded wilderness. Mud caked the boots of both. The boy wore a simple dark cap to go along with his ashen-grey work clothes. The man, however, wore a uniform, adorned with multiple medals won during countless military campaigns. He stood in front of the newly constructed town like a General standing guard over a recently conquered city. He leaned on a shovel; his rifle slung like yet another victory medallion across his back. A side-arm pistol completed the tempestuous ensemble. The boy, in contrast, was empty-handed, appearing lost and directionless in a world not of his choosing, nor of his making.

Peering closer at the familiar images, David's smile vanished. "Okay, Father," he sighed. "I'm listening now."

He stood up, straightened his uniform, put on his heavy wool jacket, and walked out the door. Finally, Koslov had summoned him to his office. And after enduring the trial of hesitation and fear that had gripped him as he stood in front of his troupe that morning, and experiencing the sublime salvation from that ordeal through the eyes of this haunting woman, David felt prepared. Although his announcement to hold a social hour for his workers was severely against protocol, he had at last done something of his own initiative that merited attention.

★

David walked into the brisk autumn air and through a flurry of hovering white flakes. In the near distance, grey plumes rose from the factory's newly erected smokestacks. Machinery huffed, whistled, and grinded in subdued tones. Those everyday sounds, so different from what he had grown up with, still unsettled him. These noises, and the sights from which they emanated, were unnatural—man harvesting elements from the earth, molding and harnessing them to serve his own devices. All of this was curious to David, and he often questioned the purpose, its end, and, even more, his place in it all. In an environment intent on industrial growth, his status as an outsider seemed even more pronounced.

But over the course of his short time in the outpost, he had discovered at least one aspect about which he was confident he knew more than anyone else: human nature. Following his father around the plains, forests, and hills of Siberia, watching him corral the tribes of the steppes, break ground on brand new villages, and implement for the first time in history the precepts of Soviet ideology, he knew the limit to which man could be pushed. He had grown up recognizing the sight of hands that had reached the point of no longer feeling pain because thick callouses had all but replaced fingers. He recognized when legs, shaking uncontrollably after an exhausting day of work, would buckle. In addition to the sounds of the natural environment, David had grown accustomed to those of man. Groans, heavy sighs, cries of both agony and sorrow—he understood them all, where they originated from, their authenticity, and their meaning. And though self-conscious about his father's deserved reputation as the famous conqueror who extinguished the remnants of Tsar loyalists in Siberia, acclaimed as the settler who brought civilization to the uncivilized, David knew his own experiences were indurate, lasting lessons in hardship the majority of his contemporaries in the factory town now lacked. True, they were all Russians. But he was of a different land then they, raised in the midst of the bitterest elements the burgeoning Soviet Empire offered.

Unexpectedly, as he began his march towards Commandant Koslov's quarters, David heard a soft crunch behind him and spun around, startled. His Assistant Troupe Leader, Maximilian, must have been almost stepping on his boot heels, as he came to an abrupt halt mere inches from his superior.

David had met Maximilian the second day after he arrived, and his initial impressions of the man were flat. Maximilian did not smile in greeting. His first handshake was matter-of-fact, no warmth or personality attached to it. Given David had made no friends amongst the other Troupe Leaders, David's sense of Maximilian—indeed, everyone—depended not on gossip or hearsay, but merely on his own limited observations and interactions. As his assistant, Maximilian did what he was asked, usually before even being asked to do it. He was, in David's early estimation, efficient, reliable, organized. But he was also quiet, almost programmatic. In fact, David had never seen him laugh.

It unnerved David that Maximilian never engaged him in any conversation or asked him about his background. But the Assistant Troupe Leader was always waiting for David in the morning prior to the formation, waiting for him right after lunch to report on production, waiting for him before he turned in at night to discuss the day's results. Maximillian was always where he was supposed to be, at just the time he was supposed to be there. And true to form, now here he was, following David at this unusual hour, at a time when very few would have known that David would be emerging from his hut. Impressed with his Assistant's prescience, David tamped down his irritation at being surprised and stepped back one pace.

"Good morning, again, Sir. I'll accompany you to the Commandant's and wait outside in case there is anything you need following your discussion, if that's okay with you."

"Yes, good morning, Maximilian. That will be just fine. Thank you. We need to keep moving. I'm due in ten minutes."

"Of course, Sir."

Both resumed their walk, this time at a quickened tempo. Maximilian followed one step behind. David, concerned with the ensuing conversation with Koslov, looked straight ahead, silently rehearsing the scenarios he suspected most likely to transpire. He had to admit he had very little idea of how things would go. Koslov, and his counterpart in the camp's Eastern Sector, Dzerzhinsky, were elusive. Much like his own father, they were both creatures of the Revolution who had found their homes—indeed their callings—in Siberia soon after the overthrow of the Kerensky Government.[32] Most of the time they issued orders and directives through a series of rotating cloaked agents who circulated as shrouded forms around the camp. One week a Troupe Leader would be designated point

---

[32] Alexander Kerensky (b.1881 – d.1971): Head of the Russian Provisional Government (July 1917 – November 1917) that succeeded the Romanov Dynasty following Nicholas II's abdication of the Russian imperial throne. It, in turn, was overthrown by the Bolsheviks in November 1917 (October 1917, Julian calendar)

man for Koslov, but then the next he would be cast aside in favor of another. In this way Koslov seemed to be able to preserve authority, ensuring the loyalties of those beneath him, eschewing predictability and habit in favor of ordered chaos, chaos only he had the power to control. In Koslov's sector, the leaders never knew quite where they stood. So they worked harder, sought to exceed quotas by greater and greater margins each day. Perhaps this was one reason they all kept to themselves, aware their fates were tied to their own success.

After a few minutes the two men reached the edge of Koslov's quarters. With the exception of the factory itself, it was the tallest building in the Western Sector. Built of wood, the original, worn panels sagged into the Siberian earth, as if they had been planted long ago, served their time, and were now desperately begging for relief. Day after day these walls continued to support three more levels placed atop the next. David wondered how long before they would collapse from the weight, crashing down, or, in a more providential act, forcibly removed, replaced by materials stronger, sturdier, more sure and lasting.

David ascended five creaking planks that led into the building. Maximilian predictably followed. Once inside, a small anteroom provided an unimpressive entry to a steep staircase winding into the upper levels. Sitting at a desk just off the doorway, bundled in a wool coat, was an Attendant. Despite multiple work spaces, rooms, and hallways branching off behind him, there appeared to be no one else inside. No scraping of chairs emanated from within, no voices discussing goals and production quotas. The only true adornment was a fading copy of Ilya Repin's canvas *Barge Haulers on the Volga* on the wall adjacent to the ascending steps.

It had been years since David had seen this painting. Glancing at it, he recalled again his father, and his own days working with him in the far reaches of Russia. Ten of the eleven men portrayed in the portrait—struggling, defeated, their backs breaking from the impossible task of pulling a massive boat onto the river's muddy shores—wore eerily familiar expressions, the torment and anguish on their faces easily recognizable. But the eleventh man, the youth in the middle, was foreign to the young Troupe Leader. Although dressed in rags and tied, like a slave, to a pulley, the man's head was raised proudly, looking determined, staring out into the future. In all his years in Siberia, David had never seen a peasant defiant.

"I'm David Zaslavsky, and this is my Assistant Troupe Leader, Maximilian. I have orders to report to Comrade Koslov at 9:30."

The Attendant meekly looked up from papers he had been shuffling through. He was an old man with kind eyes, the type who could be relied upon to perform necessary tasks, but also one to never ask too many questions.

"Yes, of course, Comrade David. The Commandant is in his office on the next floor. Please go up the stairs and turn left. He is at the end of the hall. You'll see his door is closed, but his light is on. Just knock and wait to be summoned to enter."

The old man smiled politely before adding, "Maximilian can wait down here with me, where it's warmer. Would you care for something hot, Maximilian? Tea perhaps?"

Maximilian, with his usual solemn face, shook his head. Since entering the building, David observed him subtly taking note of anything and everything, paying particularly close attention to the staircase leading up to Koslov's office.

"Thank you." David removed his coat, handed it to the Attendant, straightened his uniform once more, and started climbing the steps. Each one seemed to groan in weary protest, as if resenting the disturbance of being awoken. But it was the purpose they served until they splintered, then broke.

The higher David climbed, the colder the air became. Upon reaching the top, he wished he would have kept his jacket. As instructed, he turned left down the long hall. It was as nondescript as the rest of the building, and just as clean and orderly, albeit bare and silent. Nothing hung on the walls. Empty offices lined his way on either side.

David paused in front of the closed door of the Commandant's office, listening for any sound coming from inside. He knew it was inhabited because of the faint light shining under the doorway. Finally, he took a deep breath and knocked twice.

"Enter," commanded a deep voice on the other side.

David turned the silver knob and walked in. The office was dimly lit by a solitary bulb hanging from a wire in the ceiling, and by a few sunbeams making their way through a small, unwashed window. In the far-right corner, slumping in his chair positioned behind the desk, sat Commandant Koslov. David pivoted toward the old man, and took the few steps necessary to stand directly in front of his superior officer. Shoulders erect, hands clasped behind his back, David absorbed the reality of the figure before him. Koslov's drooping mouth slowly chewed and sucked the unlit stub of a cigar, the paltry tobacco leaves soaking into sagging cheeks. The rumors of Koslov's hideous appearance were true: fat, face scarred, teeth rotting.

Koslov's old, grey uniform was adorned not with medals, but with dark stains of what looked like spilled tea and alcohol. What hair remained was wiry and unleashed. But more than anything, David noticed his eyes. Staring back at him was not steely determination, nor the gaze of a seasoned leader possessed with wisdom, insight, or vision. Instead what David saw seemed best described as one of sorrow, a thinly disguised despair, kept carefully hidden and controlled. As he reclined behind his weathered desk in a tilting chair, Koslov did not betray fear. But at the same time, in the way his eyes initially locked onto David's before moving on to examine the contours of his face, Koslov seemed to be searching for something, perhaps a quality he had learned, through many years of hardship and war, to search for upon a first meeting. What that quality was, though, David could not guess.

David sensed Koslov's search come at last to an end, and decided to speak.

"David Zaslavsky reporting as or—."

"Shut up," the old man said, stopping David cold, midsentence. The Commandant's blunt opening salvo threw David off balance. The meeting's parameters had been set with two harsh words. Any confidence David had built just minutes before back in his room was a house of cards now being toppled by a flick of the fingers of a vastly more experienced opponent. He gulped, attention focused straight ahead at the wall behind Koslov. Out of the corner of his eyes he could see the old man move his fat hand up to his face and remove the cigar from his mouth. Placing it on the table in front of him, with his gaze fixated on David, he opened his fleshy lips and spoke.

"You listen to me, you arrogant shit." The Commandant wasn't yelling; in fact, his weathered, deep voice barely raised octaves in either direction. "I know exactly who you are, and what kind of person you aspire to be. And perhaps one of these days you'll achieve everything you are dreaming of in that pitiful soul of yours. But know under my watch, under my laws and regulations, this will never happen. I suspect you realize this already. But just in case you're not that perceptive, let me tell you straight out: I didn't want you here. And, quite frankly, you disgust me." Koslov paused, unblinking.

Numbed by the brutal attack, a lump formed in David's throat.

"While men your age are dying by the thousands in the west," Koslov continued in his flat, earthy tones, "you're here, away from the bombs, away from the artillery, away from the blood. What's more, I know you sit in your room at night, playing the victim, cursing your father—like all you children of Revolution royalty do—for the sin of being a great man, for playing a role in history, one that you'll never replicate. You tell yourself that if you had been sent west across the Urals, if you had been sent to a unit where a uniform actually means something, as opposed to here, where it's just make-believe, you could have carved your own future, away from all those who know who you are. Isn't that right?"

David barely contained himself from answering with an emphatic "No!". He bit his tongue, letting his anger cool, and decided to just take it, absorb the abuse, the lies, the slander. He would deal with his lingering sentiments later.

"Ask yourself this," Koslov continued. "When you were told you were coming here, how much did you really protest? You know which units are serving at the front. You know which ones are being sent to the slaughterhouses of Stalingrad, Leningrad, and the Caucasus. Did you once ever truly ask, truly demand to be sent to one of those places?"

A coughing fit seized Koslov. His bulk prevented him from shifting in his chair; only his hands were able to react, quickly covering his mouth. David grabbed the opportunity to sneak a quick glance at the old man, and witnessed bulging eyes and a reddening face. When the spasms ceased, Koslov managed to place his elbows and forearms on his desk, and again peered up at David.

"While you are here you will follow the guidelines and protocols of this camp," Koslov said. "The speeches, the announcements, the scripts you are ordered to read are designed and carefully crafted to support the war effort generally, and our sector's goals specifically. To veer from our narrative is sabotage. Unfortunately, although I want to, there is nothing I can do to remove you. But, do not for a moment believe I am without any authority when it comes to you. There are ways, young Zaslavsky, believe me, there are ways."

Koslov's convulsions seemed to have drained his energy, as if the Commandant had shortened his diatribe and was just struggling to make it through the main points. Apparently Koslov was human, after all.

"Have your witless social hour this evening if you choose, but know the lost time will be made up, and quickly. And as for the food, there will be no additional rations. It will come out of your current allotment. So, the choice is yours, you see. Continue with the lie you perpetuated this morning, or do the right thing, suffer the embarrassment, and tell your workers the truth. Believe me, they will eventually find out, regardless."

Koslov stopped again. Hands shaking, he reached out for a water pitcher on his desk and slowly filled a glass. All he could manage was a quick gulp before tremors threatened to spill the liquid everywhere. Finally he leaned back, re-affixing a calm gaze on David, yet breathing heavily.

David readied to be dismissed right then. Point received. Koslov would expect David to return to his room, chastened and lessened, clear about who was in charge, clear there would be no more crossing the desires of the Commandant, or veering from the official line. But apparently the few sips of water revived Koslov. He looked up at the creaking and aging ceiling, and now appeared to be addressing not just David, but visions of his past as well.

"I'm old. I've seen many things, things that haunt me, things that keep me buried here, in this chamber, *isolated* from man.

Isolated from the workers, the very people that when I was your age, I believed I was waging revolution on behalf. I know your kind and I know what entices you, what tempts you. It is what has seduced all ambitious men: recognition, *power*. Men like you have a desire to achieve something great that will alter history, putting it on a trajectory toward a paradise where all is just, all is right; a place where their portraits and utterances will forever be enshrined, guiding lamps for a lost and wandering people. Sometimes opportunities are presented—either through luck, or through their own making—that make men like you believe they can realize these truths, truths that only they possess. The temptation is too great. These men embrace the moment, creating disciples that articulate these so-called truths and turn them into sacred dogmas. There is no room for compromise, no debate. No heresies allowed! Prophets foretell the bright, shining future that lies just around the corner. Just follow your great leader! Follow your god!"

Koslov's rising, animated tones were suddenly interrupted by another bout of violent coughs. He took an almost surreptitious drink of water.

David remained still and erect. Every word Koslov spoke, every accusation he made, every insight into David's character, soaked through the young man's soul. At the beginning of their conversation David was stung by the forceful insults thrown at him, his spirit trampled by invoking his father's fame as contrast to David's own meager accomplishments. But the more Koslov continued, the more the Commandant showed his hand. The cursing, the personal denunciations, were not displays of strength. They were displays of fear. The more Koslov spouted off about power, the more David was convinced the old man possessed actually very little.

"What you are too young, too naïve, to understand," Koslov continued, "is that there are no truths, no ideals that can be perfected. And the singular, extreme pursuit of perfection, of an earthly heaven, this is when farce turns into tragedy, sometimes on a scale of epic proportions. The more the ideal is pursued, the more unachievable it becomes. But gods never fail, of course! So it is not the fault of the leader when things fall apart, or of his disciples and his prophets. No. It is the fault of the common man. He is turned into any number of things—a saboteur, an apostate, a *non-believer.* And these innocents will suffer, sometimes by paying the ultimate price, caught up in the so-called currents of history, able to do nothing but tread water in a violent storm raged on behalf of others' ambitions. But I don't think you will ever see this. I think you, and all those like you, are incapable of understanding this. That is why I despise you, why I wanted nothing to do with you, and why I'm going to let you fail. Now, get out of my office."

David executed an abrupt about-face and walked briskly out. He descended the stairs in the same fashion, and swiped his coat from where he had laid it, giving no acknowledgment to the Attendant or Maximillian. He bounded outside into a snow falling harder, into a cold quickly roughening the soft edges of autumn into sharp and biting steel blades.

David traversed the gravel path in a trance, umbrage festering with every step, manifesting into hatred, drawing strength simultaneously from every perceived slight he felt as a child, from every awkward glance and hushed rumor he had experienced as a result of being in the shadow of his father, the embarrassment and shame he felt, deep inside, from not joining his fellow countrymen on Russia's western front. Never in his life had he experienced this degree of humiliation. He didn't know where he was headed. He just had to get away from that man! He had to flee that splintering building, its foundation being expelled, slowly but surely, from the earth with each passing minute.

"Sir! Sir!" He recognized Maximillian's voice calling out from behind.

David halted, angry tears swelling in his eyes, at last overflowing from years of frustration, hurt, and confusion. He didn't dare turn around to look at Maximilian. Instead, when he stopped, gulping oxygen to stave off the emotional breakdown rushing over him, he saw in the distance those smokestacks, the iron walls of the factory, and heard the sounds of the machines. This time, however, following Koslov's denouncement, the sounds did not strike him as unnatural; the factory did not look out of place. On the contrary, the scene, the atmosphere, everything taken together eased his distress, as if the needed contrast between what was possible became sharply apparent against his sullen and unremarkable life. There, in the calm and soothing snow, the factory majestically was grinding away, churning out smoke and black soot into the crisp Siberian air unobstructed. Unstoppable.

For the first time since arriving at the outpost, David admired these machines. He recalled the trees, the bushes, and the mountains of his youth. He remembered how much he loved—indeed, cherished—the natural elements, and how much he had despised the settlements his father built out of the raw earth. But now, after listening to Koslov drone on about the temptations and faults of mankind, he saw everything—the factory, the smoke, the concrete and steel—in a new vein, one completely disproving all that Koslov said. Man's desires, his passions, his drive to be monumental, could indeed produce great things. They could indeed move history along a path, one leading to prosperity. And if prosperity could be attained, could not perfection also? What were the limits to mankind's aspirations?

In hindsight, David re-considered the old Commandant's speech. It had been listless, impoverished, lacking courage and, most of all, conviction. In fact, he demonstrated a lessening of resolve, of his own authority. Koslov was questioning his own place in history and the rightness of all he had done with his life. Why? Perhaps because of his old age? Perhaps because he wished to be waging war against the Germans, but instead found himself stuck out here in Siberia, angered that he himself could no longer be the towering figure he imagined himself to be? David did not know, nor did he care. To David, Koslov's questioning, the atonement for past deeds lacing the old man's speech—these things, not the temptation of power, not the pursuit of glory, was what should be guarded against. Koslov's loss of purpose not only signified weakness, but also a vulnerability that would lead to his own collapse, much like the building in which the Commandant hid day after day.

Maximillian at last caught up with David, breathing heavily. David turned from gazing at the factory. The tears forming in his eyes had evaporated, leaving the residue of hatred in the salt that still remained on his face. He placed his hand on Maximillian's shoulder, a silent acknowledgement of his Assistant's loyalty.

"Sir," Maximillian said. "Is the event still on for this evening?"

David considered the question. He did not have a clue how to handle the issue of the social. How could he fill the labor shortages that would occur as a result, or replenish the food stocks that would have to be borrowed? How would he keep his promise, his reputation? What should he do? He had brought this on himself. No one else was to blame.

He had no other option.

As he opened his mouth to tell Maximillian to disseminate word that the evening's events had been cancelled, his Assistant Troupe Leader spoke first.

"Sir, I know what you are about to order me to say, and I'm telling you don't do it." Maximillian spoke rapidly, his voice insistent. "If you could, please trust me. I haven't let you down yet. We can carry through with what is planned. It is a noble gesture, one that should be allowed to happen. You were brave to announce it. You took the first, most critical step, at great risk to yourself. Now I will see to it that this is completed. And I can promise you that there will be no labor shortage, and no lost food rations."

Suspicious, David narrowed his eyes, staring in wonder at Maximilian. He had said nothing to his aide about these warnings.

As if reading his thoughts, Maximillian continued in a rush. "I found a back room on the first floor, directly below the Commandant's office. I could hear everything through those old boards. Believe me when I tell you I am on your side. You are, and must remain, a hero in the eyes of your workers. It is critical. You are what we have all been waiting for. *All* of us."

David stared at Maximilian, curious at the change in his expression. Something unusual, maybe even deviant, had appeared in his face. But David acquiesced. After all, Maximilian seemed to know everything; he had the upper hand. Yet more than anything, David yearned to be everything that Maximillian just proclaimed: a hero, the savior whom all wanted. Visions of himself as such a man materialized in his mind, and the sensations of triumph, of victory, of spiting Koslov, played like a drug on his battered spirit.

"Okay. Make it so."

Without smiling or demonstrating any sense of satisfaction, David patted Maximillian on his shoulder and started toward his hut with a slumped back and depressed spirit. Since earlier that morning his feelings had come full circle: from fear to confident, exuberance to utter shame, to now being embroiled in a precarious situation, one certainly out of his control. What a disgrace to be forced to rely upon a junior officer to make things right, a junior officer who now knew everything. All because of Koslov, that old man, fat, dying, languid. David spit in disgust.

CHAPTER 10

"...we were certain of the last one too..."

T he voice of Tolstoy in the Bardo came rushing furiously atop a crest of the night's wind and invaded Arkady's dreams. Only half-awake, he absently considered the protecting overhang of the looming rock. How many days since he had last seen an animal? Or even a proper tree, as opposed to the shrubs that spotted the trails upon which he traversed? He could only guess. This region, a high valley pass in the Urals, was an icy wilderness. There was water of sorts, which he gulped up when an unfrozen puddle became visible in a crevice, but no food. Periodically, he ate plants he recognized, but those were few and far between. Hunger gnawed and permeated every inch of his being. Those aspects of soldiering he hated became even more pronounced in this inhospitable wasteland.

But each day, without fail, he saw the Thrush. Every day, like the Biblical pillar of smoke leading the Israelites to the Promised Land, it appeared, steadily guiding him.

"...And now he sits rotting, destined to die in prison, caught somewhere between the past and the future, in a village itself sitting on the edge of history's abyss."

Tolstoy's voice, continuing to rattle off the wind, shook Arkady fully from his slumber. The night was cast completely in black, save for the stars twinkling and the half-moon shining above. He sat up shivering, starving, disoriented.

"What do you want?" Arkady yelled.

He did not expect an answer. He had not received any thus far. He was a pawn, and pawns are nearly powerless in another's game. But then the unexpected happened—another wind blew, this time from a different direction. To Arkady it was clearly not of the same origin, not from the same source from which the one carrying Tolstoy's warnings came. On it rode a familiar voice, although from his distant past, not heard since childhood—his mother's. Speaking softly, it read from the Holy Book, like she had done when he was a small boy.

"Then was Jesus led up of the Spirit into the wilderness to be tempted of the devil. And when he had fasted forty days and forty nights, he was afterward an hungred."[33]

Was this the response to his petition? Sasha had implied the in-between was home to many mysteries, many souls, and wandering memories, all feasting like vultures on the fears and regrets of the living. It was a conduit for all which the physical world could not conceptualize nor comprehend, the Ural Mountains seemingly its gates. This voice was not that of the soothing Voice which had summoned him to awake already many times in the mountains, the Voice that, despite his efforts, would not identify itself. Although this new voice was in the form of his mother's, it seemed to originate from another Being, a Being that did not bring with it any sensation of peace or satisfaction. On the contrary, Arkady felt his weaknesses were being probed, the strength of his will tested. It was sinister, the

---

[33] Matthew 4:1-2 (King James)

sound of his mother serving, perhaps, as a Trojan Horse into his innermost being.

Drained, Arkady could only sit still and wonder. Perched high in the Ural Mountains, wedged between their snowy peaks, the words swept over him, and in his freezing delirium, he felt compelled to speak back.

"Yes, I am hungry, starving in this wilderness. Please, bring me relief!" he cried, swaying back and forth.

"If thou be the Son of God, command that these stones be made bread."[34]

"I am not the Son of God. I do not have this power," Arkady acquiesced. "If I could, I would surely turn these stones into food."

Again, the sinister voice, still in the form of his mother's.

"Then the devil taketh him up into the holy city, and setteth him on a pinnacle of the temple, and saith unto him, If thou be the Son of God, cast thyself down: for it is written, He shall give his angels charge concerning thee: and in their hands they shall bear thee up, lest at any time thou dash thy foot against a stone."[35]

At that Arkady found himself standing up, crawling out from beneath the stony overhang. He struggled to clamber up the rock itself, and looked down the other side. There in front of him, illuminated by the stars and the moon, was a great and expanding plain.

"Siberia!" he sighed.

Lightheaded and in awe, Arkady surveyed the magnificent wasteland spreading out before him. Never in his life had he seen anything so vast, so unwelcoming, so unearthly. Overwhelmed, a tear dripped from his eye, unable to bear the despair taking root deep within his soul.

---

[34] Matthew 4:3b (King James)

[35] Matthew 4:5-6 (King James)

Again he heard the voice, this time more powerful, more threatening. It had cast off its disguise. No longer taking the form of his mother's, it took on the air of something ancient, enveloping, transcendent in a way that caused the in-between to tremble and the mountains to cloak themselves within their own shadows.

"Cast thyself down!"

"Cast thyself down!"

Was this at last his chance? Stepping off this rock, tumbling down the mountain, throwing himself into the dark abyss below, to be swept up by angels, rescued from his torture?

There is no god. There is nothing. Only pain.

His breathing intensified, so much so he had to open his mouth wide in order to take in all the air that his fluctuating, heaving chest demanded. He threw off his coat. He peered over the edge.

"Cast thyself down!"

"Cast thyself down!"

He looked up once more at the stars. No pattern! No reason! Then he looked down at the plain.

Twinkling stars below him!

Was he himself now amongst the stars, placed in the heavens, as if the universe had swallowed him whole? Were others looking up at him, as he had looked up at the old philosophers, as the saints looked up at Christ nailed on a cross? Was he now a god himself, his own savior with the power to end all of this?

He lifted his foot, ready to step forward. But then…

…fluttering!

Out of the darkness…

…the Thrush!

The bird flew directly into his face. Arkady lost his balance and fell backward. On his back, bruised, but awake, shaken from the trance which had overtaken him, he started to cry in frustrated defeat. Another attempt at victory had failed. He was not a god after all, just a human being. He curled into himself and wept.

"But what about the third temptation!" he yelled at the stars. "In the wilderness, Christ was tempted three times! What is the third temptation? Show it to me!"

But there was nothing. The gusts died down. Clouds drifted in to cover the stars, hiding them from the ragged and pitiful creature begging for mercy. The voice of the Being on the wind disappeared. He was alone again with the Thrush, perched on a boulder near the cliff. The bird beckoned with his beak for Arkady to approach.

The weary soldier crawled forward. His scarred arms and hands left a trail of blood on the stone. Peering over the edge and down onto the Siberian plain, he sought another glimpse of the stars below him. Again he witnessed lights twinkling, but stars they were not.

"A village," Arkady murmured. "A village…," he repeated hoarsely as the world started to spin.

"…sitting on the edge of history's abyss."

He slept.

★

Arkady opened his eyes wide and blinked against the onslaught of the sun shining high and bright above him. The events of the night before rushed back into his mind. He shuddered, thinking about nearly stepping headlong over the cliff when relief might be just a few hours march in front of him. He sat up and peered below him.

The village.

From this distance up high in the mountains, it looked so peaceful. Nestled against the edge of a forest, it obviously was not one of the hastily built factory towns in Siberia Sasha had talked about. There were no plumes of grey smoke billowing out of newly constructed stacks, no flames shooting from oversized forges. All was quiet.

Arkady struggled to his feet. He felt frail, almost brittle. His head pounded and pangs of hunger still ripped through his stomach. But managing to steady himself, he walked down the boulder, retrieving his pack from under the overhang where he had left it the night before. Strapping it on his back, he greeted the Thrush making its usual morning appearance. Today Arkady required no persuading of which way to go. At last the path was clear, and he would take it to the village. Down the slopes he went, as fast as he could.

For the next two hours he maneuvered the terrain as usual, as he had been doing ever since he first entered the Ural Mountains, which seemed countless days ago. His heart lightened, his spirit lifted. The closer the sprawling plain, the more the landscape flattened, and the taller the trees grew up around him. Around a bend, as if it had been waiting to escape from the ground the whole time, a clear path suddenly appeared unobstructed beneath him. For the first time since departing the sight of the ambush, he was on a proven and discernable road.

He entered a thick forest, the one which he had seen from above, proximate to the village. Walking steadily, he admired the beauty and solitude of the woods. He inhaled, sniffing the pines' heady perfume. He took comfort in the light chirping of birds and the gentle breezes swaying the boughs above him.

But the deeper he went into the forest, the less verdant it became. Soon the birds stopped singing, and snowflakes floated like a hushed melody in the air. At first the flurries were slight and pleasant, but then thick flakes drifted through the branches, fortunately not heavy enough to obstruct Arkady's way forward. The path was still clear, and the Thrush frequently dipped and looped in front of him, urging him on despite his weariness, until at last he came upon a fork in the road. Arkady looked curiously at the bird, which had landed on the path to the right, the path heading due east, directly out onto the Siberian plain and away from the village.

The Thrush lifted gracefully up into the sky and circled, as if summoning Arkady to follow. He hesitated in place. His thoughts drifted back to his first efforts on the slopes of the Ural Mountains, when he had adamantly resisted following the creature. Then, all his efforts blazing his own trail had ended in abject failure. Whenever he followed the Thrush, however, he had survived. It was the easiest path, the path of least resistance.

Suddenly, from the way leading left, he heard noises, like a choir of triumphant music blaring from scratchy loudspeakers. When the patriotic-like tune stopped, it was replaced by a raised voice, its cadence pleading, as if urging a crowd toward something lofty, toward some unified, but not easily achievable, purpose. Arkady searched the sky for the bird, wondering if it had changed direction toward the village now that the sounds had emerged. But it had not.

"The village, food, shelter, is this way," Arkady said to the bird, pointing left.

The Thrush swooped frantically around in circles, and landed on the ground as if warning, reminding Arkady of what he experienced last time he refused to follow it.

In the far recesses of his mind Arkady heard Tolstoy's voice rolling off the night wind the evening before:

"...a village itself sitting on the edge of history's abyss."

A warning?

Arkady was too famished, too exhausted, too weak to care. Before, when he disregarded the Thrush, there was no clear path. But now there was a road clearly in front of him. The village was so close! He could hear the loudspeakers clearly, their intensity a siren's call. Arkady estimated the village to not be more than one or two kilometers farther. Just around that next bend, he should be able spot it.

Hungry, thirsty, and cold, at the end of his reserves, he made his decision. Ignoring the Thrush, Arkady stepped off to the left.

"These are simple movements, simple decisions, but still nonetheless mine," he again muttered in subtle defiance.

Sensing he was on his own, Arkady sped up. Every step he took down the road he could feel, in his promethean imagination, the fresh water on his lips, on his tongue, as it drained slowly down his parched throat. He tasted the warm meal that would ineluctably be set out in front of him. The aromas of meat, soup, vegetables, and bread were already tickling his nostrils.

A dense fog rolled in as he trudged along. Arkady could barely see in front of him. He walked faster and faster, difficult as it was in the snow, in the haze, as rough and rocky as the old road was, until he was almost running. Tripping, he fell and slid face first into the ground. Rolling over onto his back, struggling to rise to his feet, he heard the amplified sounds again: triumphant music and a man's yell blared from screechy speakers.

As Arkady brushed himself off, the fog sluggishly dissipated, revealing right before him tall and thick wooden walls. They were deep brown, made of ancient logs stacked one on top of the other. The entrance, over which was placed a guard tower, was just a few meters away. His first thought, given the fog, old road, and hand-hewn logs piled in front of him, was that he had been transported to another time, a time where tribal warlords ruled the far reaches of ancient Rus, when each village had not only its own ruler, but own army, laws, and its own fortress kremlin.

The mist lifted completely. Arkady stood, dumbfounded. He had not imagined a place anywhere in Russia that still contained ancient armature this well-preserved. As he pondered the age before the Soviet state, an historical epoch characterized by great architectural and ethereal beauty, grand battlements planted along European and Asian frontiers, onion-domed cathedrals rising from the barren earth, courts of the Tsars lavished in regal splendor, it was as if the full weight of his country's history stood starkly before him. For a moment he forgot his physical ills. He wondered if Siberia's arcane powers to seemingly move time and space had indeed transported him back to a previous era.

Eyeballing the entrance toward the town itself, and then up at the guard tower, Arkady saw no one. At least within his line of sight, the town seemed deserted. He wondered if the Thrush would appear, giving him another chance to follow it elsewhere. But there was no sign of the bird in any direction, no wind to carry it to Arkady's side. It truly was like he had stepped through a portal and into another dimension. Arkady shuffled forward, inspecting the guard tower as he passed through the entrance. Walking underneath, he noted intricately carved details in the wood: animals, plants, men, symbols of the church. All were worn down, tired, colorless.

Emerging on the other side, Arkady at last fully realized the size and depth of the village. Its wooden border walls stretched until they turned corners, their eventual connecting points hidden by the beautifully ornate but dilapidated dacha-style houses crowding what seemed to be the town's central area. As the road wound deeper into the morass of buildings, it became lost amongst structures built directly adjacent to, and at times on top of, one another, giving the sense of a dense and impenetrable maze of never-ending archaic edifices. Modernity clashed with the ancient aura through electrified loudspeakers hoisted on rudimentary poles along the insides of the wooden walls, pointing outward.

The yelling intensified, and Arkady determined the commotion originated from the center of town. A rally of some sort? Screams echoed through the streets. With heightened fear, Arkady began questioning his decision to take the road to the left. The fantasies of drink, food, warmth, and comfort in which he had indulged, faded and grew dark. This town was not the welcoming oasis he had imagined. On the contrary, here, nestled among the eastern foothills of the Ural Mountains, the dividing line between east and west, Europe and Asia, reason and passion, the village seemed indeed at the eye of some storm, locked in a struggle, but with what? Arkady could only surmise: the past, the future, its own identity, a way forward in the war...or in the new Soviet state.

That last possibility bothered him more than anything else. Nowhere among the myriad carvings and symbols had he seen the bright, red flag with the yellow hammer and sickle placed confidently in its upper left corner. In fact, he had seen no symbols of the Communist government at all. It frightened him that perhaps this was a town in rebellion, one which, upon seeing a uniformed soldier, would not be welcoming. The serene and picturesque scene Arkady had fancied from high in the mountain pass metamorphosized into something haunting instead. It was a shadow of the past, an image as observed by someone not familiar with the deeper tragedies that infect all dreams and erstwhile ideals.

"The Thrush was right after all," he admitted to himself.

He had to leave, and quickly. Something was deeply amiss in this place, something he did not want to disturb. Eating plants, bark, and berries would suffice, especially now that he was out of the mountains and on the Siberian plain. Water, too, would be more abundant. And there would be other villages, others not caught up in the baneful struggle which the reverberating cries seemed to rally against.

Arkady pivoted to exit the same way he had entered. Turning around however, he ran straight into the barrel of a rifle.

The young soldier heaved; the rifle pressed harder into his breast.

The eyes of the man holding the weapon locked with Arkady's.

Legs shaking, heartrate intensifying, Arkady noticed movement from the corner of his sight.

There were indeed two men—the one holding the rifle ready to pull the trigger at any false move, and another positioned directly behind Arkady closer to the guard tower. Before Arkady had time to examine that man, he took off running into the town; a messenger, perhaps, alerting the authorities to an intruder's presence. An intruder that was a haggard Russian soldier, no less.

The remaining man with the rifle stared at Arkady. His eyes never veered, the severity of his gaze never lessened. The muzzle of his weapon pointed level at Arkady's chest, the guard moved his finger to the trigger. Arkady's heart leapt. He stumbled backward, almost losing his balance. The man stepped closer with each of Arkady's retreating steps, who now held his hands high up in the air.

"Okay, okay. Please. No need for the rifle. I'm just here for food. I've been on the road for weeks. See, my hands!" Arkady looked at each one. "They're empty. Nothing in them. No weapon, just scars. And on my back...nothing there but what's left of my equipment."

Arkady wasn't sure if he had convinced the sentry of his innocence, of the fact that all he wanted was nourishment. The rifle remained pointed at him. The man's hands didn't shake. To Arkady it almost seemed as if the guard had anticipated someone such as himself walking through the gate, pondering the meaning of the peculiar town, and then deciding, after much consideration, to leave. And as Arkady gaped at the man, he noticed that he complemented the surroundings. The rifle pointed at him was old, worn, perhaps one of the original Mosins issued to Tsarist forces at the end of the last century. The man's uniform was also from another age, one from centuries past which must have witnessed tumultuous change in the empire's eastern fringes. The architecture, the man's uniform, his weapon, the layout and structure of the town, all these things were from history books, reminiscent of old photographs and paintings Arkady had seen in school. But the screeching speakers, the very fact that he, a man of the present, had somehow wandered into this zone, gave testament to the fact that he was still very much in the present.

Tolstoy's words echoed in Arkady's thoughts: "...caught somewhere between the past and the future."

Arkady kept his hands raised. The man with the rifle remained steady. Without a word, the guard motioned Arkady to turn around. Complying, the man pushed him in the back with his rifle, an obvious signal to move forward. Together, one in front of the other, they ventured slowly down the crooked road, deeper into the entangled wooden structures that made up the town's central core.

As they moved forward, Arkady did not see another single human being. Yet, he heard a crowd from what he assumed to be the town's main square. Noises from the strategically placed loudspeakers echoed off buildings and carried through the narrow streets. Weaving farther and farther away from the entrance gate, the outer walls disappeared from view altogether. Entering what had to be one of the town's oldest and most condensed districts, taller wooden buildings, some as high as five-stories, soared above him. They had the appearance of age, of weariness, of history, as if a strong wind could bring them suddenly crashing down.

Arkady thought to himself, "This town is not only on the abyss of history. It is on the verge of collapse."

They reached a narrow alley splitting off the main thoroughfare.

"Stop!" The guard finally spoke. "Turn right, down here," he commanded.

Arkady obeyed, entering a dark alley. The cold from the lack of sunlight became pronounced. Halfway down the passage a small, nondescript entryway led into one of the ancient clusters of wooden structures.

"Halt. Knock on this door."

He followed the guard's orders. Promptly a latch unlocked, and hinges creaked. Blackness yawned in the open portal; only a faint orange glow illuminated the inside. Standing in the doorway was the man who had run off, away from the guard tower. He beckoned Arkady to enter. Once inside, he noticed a small table and chair situated next to a fireplace radiating heat, a sensation Arkady craved. Even with a rifle pointed at his back, his heart lightened.

"Sit here," the guard commanded. Grateful, Arkady wearily dropped into the rickety chair. Lowering the rifle, his guard stood with his back against the now-closed door. As the other man ascended a small staircase discreetly attached to the room's rear wall, Arkady's attention was captured by a portrait hanging above the hearth's mantle. The old oil painting rested corpse-like in a decaying wooden frame, plated in chipped gold. Years of dirt, cracking, and flaking had worn it down, but the face of the man in the painting was recognizable. The subject was positioned in motion, eyes cast back at the viewer, dark locks of youthful hair hanging freely, frocked in silver armor covered by a blue sash stretching diagonally from right to left. Every Russian knew this face. Every Russian still, even after the Revolution, spoke reverently of this man, even if in hushed tones. The portrait itself added to the village's ambience, but its presence only heightened Arkady's swelling fear.

The man climbing the rear stairwell reached the top and disappeared from view. Arkady listened as his footsteps thumped from directly above against the wooden planks, followed by a light shuffling as a second person moved across the floor. Arkady shifted his eyes from the portrait to the stairs. Descending slowly was an old man, who was unusually, almost freakishly, tall. At one time his physical features—broad shoulders, bulging chest, muscular arms—must have complemented his height. But now, the lack of muscle, worn down and consumed through the years, made him appear gaunt and lanky, frail. Save for his head, he was completely covered in a dark cloak. His hands, peeking out from beneath, revealed the palest skin Arkady had ever seen, as if they belonged to someone who had died long ago, but was still in the process of decomposing. His hair, too, which flowed down to his neck covering the sides of his head and part of his face, was deathly white. The man's vacant and lifeless eyes sunk into his skull, and his face held a thinning, barely visible moustache. Similar to the town itself, everything about the man resembled something out of the 17th century, when the Romanov dynasty had first attained power. When the man in the portrait had announced Russia's intentions to be a player in European politics by constructing St. Petersburg out of a frozen marsh. When that city had transformed Russia into a formidable power, allowing it to project its military might throughout the whole of the West and, eventually, the world.

Followed deferentially by the attendant who had gone to retrieve him, the man reached the bottom of the steps and crossed to the fireplace. Picking up an iron rod, he began poking at the logs. Sparks flew up and into the room. The flames grew brighter, illuminating the man's snowy hair as a shimmer against his dark robe.

"Where have you come from?" the man at last asked, facing the stone hearth. His voice was neither inordinately deep nor shaky; it was sure.

Arkady decided to tell the truth. "From across the Urals. I was separated from my unit weeks ago."

"Your unit?"

"Yes. We were ambushed while looking for our comrades. They had been patrolling outside Stalingrad. They never returned. Something had drawn them east, to the foothills of the Ural Mountains themselves."

"So...you found your comrades, then?" The old man angled slightly away from the fire; Arkady flinched at the full profile of this ghostly figure against the orange glow of the flames. The black garments hanging from his thin body, and the way his skin appeared to be loosened from his bones, reminded Arkady of the elderly philosophers. The old man turned to face Arkady, moving in such a fashion that allowed

Arkady an instant glimpse of the portrait, before blocking it again from view. Arkady's heart jumped, startled. What had he seen? Perhaps it was only a trick from the light, or perhaps from the effects of the cold, the hunger, the thirst. Perhaps—

"I asked you a question!" the old man barked. "Did you find your comrades?"

Arkady snapped out of his swoon.

"We did!" he answered, attempting to look past the old man for another peek of the portrait.

"Well, what had become of them?"

"They had been slaughtered by a German patrol. It was probably the same patrol that attacked us."

The old man scowled.

"Germans...," he said, as if reflecting on the word. "Why would Germans draw a Russian unit that far east?" For the first time the man looked directly at Arkady. Flames reflected brightly in his eyes. Five minutes ago they appeared vacant, lost. But now, they were alive. Suddenly the old man seemed not quite a ghost, as if the longer he was in the room, the longer he conversed with Arkady, the longer he stood in front of the fire, the more mortal he became. A sharp chill shot through Arkady's spine. He needed one more look at the portrait...

"I really don't know," Arkady at last said, speaking the truth. He had never thought about why a German patrol might lead Russians deeper into their own country. It didn't make sense. What evidence, after all, existed that it was a German unit?

"*...and it came to pass, when they were in the field, that Cain rose up against Abel his brother, and slew him.*"[36] The old man spoke in bitter tones into the darkness, seeming to grow straighter, more erect with each passing second.

---

[36] Genesis 4:8 (King James)

"…the voice of thy brother's blood crieth unto me from the ground. And now art thou cursed from the earth, which hath opened her mouth to receive thy brother's blood from thy hand,"[37] he continued.

Perhaps it was just the shadows bouncing in odd forms off the walls in this small, enclosed room, but this man, the one who just a few moments ago seemed frail and on the verge of death, seemed to be morphing into something very different before Arkady's eyes.

"Tell me, what led you through the Ural Mountains? How did you make it over with nothing besides an empty pack?" the old man persisted in a more sensible tone.

Arkady recoiled. If he told the truth, that he had blindly followed a bird, the old man would laugh and mock him; he would surely be called a liar.

"I was lucky. I knew enough about navigation in the stars to find my way. I barely made it! Can't you see how hungry I am? I'm on the verge of death!"

The old man shook his head.

"You are not lucky. Something led you here…the same as the last one, perhaps. Why don't you tell me the truth? Is it because you are afraid that I won't believe you? Trust me when I tell you, there is nothing in this world, or the next, that I have not seen, nor felt." The two attendants guarding the door laughed. The giant smirked, seemingly unamused.

"I have no idea what you're talking about," Arkady said stubbornly, but he suspected he would not be believed. The old man, this village, was somehow caught up in whatever was going on. He had perhaps seen more than Arkady, and was now only toying with him, stretching out the conversation, making sure it continued until…until what?

---

[37] Genesis 4:10b-11 (King James)

"Who is the *last one?*" Arkady continued to protest. "Who or what would I have followed over the mountains? What is this place? Has everyone lost their mind? I'm a soldier! I need help! Please help me!"

The old man turned back toward the fire. He seemed to breathe in the flames, inhaling the life the fire exuded. Again his figure completely covered the portrait; Arkady could not get a clear glimpse.

"Men do not end up in Siberia by chance," the old man said. A sense of wandering, of distance, laced his voice. "No. They are always sent here, banished and cursed. For centuries this has been the case. What was perhaps my greatest military defeat[38]—the one I did nothing to avenge, the one I ignored, the one that kept our armies guarding the fringes of our empire for another century—was in this land. Oh, Siberia. You are indeed a graveyard."

"I tell you, I don't know what you're talking about," Arkady sputtered. Tears of panic rolled down his face. He should have followed the Thrush. He should have turned and run, as soon as he heard the violent screams in the village's central square.

The man, still staring into the fire, continued, his voice growing adamant and unyielding.

"All this, this ancient town, these walls, the people who inhabit it, were once part of a vast bulwark of defenses. Now this is all that is left, this small village, a sister to larger cities like Verkhoturye, Tyumen, Tobolsk, and of course Yekaterinburg. I built them. Together, along with others, they formed a network of fortress cities stretching north and south, east and west along the mountains. They were symbols of the might of the Romanov Dynasty projecting the splendor and power of Holy Russia into the heathen east. Like gravity fixated against

---

[38]   See endnote 10.a.

the ocean, they were the forces of civilization pulling the waves of history toward the unsettled and uncivilized shore, leveling all before them, drowning those who would not voluntarily submit. And now we, the remaining few, are fighting, rallying every day against those who have surrounded us, against those pining for the next revolution, against those who believe their vision, not ours, is the way to ultimate power."

Having finished breathing in the fire, the man slowly turned toward Arkady. Like the old philosophers, Arkady felt a surreal and unexplainable connection to him, as if this man had somehow, long ago, affected his life in uncounted ways, ways whose inflection points were removed by time and space, but nevertheless critical to all that Arkady was, had seen, and experienced. This giant, reminiscing about the height of a ruling dynasty long since passed, seething about enemies surrounding him, about enemies wanting to take what *he built*...

"Your presence here is not unexpected," the old man continued. "The only question is how much you yourself are involved. And that, we will soon learn."

The man now fully faced Arkady, towering above, looking directly down at him. Arkady knew he was broken, powerless, just as he had felt amongst the old philosophers that night on the mountain slopes. All of the pieces were there, the signs pointing to who this man was. But it couldn't be! Yet, in some fantastical way, it all made terrifying sense.

"The future is a variation improvised on a theme of the past..."

The words of Herzen from that haunted night rushed into Arkady's mind. This village, in all its ancient and ornate beauty, once grand, once great, once conquering...now in its last throes, now beset by revolution, continued to rally, pitting itself against the tidal wave of history sweeping over the whole of

Russia and Siberia. This village, representing the past—or was it the future?—now in the midst of being replaced, succumbing forcibly to something else, more confident, perhaps unnatural.

"...caught somewhere between the past and the future."

"Is it you?" Arkady asked in a trembling voice. The man's eyes lit up. A pleased but deviant smile crept across his face, as if triumphant that he had been recognized. At last the man stepped fully away from the painting, and Arkady saw what he had feared all along. The figure in the portrait was no longer the prisoner of some artist's impression, destined to spend eternity existing only as the composite of green, black, red, and silver. Instead, there he stood, young, vibrant, in armored regalia, in living, breathing form. The incorporeal portrait had consumed the man, and the man had consumed the portrait. He threw off the dark cloak. His white hair had turned deep brown. A breastplate of silver armor sparkled in the glow of the flames, and a blue sash stretched from shoulder to waist. Although centuries removed, Arkady recognized him.

Lowing his eyes, Arkady's limbs shook...submission, indications that this ancient but powerful sovereign still ruled his subjects from the grave, from the Bardo. Arkady grew dizzy. The wound on his forehead began to trickle blood. This wound would never heal! He felt himself flanked by the two guards. Together they put their hands under his arms, hoisted him up from the chair, and forced him down onto the floor, his face pressed against the hard wood, his blood seeping between the cracks, fertilizing the unholy ground upon which this village, this man, unnaturally existed.

In a daze Arkady heard the attendants yell at him, "Bow down! Bow in the presence of your sovereign, Peter Alekseyevich Romanov,[39] Emperor of all the Russias!"

---

[39]   Peter the Great, Tsar of Russia; ruled May 1682 – February 1725

The sight of the giant, the founder of the Romanov Dynasty standing before him, for almost four hundred years a symbol of order, law, and violence throughout Europe and Siberia, was the last image Arkady saw as he slipped once more into unconsciousness.

CHAPTER 11

Natasha could not prevent herself from looking up every few minutes at the clock. The early release was just an hour away; she could sense the excitement for the festivities building. Everyone went about their tasks in their usual silence, but more quickly than ever before. There was a looming sense that at any minute the social could be canceled, their spirits let down, hopes dashed. But the lunch hour had passed, the afternoon shift began, the time grew closer, and still no disappointing notification. In fact, although David had not been seen since he made the announcement that morning, Assistant Troupe Leader Maximilian rushed about, looking for volunteers. They left their posts and returned smiling, grinning, with news that one of the huts was being transformed into a makeshift dance hall, with a small band, and food of the sorts they had not seen in many months. Although eagerly anticipating the evening's festivities, Natasha's best instincts told her all was not as it seemed. Her troupe was the only troupe holding such an event. Everything else around the camp proceeded as normal. Something was not quite right.

Rachel had been one of the workers called to support the set-up for the evening's gathering. Shortly after lunch she returned to her place on the factory floor. Natasha had never seen her shy friend glowing as she did now. Discreetly moving closer, Natasha nudged Rachel.

"What did you see?" she asked.

Rachel's lips curved barely upward. "Exactly as announced this morning. One of the empty storage warehouses is being heated. Tables are being brought in, along with food. Maximilian said that the food is from the Troupe Leaders' mess, that Comrade David procured it himself."

As Rachel mentioned Maximilian, Natasha noticed a forlorn tinge in her friend's voice.

"So you spoke to him, then?" Natasha gingerly inquired.

"Who?"

"Maximilian." Natasha suspected Rachel knew full well who she was referring to.

"Yes, yes I did," she responded and blushed.

"What was he like? He seems so serious whenever we see him, no emotion at all."

Rachel nodded. "He is serious. He was very focused on what was going on. And very organized. At least from what I observed and how he interacted with me, he was no different from how he acts in front of us. I've heard people wonder if he might be cruel. I didn't get that feeling at all. Just the opposite, actually. I don't know for sure."

"What did he say to you, specifically?"

Rachel looked down at the casing she was polishing, not saying anything. A slight smile crept across her face.

"Well, he just asked me my name. That's all. He didn't inquire about anyone else that was with us, though. Just me." Her eyes remained focused on her work.

"That was very nice of him," Natasha said. To her knowledge, Rachel had never been romantically involved with anyone in her life. Her shyness, her awkwardness, the things she delved into—books, history, art—represented walls she had built around herself, walls that over time had become nearly impenetrable to all except those chosen few who earned Rachel's trust, as Natasha had done the first night on the train. To Natasha, Rachel seemed to be the type that, in her home village, secluded herself in the local library for long periods. The type that had been so average as a girl that she had become an anomaly, someone not so average after all, a person whom others had left alone, perhaps in the fear of succumbing themselves to the lonely world in which Rachel dwelt.

Natasha decided to drop the topic for now. Maximilian was in a position to pursue Rachel further at a time of his choosing. Even if Rachel wanted to, even if she had Lara's instincts when it came to men, there was little she could do to encourage future encounters. Perhaps if the evening social went well, though...

"One hour to go!" Natasha said, forcibly breathing some excitement into the approaching event, despite her own instinctive misgivings, trying to nudge her friend out of her melancholic thoughts.

Rachel finally raised her head and smiled. On the rare moments when she was inspired to do so, the expression softened the hard edges already developed in her young face, revealing a dimension to her personality, to her soul, rarely seen. If Maximilian could see that smile, Natasha thought, there would be nothing left for Rachel to do.

★

The clock's hands reached the appointed hour, and, as promised, the horn sounded. Members of David's troupe quickly put away their work aprons, gloves, and other articles. Within ten minutes the factory floor had entirely emptied.

The workers were on their way. Natasha listened to the excited whispers and speculations as they headed toward the distant, transformed hut, a promised land, of sorts.

They had at last been rewarded, recognized for their efforts in trying to win the war, a victory, they had been assured, that was not far off. This simply had to be, finally, the truth. There was no other way to interpret it, no other explanation for this aberration to their daily routine. Other work troupes might not be doing the same, but that's because their Commanders were not as thoughtful, not as inspired, not as influential nor forward-thinking as David. In their minds, they had become the chosen people, the ones who had been anointed the vessel for this talented and handsome young man.

Natasha marveled at the change in their attitudes, and as she did so, she heard faint hints of a familiar voice—Father. When he was alive, wisdom he had gleaned from his art, from that which could be touched, polished, and physically changed, would often spill into his insights on the intangible. In ghostly appearances and whispers, this attribute of his had not changed. As if confirming her own earlier apprehensions, he spoke.

"Is it not telling," he said, "the speed with which people, especially those undergoing hardship, and based on little evidence beyond their own hopeful projections, can arrive at conclusions about those in whom they vest all hope? Is it not providential of the human condition the ease with which the recipients of this collective admiration so quickly and completely succumb to the corruptions of these exaltations?"

It was true, Natasha thought to herself. Within a few short hours David, who had arrived just two weeks ago, who simply had made one announcement during the course of one short speech, became the fixture of everyone's admiration. As the word of his gesture spread throughout the camp, he had become a minor, but consequential, celebrity to those who yearned for hope, who dreamed of freedom and victory, detesting the squalid conditions in which they were forced to live, and the long hours they were forced to work. Many, Natasha reflected, in their private whispers, even fell to the temptation of lacing together more vacuous and superficial matters with the profound. David was attractive. He was young. Hence, he was a shining light guiding the way around tired, old men and their exhausted methods.

"No need for experience! Details do not matter! What are those trivialities when we have one that will allow us to be ourselves?" Natasha's father proclaimed, his cynicism on human beings' need for importance shining through.

But Natasha also intuited the true depth of her fellow workers' sentiments, overheard and captured in one disturbing murmur, "At least for one night, one that is free of consequences, we can bask in our truth, we can bask in the privilege that David has bestowed upon us."

She joined her comrades as they filed, smiling, talking, and laughing, into the warehouse. As the first ones stepped through the door, members of a five-piece ensemble, grinning with joy themselves, started to play traditional music from the hastily assembled stage. There was the accordion-like garmon, the buben swatted like a tambourine, the stringed gusli, the Russian guitar, and of course the balalaika itself. In harmony these ancient instruments carried everyone instantly away to other times, other places. The tables were uncovered and there before the gathered mass was food, the likes of which they had not seen since arriving in Siberia. Laid out in front of them were sweets, breads, jams, fish, cheese, various types of meat, drink, fruits, and vegetables. Never had these workers imagined these delectable treats were within a thousand-kilometer radius of this desolate place, especially when things as simple and critical as soap were hard to come by. Never in their dreams had they even dared imagine that these items might be in a storeroom next door, separated merely by a thin wall, a few centimeters between them and a full, satisfied stomach. But when they saw this feast, surrounded as they were by the simple orchestra strumming music in the background, comforted by the glow of warm fireplaces projecting the shadows of dancing flames on the walls, they were not embittered, they were not jealous. As long as David was their leader, as long as he was in charge, these things would be theirs now and in the future. They quickly forgot any grievances with the ruling class; they quickly forgave any perceived slights. They strolled up to the tables, ate, and then danced, forgetting where they were, what they were doing, and even who they were with, so enthralled in the moment that their fears regarding loved ones at the front faded into the fireplaces themselves.

Rachel and Lara arrived a few minutes behind the others, having agreed to meet near their living quarters in order to leave together. Rachel apologized that it was her fault for their slight tardiness, and Natasha immediately discerned why.

"You look very good tonight, Rachel," Natasha said with an approving nod. Her friend had brushed her long hair, tied it behind her, and clearly gone to great lengths to use what she had available to brighten her eyes, accentuate her lips, and generally liven her face. "If she would just wear that smile I saw earlier," Natasha thought, "she would be radiant."

"I'll ask again, who is he?" Lara asked, laughing.

"Lara! Stop," Natasha scolded.

Rachel blushed at her transparent efforts.

"Maybe I shouldn't be here tonight. I'm not feeling too well, after all," she said, dejectedly, looking down.

"No, no, no!" Lara answered, apparently regretting her earlier quip. She smiled, and assured, "I'm just kidding, of course. You look wonderful. Stick with me tonight."

Rachel smiled and raised her head. Natasha beckoned them in the direction of the music, the delicious aromas of food, drink, and fire wafting from the chimneys of the formerly deserted warehouse.

When her two friends entered, they were speechless. Like the others who had arrived before them, they had not imagined that something on this scale could, in a matter of hours, appear in an abandoned building in this frozen desert. It was as if they had walked through a portal, leaving a land of loneliness and entering one of plentiful abundance, as if they had left a realm of despair and walked into one depicting what was possible, what was right around the corner, what *could be* if only the right leadership were in place. Rachel's eyes sparkled as she took everything in. Lara's mouth gaped open. She laughed aloud, clapping her hands, spinning around in the makeshift foyer.

"Let's go!" Lara said, grabbing Rachel by the hand, leading her excitedly over to the food. Natasha remained where she was, smiling, but silent. She wanted to burst into laughter, just as Lara had, to forget everything, if only for a few minutes, lost like the others in the joyousness of this much needed release. But something kept her restrained, from being overtaken completely by the moment. Avoiding the figures moving in unison on the dance floor, she made her way to the far side of the building and found a seat. Instead of losing herself in the food, drink, and dance, she would sit and listen to the music, absorb the smiles on the faces of her comrades, and try and make sense of her nagging uncertainties.

Natasha noted the couples' methodical movements around the dance floor. She observed how, with no practice, with no rehearsal, some having barely just met, the men and women knew their partners' next moves; where the others, circling around them, would proceed. They resembled the stars in the skies: seemingly random and chaotic, but nonetheless ordered, each spinning, traveling in a set path, but kept just far enough apart to ensure self-preservation. With no other explanation than just the smiles on their faces and the laughter in their voices, the couples each maintained their unity, oneness, in rhythm with the music, that enigmatic force keeping all those on the dance floor in balance, all in motion. Was there similar music in the universe that the stars danced to? Was there a comparable beautiful force, one perhaps only heard by a few, by those who chose to listen, that knit the stars together into perfect union? To Natasha the existence of such celestial music was self-evident because, despite the rejection she had known growing up in her village as an outcast, she had known Arkady. She had known love, a force of passion she had allowed to occupy the deepest recesses of her spirit, severing attachment to the pain and regret brought down on her by more powerful and unforgiving forces.

In her encounter with love she, an innocent, had been able to forgive all that had tormented her, bringing to her soul reconciliation with experience, with history. Reconciliation— that state of being required to live a life of peace, a recognition that the beauty she observed in the dancing couples and heard in the accompanying music was sovereign over all the pain she had suffered.

Natasha sighed as her thoughts turned to Arkady. Despite his own insecurities and regrets about his mother, despite his bitterness at having to leave for a cause he ultimately did not understand, he had recognized in her something others had not seen. Perhaps someday she could repay him for all he had done for her. Perhaps someday she could save him from a demise she felt certain would destroy him if he did not choose to forgive, as she had done. But for now she would have to wait, wait and hope that he would come back to her. She prayed that after the war they could start fresh and new, exploring these and other mysteries together as man and wife were meant to do, together as one person, both in the flesh and in the spirit.

A cold wind swept through the warehouse, so biting it snuffed out one of the fires. The music abruptly ceased, and the musicians leapt to their feet accompanied by a rattle of tumbling instruments. All stopped dancing; those at the food table turned at the disruption and stood stoically at attention. There in the open doorway, snow swirling around him, was David. He quickly stepped inside followed by Maximilian, who closed the door behind them.

"Comrades! Comrades!" David smiled and waved a half-salute. "Please continue. Do not mind me. There will be no speeches tonight. Nothing. Just enjoy yourselves for as long as you are able. I am one of you this evening."

Maximilian signaled to re-light the extinguished flame, while David motioned to the band to start playing again. Instead of their previous jubilant selections, the musicians struck up a somber tune originating from east of the Ural Mountains, the lyrics which were said to have been imagined in a dream. A young woman stepped to the front of the stage, filling the hut with her clear, dulcet voice.

Ah, it is not yet evening, but I have taken a tiny little nap, and a dream came to me;

In the dream that came to me, it was as if my raven-black horse was playing about, dancing about, beneath the bold, brave youth.[40]

---

[40] "The Cossack's Parable", or "Stepan Razin's Dream" by Alexandra Zheleznova-Armfelt (1896). See endnote 11.a.

Natasha observed David as her fellow troupe members crowded around him, offered their hands, and poured him vodka. The hands he shook, the alcohol he refused, albeit always with a smile on his face. In contrast, Maximilian stayed close to his master's side, wearing his usual dour expression. Every time someone would shake David's hand, slap him on the back, and then depart to continue eating, dancing, and talking, David would take a moment to allow his gaze to scour the room, as if he were looking for something—or someone—specifically. Natasha, her curiosity piqued, found herself following the direction of his searching eyes. Did the decorations meet his high expectations? Did he seek a subordinate to scold, or congratulate?

Ah, and there wild winds came flying out of the east, and they ripped the black cap from that wild head of mine.

David turned to his left, peering across the dance floor and through the couples waltzing slowly to the music. His eyes met Natasha's and stopped, fixed in place. Natasha was unable to look away, her suspicions from this morning confirmed—he had, after all, been searching for her. A sense of exposure and vulnerability easily toppled her usual stalwart façade. That wall breached, the uneasy feelings she had sensed while looking beyond the city's fences into the vast Siberian expanse washed over her, even in this warm, welcoming atmosphere. The caution she had felt before embracing the celebration like the rest, now seemed justified. But there was nothing she could do. He had spied her staring back at him. If she were to get up and leave—no, to get up and run!—no telling what would happen. She would have to remain where she was. She would have to endure his stare, his approach. She would have to consider the possibility that he might be everything that people thought he was—generous, insightful, courageous.

Ah, the sounding bow was ripped off the mighty shoulder, ah, the tempered arrows were scattered on damp mother earth,

Pinned in place and squirming like a captured butterfly, Natasha watched David whisper to Maximilian. The Assistant Troupe Leader nodded his head and departed his master's side. David stepped to the table, heaped food on his plate, and nonchalantly walked across the dance floor, directly toward Natasha, pausing periodically to shake hands with couples as they waltzed passed him. A vivid memory washed over her of how Arkady first came up to her in the market: cautiously, reservedly, not with David's self-assurance. Arkady had approached her as one who was humbled before her. In stark contrast, David strode toward her as one who possessed power, exuding the confidence that accompanied his exalted position and sudden fame.

Ah, who will be there for me, that he would interpret this dream? Ah, the esaul was a clever one, the esaul unraveled all of that dream:

As David drew near Natasha, she rose on trembling legs.

"Good evening, Sir," Natasha said.

"Good evening," David smiled in return. "Would you care for a bite?" He handed her his plate.

"Oh, thank you, Sir. That is very kind of you." Natasha accepted the plate, touched he had procured it not for himself, but for her.

"I saw you sitting here all by yourself. I also noticed you were the only one not dancing or talking with someone. Why?"

"I'm just enjoying watching everyone else. Their smiles are infectious. Don't you think, Sir?"

David's mouth curved up at one corner. His eyes softened, but to Natasha they became even more penetrating, as if he interpreted her off-hand comment as some sort of signal that she was neither lonely nor vulnerable.

"I do," he replied, a speculative expression flickering across his face, as if wondering if she was, in fact, more formidable than he expected. "Please, enjoy your meal." He politely pivoted and focused his attention on the dancers twirling by.

"Stepan, our dear, Timofeyevich, you whom they call Razin, off of your head fell the black cap: off will come that wild head of yours.

"Ripped away, alas, was the sounding bow: for me, the esaul, there will be a hanging. Ah, scattered were the tempered arrows: our Cossacks, alas, they will all turn to flight."

The original seven stanzas of the song ended, and the band launched into its refrain. Applause thundered from the crowd. The musicians and singer bowed and started over, repeating the story of the Cossack leader whose great and glorious victories would all culminate in devastating defeat, he himself put to death in Moscow's Red Square.

David remained at her side, and Natasha had no choice but to eat what he had brought her. Each bite brought a new and unexpected flavor, as she tasted the various cheeses, meats, fruits, and vegetables.

"Tell me." David looked directly at her now. "What is your name?"

"It's Natasha, Sir," she said, averting her face.

"It's my pleasure to meet you, Natasha. And please, my name is not 'Sir,'" he chuckled. "It's David. Please call me that from now on. I have something to tell you…" his voice drifted off, as if he was hesitating over how to proceed.

"Oh? What is that?" Natasha prompted, lured by the vulnerability in his tones.

"Well, it's just that, when I was up there this morning, on the stage, and I was looking out over the entire troupe, it was only you that caught my attention. I'm not sure why that was. And then when I saw you alone again this evening, over here, I thought to myself, 'there is someone I need to talk to. There is someone who might understand the loneliness that must be borne even in times such as these. Perhaps she has an insight into the other members of the troupe, an intuition that would be valuable for me, as their leader, to have.' Am I right?"

Natasha was taken somewhat aback. "Well, I don't know, Sir…I mean, David. I'm not sure I have any unique insight into anything. I'm like many of the other women here, and, I suppose, similar to the few men we have in our troupe also." She trailed off, searching for the right words. "We were sent here, so far away from home, away from those we love, wondering, like everyone else, what is going on thousands of kilometers away. Especially in this foreign land, our imaginations run wild as to the whereabouts of our loved ones, and what will become of us after the war. These are thoughts, dreams, nightmares, really, that we all have. I'm not different in this regard."

"Yes. This is what I need to hear," David readily replied, "not only now, but regularly, weekly perhaps. Maximilian is efficient, but he is as separated from the daily lives of the workers as I am. You…well, you can provide a different perspective, one sorely needed."

"I'm happy to help as I'm able to," Natasha answered.

David nodded, and the two continued to watch the dance floor for a few more minutes.

"You know," David said, his attention still riveted to the dancers, "I'm not as unlike you, or the others, as you might think."

"Oh, really?" Natasha asked, curiosity piqued.

"Yes. Well, one difference perhaps. I was born out here in the east. I've actually never stepped foot in western Russia. My father was in the Revolution. He loved the west but had a passion for the east. And when there was need, following the overthrow of the Provisional Government in 1917, for a campaign to finish off what was left of the imperialists who had fled here to Siberia, he eagerly joined up. He was in the leadership that pushed Admiral Kolchak's army all the way to Lake Baikal. And when the Whites were finally defeated, by that time my father had fallen in love with this land."

David's voice, along with his gaze, drifted. Darting a glance, Natasha glimpsed regret in his eyes, and a touch of sadness and longing.

"He had also fallen in love with my mother," David added. To Natasha, that afterthought appeared a much more significant confession.

"I see," Natasha said. She joined David's study of the dancing couples on the floor, weaving arm in arm, hand in hand, and in between others, staring intently into their partners' eyes as they created beautiful, invisible patterns.

"Shortly after they were married," David continued, "my parents were among the first settlers at Birobidzhan."[41] David glanced down at Natasha, as if to garner her reaction from revealing this telling fact.

Natasha widened her eyes in surprise. "So, you're Jewish, then?"

"Yes." David smiled.

---

[41]   See endnote 11.b.

Inexplicably reassured, Natasha relaxed, and allowed herself to respond with a faint smile of her own. "My parents had considered moving there as well. The idea of a Jewish homeland was always so appealing to them. Many times, I remember, my father saying to me when I was little, 'this time next year, we'll be among others just like you and me!' But, of course, it never happened," Natasha added, with a note of dejection, remembering how her father had returned home suddenly after his tenure in Moscow, sullen, bitter, lost.

David nodded. "Yes, we all had the same dreams. But as I'm sure you know now, things there were not as they appeared. I can imagine some of the hardships you probably faced in your village, but it was probably for the better you never made the move. My mother died a few years after I was born. The disease, the hardship of that place, it was too much for her to bear. And once she passed away, my father was once again free to pursue his calling. There were still pockets of White resistance in Siberia, still tribes that gave refuge to those disloyal to the Soviet Government. He was tasked with finding every last traitor, and he did. Then, under what seemed insurmountable odds in those barren lands, he set up local networks of governments, ruling councils that could bring Marx, Engels, and Lenin to these backward lands. If there is any man responsible for claiming the whole of Siberia for Comrade Stalin, it is my father."

Natasha shook her head in wonder. She had heard of the campaigns in eastern Russia to vanquish the remnants of resistance to Moscow. Within the deepest forests, and most hidden valleys, many of the region's natives refused to let go of their pasts, their beliefs, rituals, and traditions. And even though the Civil War—and the efforts to tame the east—had ended close to twenty-five years ago, the cultural struggle remained.

Siberia was still, in many ways, a land to be conquered. The terrain, villages, and cities may be Soviet, but many minds remained untouched, vast, uncorralled, resembling the wild land in which they had been born, bred, and in which they intended to die.

"So," David started again, this time a bit more light-heartedly, "I, too, am away from what I know, here amongst these factories, confined to these walls instead of the open forests and rivers that I grew up knowing so well."

Natasha, acutely aware of his figure towering above her, looked up and locked gazes with her leader. She perceived something familiar, but not the similarities David perhaps wished her to see. Yes, like her he was Jewish, he had experienced the loss of a parent, he had perhaps felt isolation and neglect unfairly at the hands of others. But his pain seemed to be of a different sort, originating from another source. Natasha knew more about David then she could have hoped just a few minutes ago, yet he seemed as distant, and as inaccessible, as ever. He remained a mystery, luring her to explore further given his personal disclosures.

"It's good to know we have someone looking after us who understands our situation so thoroughly," she finally said with a quick flash of a smile. "That's truly a comfort." She didn't know what else to say. Her eyes surveyed the dance floor. She caught sight of Rachel standing next to Maximilian, both unspeaking. Nonetheless, Rachel's radiant smile lit up her face, just as Natasha had hoped.

"The two of them seem to have found each other," David said, following the direction of her eyes and grinning.

"Indeed they have," Natasha laughed. "It's amazing how two souls, amongst all the others in the world, can somehow meet, recognizing some complimentary point in which they can find happiness or…solace. It was like that with me and my husband. There was nothing but the sight of each other, the expressions on our faces, the tone in our voices, our words, that triggered a connection. Even to this day, it's still a mystery to me, one that I'll always wonder about."

"If you don't mind me asking, where is your husband now? Do you know his whereabouts?" David inquired cautiously, a serious expression painting his face.

Natasha's moment of gaiety evaporated. She dropped her gaze to her fingers gripping tightly together in her lap.

"Stalingrad." Natasha barely managed to choke out the word. "The last I heard he was in Stalingrad." Just to utter that city's name was tortuous. It was merely another term for death itself.

"He'll be in my thoughts. Please let me know if there is anything I can do." David smiled kindly at Natasha. She forced a polite, but grateful, smile in return.

David and Natasha watched their comrades in silence. Natasha took comfort in David's continued presence, especially since he was staying longer than obliged to. Was it concern for her since she had confided the unlucky location of her husband? She glanced around the hut. The food on the tables was nearly gone; the singing stopped. A couple of the band members remained, determined to keep the festivities going until ordered to stop; their comrades had already retired to the dance floor themselves, devouring what was left of the buffet. Those who had consumed too much alcohol, exhausted from both the day's work as well as the dancing itself, sat slumped in chairs, intoxicated smiles still beaming, lost, for a moment, in the emotional freedom that drunkenness can deliver.

"I must be going now, Natasha." David said. "It's been a pleasure speaking with you. I appreciate it. I'll be in touch soon about future meetings, ones where you can give me insight, from time to time, on our troupe's goings-on."

"I would be happy to," Natasha reiterated. She rose to her feet and shyly bowed her head. David smiled once more and stepped off. He did not seek out Maximilian, who had been replaced at the still-beaming Rachel's side by Lara. He did not shake any hands, nor speak to anyone. Instead he headed straight toward the exit door, cracking it open only a bit, almost as if to slip through unnoticed, unobserved.

Natasha stared unseeing at the floorboards. On first encounter, the patience, wisdom, yet invigorating youthfulness that she and others believed David to possess were, indeed, present and genuine. But having spoken with him, learning of his past, the death of his mother, the isolation and loneliness he must have endured as his father marched through the east, Natasha felt kindled within her a fledgling connection to this young man. To her—as one upon whom Rachel and Lara constantly relied for strength—it was reassuring. Comforting, in fact, to know there might be someone else in her situation with vulnerabilities similar to her own, spiritual vacancies left bare by the long dearth of belonging, love. She had yet to learn how to fully cope with Arkady's absence, except by writing letters to him—the only man she felt ever filled this empty space. But with no responses, no reciprocation, what was she to do?

Natasha sighed pensively, standing up to at last leave the party. Arriving back at her hut, she slid immediately into her bed, attempting to cast out from her mind questions that had tormented her of late. Surprisingly, welcome sleep found her quickly, her happenstance meeting with David providing a needed equilibrium, one that induced calm, peace, and blissful dreams.

★

David fled outside, craving the cold wind, the snow dropping in heavy flakes, needing the frigid elements to wake him from his building, passionate desire. The longer he spoke with Natasha, the more her soothing presence ushered in peace, a peace that he had suspected could only be felt in the presence of a woman. Growing up in the harsh surroundings of Siberia, with a father whose passions in the absence of his dead wife had become unrestrained, David had never known this feeling. There had been other women, of course, ones he had tried to embrace. But they were uneducated and simple, in his mind so typical of the kind that mostly hailed from the east. But in Natasha…ah, Natasha! What stoicism, as well as bravery and insight. Given the torment of her childhood, she must empathize with him, had felt what it was like to be shunned, to be an outcast, a stranger. Here was someone who could understand him and not judge, while also help deliver to the world all his potential, all his worth. His devised plan asking for her advice in order to see her again was clever, but it would not be enough, for the simple fact that she was clearly in love with someone else.

"Poor soul," David thought, uncertain whether he was referencing Natasha's husband's, or his own.

An obvious solution to his dilemma tantalized him. He shook his head in denial. "No, I can't wish that on anyone. I can't wish her husband—whoever he is—death. That's inhuman. And am I not, after all, human? Do I not have some base responsibility to my fellow man? To care about an individual, as I care about Natasha, is to wish only the best for them, to strive for their happiness, regardless of my own desire. Is this not truth?"

But the stark fact that Natasha was married troubled David. As much as he tried otherwise, he could not imagine a reality where he and she were not ultimately together.

Deep in thought, considering his interactions with Natasha over the course of the day and the feelings now tormenting him, David suddenly realized he had reached the outskirts of his quarters' perimeters. Approaching the gate to enter the courtyard, he spied a figure bundled in a cloak waiting just outside the entry way, yet a full step away from the light, hidden in darkness. As David drew closer the mysterious man started toward him. The distance between them quickly closed.

"Maximilian? What are you doing here?" David asked, surprised. His Assistant Troupe Leader was timely, but this appearance seemed extraordinarily opportune.

"Sir," Maximilian said in a hushed tone. "I have a message. A message from the Commandant."

David scowled. The thought of having to appear before that wretched and disgusting man again nauseated him. Koslov was probably upset that his plan to sabotage David had not worked as intended. The celebration had proceeded as David announced, defying everything Koslov had set out to do. David still hadn't a clue how he would make up the production shortage in the coming days. Nor had he considered just how Maximilian had secured such a splendid feast that evening, a feast that somehow must be replenished. But he would figure all of this out later. Learning about Natasha's past, feeling her spirit in contact with his, had renewed his strength. It made all of the potential problems worth the effort.

Maximilian must have read his expression accurately, as he quickly added, "No, Sir. Not Commandant Koslov. The other one. The Commandant of the Eastern Sector. Commandant *Dzerzhinsky.*"

David felt the blood drain from his face. Maximilian had a look of apprehension, as if he were holding his breath, waiting to see how his Commander would react to this request, this revelation. Unexpectedly on this cold, unremarkable hour following the social, a potentially brilliant but uncertain and dangerous future could pivot on David's next few words.

Staring at Maximilian through the heavy snowfall, David tried to gather his careening thoughts. Suddenly so much that had been confusing and inexplicable throughout the day made sense: the insistence by Maximilian to hold the event despite Koslov's threats, the abundance of food, the lavishness of the venue, the assurance that nothing would be lost in production. David gleaned its hidden meaning, finally. He was being given an opportunity by someone whom he had never met, but who clearly had plans, plans whose practical results perhaps paralleled his own ambitions, ambitions he had dreamed about, but not understood exactly how to achieve.

"Okay, Maximilian," David said cautiously, "continue with your message."

"It's simple, Sir. Meet me out here in one hour. We'll go to the Commandant together. He'll explain everything."

David did not acknowledge the plan right away. A million alarms were still going off in his brain. What was Commandant Dzerzhinsky's ultimate objective? And what role was David intended to play?

Among these hurried and panicked questions, an image floated through David's mind, one that calmed him, melding naturally with his earlier epiphany that morning when he looked at the factory; when he, for the first time in his life, saw potential for perfection in all that man had built, created, and dreamed. The image was that of Natasha. Did not her flawless beauty and sublime spirit represent incarnate perfection itself? Was she not a living symbol that the ideal could be achieved? Now, as the opportunity to perhaps realize that ideal was laid before his feet, it seemed that acquiring Natasha was not just possible, but necessary, husband or no. After all, did not the achievement of the ideal in the name of the masses, those masses who now looked to David as their leader, their savior, outweigh the interests of the individual? How things can change so quickly! If David was indeed the chosen one, if he was indeed the one who would lead his troupe, perhaps even the whole of this burgeoning city, to paradise, then sacrifices must be made. Did the interests of the one truly outweigh the interests of all others?

"Agreed. It will be as you say, Maximilian. I will return here in one hour." Confident at last, David imbued his voice with a sense of command, and notched his chin up the tiniest bit so he could stare down his nose at his Assistant.

Maximilian spun around and disappeared into the darkness, no doubt to relay the news to Dzerzhinsky that the meeting was on.

David watched his footsteps fill with the falling snow, wiping out the tracks as the clouds covered the stars.

CHAPTER 12

Arkady's head was propped up, cradled in another's hands. He felt a damp cloth wiping his face. The lap in which he lay was soft, but the ground underneath his sprawling body was cold and hard. He opened his eyes to utter blackness. Was he blind? Panicked, his body spasmed. The hands holding his head slid lower and pushed their weight on his chest, holding him down; not forcefully, but soothingly, signaling that everything was alright, that he was safe.

"Where am I?" Arkady said. He sensed a familiar presence, but it did not originate from whomever was holding him, wiping his forehead, caressing and soothing him. Rather the familiarity was from an echo of the past. Sasha's words repeated in Arkady's head.

"The Buddhist natives of the steppes compare Siberia to the Bardo, the realm between death and rebirth. Some perceive it literally—a place where wrathful spirits dwell, condemned to plot, scour, and roam until they attain enough merit to re-enter the world of the living. To others it is a reflection of our own fears and unholy desires—a haunted realm where our regrets wander in human form, where our grandest dreams and ambitions confront us in a manner that strips them of any noble pretense, revealing, like a mirror, the grotesqueness of mortal ambition"

The scenes and images from before Arkady had slipped into an unconscious delirium slowly came back to him. He remembered the town, the ancient structures, the yelling, screaming; being brought to the small, dark room where, before his eyes, he witnessed a near lifeless corpse take on the attributes of a portrait.

"Where are you, you ask? Sasha has already told you."

At last, a voice from a Being in the present. Yet judging by where the sound of the voice came from, the Being must have been a few meters away. The sound of it sent a chill all the way through Arkady. The hands and body holding him suddenly became motionless, as well.

"Who are you? How do you know Sasha?" Arkady asked, still feverish, dizzy and disoriented.

"I am someone who can bring everything into focus. All that you've experienced, all that you suspect or think you know, I can provide an explanation. The in-between, your visions, this town in whose prison you now sit, resting on the edge of history, there *is* an answer. I can put everything into context. This is something I have done for ages past. You could say, in fact, that it is what I was created to do. It is my purpose. But you must be receptive. You must listen. You must *want* to believe," the Being said.

"Why must I want to believe? You sound as if you need my approval. What power do I have over you, over anything in this haunted place?"

"You have power because you, Arkady, are favored above all of God's creations. You were created in His image. Do you not remember the stories your mother told you from the Holy Book, the story where Jacob was visited by an angel, how Jacob wrestled that angel, how Jacob defeated that angel? *Yea, he had power over the angel, and prevailed...*[42]"

"I remember," Arkady answered wearily, his voice shaking.

---

[42]   Hosea 12:4 (King James)

"Oh yes, I almost forgot…you are famished from your journey, aren't you? You are famished in so many ways. May I help you? May I ease your suffering?" the Being asked in a suspiciously compassionate tone.

Whoever was supporting Arkady seemed almost paralyzed by that voice. The hands flinched and gripped Arkady tighter. In fear? Or as a warning, perhaps, not to let this Being, whose voice dripped with a soothing kindness, get too close.

Much like the echo from the past, the first temptation Arkady had heard that night in the icy wilderness of the Ural Mountains now rippled through the stale air: *"And when the tempter came to him, he said, If thou be the Son of God, command that these stones be made bread."*

"Yes, please help me," Arkady moaned, relenting. He could resist no longer. He yearned to return to the warm seat in front of the fireplace; he could almost taste the food he had been dreaming about as he approached this village. He was starving, and the pitch-black was unnerving.

The dirt on the hard floor crunched as the mysterious Being moved closer. Tension built in the arms and chest of the one embracing Arkady. With no warning. Arkady was released as the caressing figure scrabbled away in the opposite direction.

Startled, Arkady stretched out his arms to break his fall. Weak and unsteady, they wobbled from his full weight. Inches from the floor, another strong set of arms caught Arkady, first lifting his torso, then his legs up into the air. He was carried a few steps away, set down on the floor, his back propped up against a wall. Eyes adjusting to the gloom, Arkady made out shadows dancing in slow, methodical, rhythmic motions. It was as if they were being directed by the hands of a skilled maestro conducting a hidden orchestra. The shadows surrounded Arkady, but as of yet they had not touched him.

Arkady ached to repeat his question, to know where he was, to understand his situation. But he couldn't speak. His mouth was dry, his stomach in severe pain. Unexpectedly the smell of soup wafted into his nostrils.

"Drink!" the Being said. The shadows approached Arkady. A cup was pressed to his mouth. Water seeped its way past his cracked lips, moistening his tongue, finally sliding down his throat. Arkady couldn't get enough, inhaling and gulping as fast as he dared.

"Eat!" the Being commanded. Another dark form pressed a spoon against his lips. The soup followed the path of the water, entering Arkady's body, relieving, bit by bit, the hunger that had overtaken him.

"Here, bread," the Being continued, as a stale chunk was pressed against the back of Arkady's fingers. He grabbed it. He had dreamed about it for so long, and now at last something of substance, something hearty was in his hands. He devoured it in seconds.

Refreshed by even this miniscule sustenance, Arkady leaned his head against the wall as memories came flooding back.

"I remember," he started, mostly to himself, but loud enough to be heard, "I remember a man, a tall man, almost a giant. He was ancient. His voice, the way he spoke, seemed to infect my soul."

"Hmm," replied the Being.

"I remember a village, a village that seemed to be caught somewhere between the past and some future. I don't know. I remember hearing yelling, screaming. Like a crowd under siege. I remember a portrait. The tall man became the portrait. I bowed to him. And then nothing more. I remember nothing more."

Water, soup, bread. One after another were offered while Arkady recounted his memories. It was as if the owner of the voice had heard it all before. Arkady's body soaked up the nourishment like a sponge.

"I see so many injuries," the Being said soothingly. "Your arms, your legs, and here, probably the most severe of all, on your forehead." As the Being referenced each part of Arkady's body, the corresponding wound flared up as if a flame had just been applied directly to the gashes. But after the heat dissipated, Arkady felt incredible relief. He wanted more.

"May I try and heal them?" the Being asked, taking on the air of eagerness, but also of a refined and genuine concern.

Arkady remembered again that evening in the Ural Mountains as now the second temptation was carried to his ears through the stale air: "...*for it is written, He shall give his angels charge concerning thee: and in their hands they shall bear thee up, lest at any time thou dash thy foot against a stone.*"

Arkady's head pounded. He felt the gash on his forehead dripping blood once again.

"Yes, please heal me."

The shadows went to work. They touched Arkady's forehead. The throbbing stopped. The pain ceased. Arkady's mind, his stomach, his senses now felt more rejuvenated than they had in months. He breathed easier. He blinked his eyes wide open.

"I want to understand everything," he said. "What is this place? What is my role? I want to *believe.*"

"Where you are now, this village, this town, this prison, this is not a place you were intended to be. You veered from the path that was put before you, the path that was chosen for you by the old men, by the Thrush," the Being spoke, not harshly, nor condemning, but rather sympathetically.

Arkady sighed as he thought about the fork in the road. The Thrush had urged him one way, but he chose the other. A tear rolled down his cheek. He had been so foolish, so selfish.

"Oh! Do not cry! Do not worry! Mankind often makes choices along the way that are not the correct ones. Man often finds himself in situations beyond his own control where he requires, shall we say, *divine intervention* in order to be rescued, to be put back on the correct path. But you must promise me that when you are released from this place, when you are at last breathing the clean air of Siberia once again, marching east across its frozen landscapes, through its low valleys and dense forests, you must promise that the Thrush will be your guide. You must promise to follow it. Has it not brought you already through the Mountains? Has it not already led you away from the violence of the war?"

"Yes, yes it has," Arkady answered regretfully, fitfully. "I promise. I will follow it."

"Good, good," the Being responded. The shadows hovered once again, offering more food and attending to his wounds. A faint twinkle of hope rose within Arkady. Maybe this Being could be trusted, despite the obvious apprehension of the one who had been holding him. Wary, Arkady decided to probe deeper.

"You said," Arkady started, "that you could provide an explanation, that you could provide focus—"

"Say no more!" the Being interrupted. Arkady waited, holding his breath in anticipation for what would follow.

"Imagine," the Being began, "there are two shores divided by a great river. There is no bridge connecting the two shores, and the river is too deep and too turbulent to cross. But you have heard there is peace, that there is perfection, and love is on that other shore. The only way to get there is to cross that river. The only way to realize peace, love, your true *potential* is to reach the other shore. So you set off. First you step into the water, and it seems fine, warm, calm. You push farther and farther, deeper and deeper into the water. Never do you realize that you are being swept away. Never do you realize that you do not have the power, on your own, to make it to the other shore. So you don't. You never even get close. You even lose sight of the other shore, and begin to believe that everything that you ever knew, that you perhaps ever wanted, is swirling in the river. Eventually you might even forget about the other shore, content to stay, to fight, to haunt others who themselves attempt to cross the river."

The Being paused. Arkady could hear nothing but his own breathing. The shadows, too, had ceased their work. Their hands left his body, neither food nor drink offered to him.

"When you left the ambush site, when you turned your back on all those in Stalingrad, you left your shore and entered the river, Arkady. You took that first step searching for peace, for perfection; you followed the Thrush. You encountered the old philosophers of your country's past, they who are still caught in the current, still caught in the in-between, looking for a path out, their own path to the other shore. Last night you encountered yet another figure, a figure more ancient than you have yet seen. He too is fighting, fighting to achieve what he believes will bring him the peace he so desperately needs. And there are others roaming in this realm that you have not yet encountered. Others more dangerous, more ambitious, more ruthless. They are, all of them, searching for the same thing, searching for the path through to the other side."

The voice of the Being drifted off. Arkady sat in a quiet stillness. The world had seemed to stop rotating. Time itself was now of another dimension.

"Do you understand God?" the Being asked, growing deeper, more profound.

"I don't know," Arkady answered in the faint, stilted tones of a trance. Another verse from the Holy Book echoed into his ears:

"I am Alpha and Omega, the beginning and the ending, saith the Lord, which is, and which was, and which is to come, the Almighty."[43]

"Truly He is, Arkady," said the Being, answering the echo from the scripture. "That is the nature of God. But who is this God? Some believe man has fallen out of favor with Him, whoever He might be. Man—stuck on one shore, with no bridge to connect him with what he so desires. Thus man exists in an abnormal and unnatural state in relation to his Creator, the only being that many believe can make him complete and perfect. Do you understand what this means?"

"No. What does it mean?" Arkady asked. The voice had lulled him, slowly but surely, into a dream-like state.

"It means that, if this is true, then man is indeed on his own. Man must, after all, make his own way across that river. It is incumbent upon him to right the universe, to find God, to fix what was broken. Do you believe this?"

"I do. I do believe it," Arkady answered.

"Good, good. But why would man want access to Him, this God whom, it seems, has no desire to touch His own creation, who Himself has no desire to be in communion with mankind? If it is up to man to build his own bridge to God, if it is up to man to realize on his own the spiritual and psychological unity with the all-powerful, is this a God worth serving, worth pursuing? After all, if man is able to reach that opposite shore on his own, if he is able to create perfection, is man not God Himself?"

---

[43]   Revelation 1:8 (King James)

Arkady's eyes glazed over, sinking headlong into the hypnotic aura enveloping the cell.

"So, these offerings of bread, of healing—you call these temptations? Ha! These are not temptations after all, as you have seen, are they? No, they are steps intended to open your eyes..."

"Open my eyes to what?" Arkady intoned.

"To your potential, of course."

"What is my potential? What is my purpose in all of this?"

"You were chosen by the old philosophers to be their bridge out of the river and onto the other shore, carrying their ideas, passions, dreams, and ambitions, the residue of their mortal existence now left wandering in this realm. You are to carry it back out into the world so that they may be redeemed."

Off the wind rolled another sentence spoken by the old men that night in the mountains, this one from Herzen.

"Modern man, a mournful pontifex maximus, merely builds the bridge. The unknown man of the future will cross it...Do not stay on the old shore!"

"And you? What is your interest in this? How does this benefit you?" Arkady begged the Being.

He heard a ripple of whispers, and from the Being a shrill laugh emerged, reaching octaves that seemed to burn forth from another dimension. Arkady's breathing intensified.

"Well, Arkady, my interests are, shall we say, more *long term*. But I have been trying to help man find what he is truly capable of for so, so long. Man, being created in the image of God...well, from my perspective, he has no limits. I have made it my mission to be his humble servant. Tell me, do you remember the final part of the story of Christ in the wilderness? The 'third temptation' I think you called it?"

"Yes, the third temptation. What is it? Tell me what it is!"

Over the lurid air rolled another verse:

"Again, the devil taketh him up into an exceeding high mountain, and sheweth him all the kingdoms of the world, and the glory of them; And saith unto him, All these things will I give thee, if thou wilt fall down and worship me."[44]

"This third temptation," the Being whispered, "is quite literally, the realization of your own power, your own will. The potential offered to you to cross the river, to reach the other shore. To not only touch God, but become God."

The shadows returned. Multiple sets of hands came from all directions, some from above, some from the ground itself. They surrounded Arkady, giving him comfort, feeding him confidence, as if, in some superficial way, flesh to flesh, he was being exalted, praised.

"Throughout history I have offered this insight to many men. But so far, in all of human history, only one has refused completely my wisdom, my knowledge."

"And what happened to him?" Arkady asked.

"What happened to him? What do you think happens to any man who doubts his own abilities in this universe where power reigns supreme? In this universe where, after all the debates, all the arguments, all the violence over noble ideas and principles, the only thing that matters is strength, influence, power? He was killed, of course. Crucified!"

Arkady pushed to regain his senses, to battle back the trance-induced fog hampering his brain processes. He noticed that the strange hands caressing his body, healing his wounds, feeding him, worshipping him, had been everywhere except his chest, everywhere except for the area where the icon of the crucifixion was kept, wrapped in his jacket. Out of sight, but apparently not out of mind.

---

[44]   Matthew 4:8-9 (King James)

"You speak in riddles. I still do not understand my role in this. I do not have ambitions like this. All I have ever wanted was to be left alone, to be left in peace. That's why I left the site of the ambush, followed the Thrush, crossed over the mountains."

"I have opened your eyes, Arkady. But all has not yet been revealed. The time has not come for you to make any decision regarding this last temptation; the time has not come for you to prove whether or not you are indeed the bridge to the old philosophers' woes, the redeeming key to their salvation. But know this: when the time comes you will have an unambiguous choice. Will you accept the opportunity to take power, to take the world, to cross the river, to make right what you perceive to be wrong? Or will you take the path of that man whose image lies hidden away in your breast pocket? Who refused the world I offered to him, and who is now remembered best as a corpse hanging limply and powerlessly on a cross? Will you forego what is being offered to you in favor of death and, perhaps, *the death of the one you love?*"

Arkady's heart sank. Natasha. It was as if the Being, having said all it had to say, still needed some catalyst, some instigation to spark a flame within Arkady. It was true. Arkady had never had ambitions for power or dreams of greatness. It was true, all he had ever wanted was peace. But are there not multiple ways by which human beings can be ensnared? Do we not all have weaknesses that, when the time comes, we cannot resist? It seemed the voice had found Arkady's.

He scowled and spit. The physical touch of the demonic hands reaching for him, wanting him, recognizing him as unique, special, blessed above all others, had emboldened him. The dark Being, laying bare before him the brutal reality of life, a reality of pain, suffering, struggle, a reality he had always suspected to be true, had hardened him. And now coupled with a belief that his wife, the one whom he felt was the source of all that was good in his life, was somehow in danger, Arkady's anger swelled. The bitterness that brewed from the war, the loss of his mother and Sasha, fused with rage at the thought of losing Natasha completely. He jumped up and threw himself against the wall. It wouldn't budge! He raced toward the other side of the cell, hitting it squarely, knocking himself down onto the dirt floor. In frustration he cried. In frustration he yelled, "I must leave at once! Tell me how to get out of here!"

But there was no response. The sinister Being quoting verses from the Holy Book, explaining all to him, putting into context everything Arkady had so far experienced, did not answer. The soothing sets of hands, the food, the drink, had also disappeared. Arkady was left alone in the pitch-black, imprisoned within a town still caught somewhere in the in-between.

"You promised!" he screamed. "You promised to release me from this prison, from the Bardo itself if I would follow the bird! Let me out of here!"

Only deafening silence replied. Arkady lay on the floor, once again bleeding. The final image he had of Natasha flashed through his mind. He saw her sitting on their bed, looking blankly out their window into a darkening sky, the mobilized Red Army transports below on the streets departing for the front, one-by-one. He saw himself grabbing his coat, preparing to join them. He had refused to look at her, choosing not to touch, not to kiss her one last time, as he left.

Tears streamed down his face. He was completely isolated from anything real, isolated from the earth, from life, from love, from God. In the darkness of the cell, he could not see the stars. He could not make out the constellations that gave him comfort from above, the chaotic but still-ordered patterns that gave him hope of something all powerful, all controlling.

Through his anguish the sound of rustling along the dirt floor, a few meters away on the other side of the cell, captured his attention. He remembered the set of hands that first held and comforted him in the prison, before he had invited the mysterious Being into his life, into conversation and communion with his soul. After the Being had left, along with the shadows, this figure remained, not disappeared as well. Probably a man, like Arkady himself. Real, a living being caught in the in-between, struggling to escape the violent currents of this spiritual river.

Tolstoy's whispers, as if speaking through time itself, permeated the cell...

"...we were certain of the last one too. And now he sits rotting, destined to die in prison, caught somewhere between the past and the future, in a village itself sitting on the edge of history's abyss."

CHAPTER 13

*A*h, it is not yet evening, but I have taken a tiny little nap, and a dream came to me; In the dream that came to me, it was as if my raven-black horse was playing about, dancing about, beneath the bold, brave youth...[45]

As night fell, David dreamt he rode on a galloping black horse like Stepan Razin, the wind on the Siberian plain grazing his face. The horse slowed to a trot, then halted. There was no one in sight—no village, no town, no factory, just mountains in the distance, thick patches of forest spotting the countryside, and a large river that sprawled endlessly before him. David could not identify a way to bridge it, no point narrow enough to forge through. He took out a pair of binoculars from a side satchel. Peering through them up and down the turbulent waters crashing against steep banks, his heart sank. It could take days, perhaps weeks to find a safe crossing point.

Out of the corner of his eye he spotted the figure of a woman moving along the opposite shore, slowly tracing the edge of the river with delicate steps and graceful shifts. Dressed completely in white, she gleamed in the twilight of the setting sun, animated against the greenness of splendid fields. The wind ceased. Every rustle and motion in the vast Siberian

---

[45]   See endnote 13.a.

landscape seemed to stop abruptly. Even the river slowed. The woman gestured to him, swinging her arms delicately but obviously inviting him onto the other side.

"But the river...how am I to cross it?" he asked.

The woman only smiled. Her hands dropped in front of her, clasping one another against her clean and sparkling dress. Her bright eyes looked down to the grass, then she lifted her head, her lips sweetly and softly mouthing "Hurry..."

"I will. I will! But first, I must build the bridge." David recognized her mouth, her eyes, her sway, but most of all he recognized the feeling washing over him. It was home. Peace.

Anxious to join her, David lifted himself above his mount's withers, searching for fallen logs, anything useful to construct it. How to begin? Where should he start? Above, out of the sky, he heard knocking, as if someone was pounding on a door in the sparse clouds scattered above, beckoning him to another place, another realm where, perhaps, he might receive the answer...

David startled from a sound sleep in his warm room. The soothing crackle and dry warmth emanating from the small wood stove had lulled him into that dream. He leaned forward on his bed, resting his elbows on the soft mattress, his legs hanging over the side.

Knock, knock, knock.

Someone was at David's door. He looked at his watch. An hour had passed since he had seen Maximilian, when his assistant had revealed in cryptic language a plan brewing on the other side of the city, a plan David was perhaps being summoned to fulfill.

The Eastern Sector, as those in David's command called it, was an enigma. Small, distant, forbidden, its function was unclear in relation to the Western Sector under Koslov's command. And David knew no one who had ever set foot within its perimeters. Isolated from the Western Sector, which was home to the main factories, warehouses, supply points, and the vast majority of the workers, the Eastern Sector still, however, provided a vital function of some sort to the city's overall operations. How the two sectors had come to be split, growing up separately alongside one from the other, and how they barely had any noticeable interaction, was a source of mystery. Koslov's constantly rotating point-men, those Troupe Leaders who would be in his good graces one day, only to soon be cast aside in favor of another the next, had very little information themselves. The few who had been tasked with visiting the Eastern Sector were only allowed to approach its outermost gates, where they would then be met by an Officer who reported directly to Dzerzhinsky, the Eastern Sector's Commandant. Even then, they only did so at night when the Eastern Sector's main area was concealed by darkness, when only a few lights from its buildings shone through crowded trees in the distance.

Knock, knock, knock.

The rapping remained furtive, but David sensed an urgency in its tempo. He lifted himself off his bed, donned his coat, hat, and gloves, and opened the door.

"My apologies, Maximilian," David said to his waiting Assistant Troupe Leader.

"We must get moving, Sir. Commandant Dzerzhinsky is expecting us, and we have a long walk."

"Of course. Let's go."

With Maximilian leading, the two men strode swiftly down the deserted hallway. No sounds came from any of the other rooms. Hopefully the other Troupe Leaders were fast asleep. Upon reaching the door to the outside, Maximilian pressed down on the latch, clicking it open. The snow had lightened some over the last hour since David had returned, but he still grabbed his jacket and pulled it tight around him. Once outside, the men walked closely together out of the courtyard, a single dark mass disappearing into the icy morass. Instead of taking the path that led directly to the city's main square, Maximilian unexpectedly turned right, onto a little-used trail stretching to the northern section of the compound.

Alongside their route, nascent branches and tall overgrown weeds protruded from the drifts and the close-in forest. The men tread lightly, plodding forward without making noise. Soon David felt that a comfortable distance separated them from any populated areas in the Western Sector. As they pushed deeper into the brush, David felt closer to Maximilian than he ever had, the two of them now enjoined in a pursuit which transcended—indeed, was much larger than—the immediate concerns of their troupe.

"Maximilian?" David asked through his upturned collar, his voice muffled.

"Yes, Sir?" Maximilian responded. David appreciated the fact that Maximilian still addressed him as "Sir." After all, which of the pair was privy about what was really going on? Who was working for whom?

"What were you before the war? Before you came out here to Siberia?"

"Me, Sir?" Maximilian paused, briefly bowing his head. "I was nobody. A simple laborer in an obscure mercantile shop. That is all." His voice carried a wistfulness as if he were talking about not just another time in the distant past, but another person completely.

David considered his own motivations for accepting Commandant Dzerzhinsky's invitation. He tried to isolate just what it was that drove him to be here, on this specific path, tonight of all nights. Why this zeal to pursue the ideal, the perfect?

Was it his father? A desire to not only please but also surpass him, to prove to him that David was, in his own right, a great man worthy of recognition?

Was it hatred of Koslov? The need suddenly to spite that tired old man, exact revenge, eventually seeing him off to a much-deserved tragic end?

Was it Natasha? A passion to unite with her, protect her, be the hero he believed she needed?

Or was there something else, something at the root of all of this, tying these myriad motivations together? What was this spiritual and emotional longing he felt, but could not quench?

These questions intrigued him. This moment of self-reflection demanded an answer, one he did not yet know. Perhaps someone as introspective as Maximilian had the answer.

"A laborer?" David probed. "So why become swept up in this, whatever it is...this...this intrigue between Commandants Dzerzhinsky and Koslov?"

Maximilian didn't respond. David decided to cease his disquisition. Perhaps the answer would reveal itself naturally in time. Besides, the two men had started up a steep incline, causing their breathing to intensify in the frigid air.

Cresting the hill, David could at last see beyond the thick evergreen trees crowding them. In the near distance low, flickering lights shone: The Eastern Sector, not more than five hundred meters away.

A roar of engines thundered above. David turned his eyes upward, and through the clouds he caught a glimpse of the lights of at least four planes ascending. They soon disappeared into the foggy heavens, heading west. Delivering supplies to cities under siege further abroad?

"We have to approach via a hidden path that goes around to the south, Sir. We cannot use the front gate. It's just a little farther. Please, keep close."

Maximilian started down the hill. A few meters later he ducked into the woods; an even narrower, secluded pathway bent away from the main trail. David could see nothing in front of him, but to his left the faint lights again glittered, this time closer. The men continued on until a barbed wire fence blocked their way forward. After a few more meters of walking parallel to the barrier, Maximilian stopped afront a makeshift gate, well-camouflaged and barely visible within the barrier.

David stood slightly behind Maximilian, both cloaked in the shadows of the muting vegetation. A faint light emanated from their position. Surprised, David followed its trajectory to its origin and watched Maximilian signal: one short flash, followed by two longer ones. During the silent communication to whomever else was watching, all was still. Only the wind blew. Every so often he heard the gentle sway of the towering trees and the accompanying splat from clumps of falling snow.

Out of the darkness, two men emerged from behind one of the buildings inside the perimeter. They crossed the alleyway separating the fence from the main part of the Eastern Sector's structures and approached the gate. One of the men took a key from his long overcoat and unlocked it. Maximilian stepped through without glancing back. For once oblivious to his Troupe Leader, he marched away, chin held high. He seemed relentless, guided by an internal compass pointing to a north only he fully understood. Maximilian's look and cavalier posture struck David as familiar. He had seen this somewhere before; not in the expression of an actual man, but as a painted figure, emblematic of what the Revolution, and now the war, had set loose upon Russia. David at last made the association—the laborer in the painting, *Barge Haulers on the Volga:* the youth's head raised, stoic, proud, eyes fixed on the future, having thrown off the chains tying him to a life of anonymity, indignity.

The earlier unanswered question posed to Maximilian now seemed evident. David grasped that tonight's self-described simple laborer had made a decision long ago to become something more, something consequential. Someone who mattered. David's motivations for this surreptitious, unorthodox meeting were varied, still lacking that unifying element that put everything into focus. But Maximilian? The man's cold, calculating eyes, his singularity of purpose, pointed to a desire to never again be "just" a laborer. David's father had always commented that the seemingly most quiet and harmless among men, if given the right circumstances, could slowly reveal attributes and traits overlooked in normal times. But when the moment was right, when the forces of hell unleashed upon the world, ripping and tearing to shreds the institutions, laws, customs, and norms mankind had spent centuries constructing and refining, these simple men—quiet, ignored—revealed themselves to be the most consequential of all. Maximillian was the spirit driving history relentlessly forward, keeping all on track, all in sync towards a carefully crafted vision. But who, then, was the architect of this vision? Whose orders did Maximilian ruthlessly carry out?

The men at the gate impatiently waved David inside. With a long breath, he slipped through the fence. After all, by entering the Eastern Sector, he was committing, for all intents and purposes, a treasonous act. David soon lost his bearings among the morass of buildings. Fortunately, by tracing the footsteps of Maximilian, he quickly caught up. It did not even seem that Maximilian had noticed his absence.

As his fellow conspirator led him deeper into this foreign land, David took note of his surroundings. Except for that barest hint of life, the whole of the area seemed isolated, void of activity, *dead*. In the Western Sector construction was constant. Buildings, housing, medical facilities, were rising from the earth, as if challenging the distant mountains in the race for the stars. When he walked along the paths of the Western Sector at night, David could see lights in windows, feel heat reaching out from the huts, and hear the subtle chatter of conversation through the walls. And the factory itself was his constant companion, that steel cathedral built to realize the ultimate potency of the industrial divinity: belching noise and acrid smoke, manufacturing the future all night long. But here in the Eastern Sector? Nothing but dark wood shacks and flickering, disused spotlights. As David passed the numerous buildings, he heard no conversation, felt no warmth. Maybe the storm had subdued a usually jovial atmosphere, the thickening flakes concealing windows, the intensifying wind deadening sounds. But where was the factory? Where was the work performed? What function, exactly, did this sector serve?

David and Maximilian entered what seemed to be the center of the encampment. All of the buildings were only one-story high, crumbling timber. They slouched exhaustedly toward the earth, each one indiscernible, as if a replicate, leaning against each other for support. David imagined they stood in the midst of the original settlement of both sectors, the seed from which the rest of the thriving industrial city had sprung. These forgotten structures had rotted, their remaining inhabitants condemned to view from afar the development, progress, and burgeoning authority of their western neighbors.

"Isn't that just like Koslov," David thought to himself. "While we are enjoying the fruits of the factory in the Western Sector, that decaying old man has left our fellow countrymen over here in squalor."

Halting directly in front of one of the nondescript dwellings, Maximilian knocked twice on the door. David heard a bolt release and a latch click open. As the entry door creaked ajar, a warm, low light appeared in the room behind. They stepped inside, and an armed man dressed in a wool cloak greeted them.

David, still gripping his jacket close, stole quick glances of his surroundings. At first it appeared to be a simple anteroom serving four dimly lit, directionally opposite hallways, spreading out indefinitely within the morass of clustered buildings David had observed from outside. From the exterior, though connected, the unimpressive shacks had seemed lonesome, barely standing. But now inside, David's view became clearer, his understanding of the complex grew more comprehensive. These buildings were not slouching against one another. To the contrary, they were as intertwined as a spider's web, as entangled as a knot in the finest thread. The headquarters in which Koslov lived and worked was tall. Somewhat imposing, yes, but isolated, its foundation cracking. From inside this structure, however, David perceived something quite different: unity disguised beneath rotting, one-story structures. It was as if the buildings were crouching together like a pack of wolves in order to withstand the storm, ready to rise up, pounce, and devour their prey when the opportunity became ripe.

"How is the Commandant doing, Semyon?" Maximilian asked the man in the cloak.

"He's getting along. This development has encouraged him. We were all afraid this moment might come too late." Semyon nodded and reached out his hand to David. "It's good to meet you finally, Comrade." No smile adorned Semyon's respectful salutation, but his eyes were genuinely welcoming. David reached across and shook it. For the first time throughout this whole episode, he felt important, not simply Maximilian's tag-along.

"Is the Commandant ready for us? We don't have much time. We need to return before sunrise," Maximilian remarked.

"Yes, follow me." Semyon started through the far passage leading to the right.

The three men processed in single file; David last in tow. In even intervals small lamps on the low ceiling and along the sides lit the otherwise dark hallway. Every so often, the halls would empty into another anteroom, and additional passages would spread out in a multitude of directions. Semyon never hesitated; his step never faltered. He knew exactly which way to go.

Finally, the men turned down a passage lit by only one light, with only one door ahead of them. Semyon stopped and thumped on the door with his fist.

"Enter," a voice called out. Semyon opened the door, and the three stepped in.

The room was small, but large enough for all present to stand comfortably. A low fire blazed in a stone hearth at the far end. Placed adjacent to the fireplace on the adjoining wall was a desk, draped in shadows. And directly in front of the men, sitting up in bed as if trying to absorb all the fire's heat, was Dzerzhinsky. Unlike the heavy and grotesque Koslov, he was of slight build. His eyes appeared kind as they shifted in examination from one man to the other, yet shadowed by the reflection cast by the dancing flames.

"Maximilian, it's good to see you," the old Commandant said. Maximilian nodded and smiled. David had never seen a reaction resembling pleasure from his Assistant Troupe Leader.

"And you must be David, I presume?" Dzerzhinsky added, his attention riveted onto David even though he stood farthest away.

"Yes, Sir. Thank you for the invitation." But in his heart David was confused. If this was Commandant Dzerzhinsky, then he had been misled. This was not the man whom he had envisioned, a man who was the complete foil in purpose, stature, health, and vitality to Koslov. This man appeared just as sick, if not more so; just as fragile in spirit, if not already completely broken.

"You may have expected someone different tonight. Someone who could at least stand up to greet you?" Dzerzhinsky grinned at David's evident bewilderment, as if he took pride in being the cause of David's perplexed stare.

David was taken aback.

"I...I...honestly, Sir, I had no expectations. None of us in the Western Sector know anything about what goes on over here. We know nothing about you." He added, "Only your name."

"That's the fault of Koslov." Dzerzhinsky sighed, and shook his head. "Many, many months ago he built these walls between us. Surely you must know the critical function that we provide to this camp?"

David shook his head.

"The airfield, David." The old Commandant stared at his wrinkled hands clasped neatly together in his lap. "We control the airfield. Have you or your colleagues never wondered where the flights land, where they are fueled, maintained, prior to departing this desolate place?"

A hot wave of embarrassment swept through David. He had never considered this.

"I haven't been here long, Sir. And, honestly, the Troupe Leaders...we don't communicate much with each other. We are so cut off from everything else, and the air operations always seemed so distant from what we are doing in the factories. I just don't think it crossed anyone's mind."

"I see," Dzerzhinsky said. A cough broke free from his chest. He took a series of deep breaths before again looking up. "Come closer, David."

David took a few steps forward, placing himself right next to the Commandant's bed.

"Behind you, on my desk, are three pictures," he said in a thready, weak voice, a pointed finger wobbling a few inches above the coverlet. "Bring them over here, please."

David turned around and crossed the room. On the desk, amongst a variety of stacked papers, three framed photos perched on its far edge, out of range of the flickering light. Unable to make out who or what was in them, David carried the items to Dzerzhinsky. The old Commandant carefully grasped each frame in turn, studying the images with a forlorn expression on his face. He gestured for David to sit on the edge of his bed. David obeyed, resting uneasily next to a man he felt certain could die at any moment.

"This first photograph," Dzerzhinsky began, handing it to David, "is of me at the Finland Station in Petrograd. 1917. When Comrade Lenin returned from abroad in exile. Once the Bolsheviks demonstrated a resolve to rule—a resolve that none of the others vying for power at the time showed—he saw his opportunity, and he grabbed it."

David examined the picture, faded into shades of sepia tones. The cameraman had caught Lenin striding away from the locomotive, surrounded by supporters. Close enough to Lenin to be recognized as someone who mattered was a youthful Dzerzhinsky, following dutifully behind.

Dzerzhinsky continued. "You know, David, the term 'Bolshevik' refers to those who are members of the majority. Of course, in reality we were anything but. The Socialist Revolutionaries, the Liberals, even the Mensheviks counted more members than we did. But do you know what set us apart? Do you know why we were feared?"

David didn't answer. He continued to stare at the photograph, trying to recreate a mental picture of that historic, triumphant day.

"It was because of our willingness to seize control at any cost. Others talked about power. Others talked about what they would do if they had it. But while others debated and dreamed, we set to work to realize our goals. We were the only ones who truly wanted power, to wield it, to put our ideas and ambitions into practice. It was this zeal, this drive that propelled us forward. This passion and sense of destiny allowed us to wrest the reins of government from the inept parliamentarians and those loyal to the monarchy. It allowed us to establish something new, something the world had never seen before! But, of course, it wasn't easy. We came close to losing what we had fought so hard for. In the beginning everything was so very often at risk…" His voice faded away into a hard cough.

Dzerzhinsky waved the second photograph under David's nose, his gesture a mixture of imperiousness and impatience, as if he must divulge this story now, this saga of the Soviet Empire and what it took to convert Bolshevik idealism into a reality.

"Lenin might have been able to sustain and build upon what he birthed, but his health prevented him ultimately from seeing his project to fruition. So, it fell to others to solidify, to expand, to promulgate the hard-won victories. And in the end—amidst the squabbling of the leadership over ideas, processes, methods—there was only one man who saw through it all, who realized that, in order to make everything realizable, raw, brutal power was needed most."

David grasped and steadied the second photograph. Stalin pictured prominently in the foreground, while again in the background, amongst a few others, stood a middle-aged Dzerzhinsky. Much like the photo with Lenin, the Commandant was never front and center. Much like Maximilian, he always seemed to lurk behind the scenes; ultimately a functionary, but with influence, and an obvious ability to adapt and survive.

"Stalin understood fear. He understood violence, and he used it, perhaps more effectively than anyone since Peter the Great himself. I was right there with him from the beginning." Pride infused Dzerzhinsky's trembling voice. "Right there with him to consolidate his gains, weed out those that would have become mired down in their own writings and speeches. Through Comrade Stalin's leadership we realized that the only effective words are those that are combined with immediate action. And so, we acted."

At this Dzerzhinsky picked up the third photograph. David caught his breath. In shades of black, white, and grey, three men posed against an immediately recognizable backdrop: the forests of Siberia. A churning river ran behind them, placing the season to summer. On the left was Dzerzhinsky, in the middle, Koslov. And flanking him, farther on the right, was David's father. David couldn't tear his gaze away. He had played in those same forests, next to that same running river. He had smelled the pine, the sweat, the blood. He had heard the moans, the cries, and seen the misery his father's actions had triggered within the locals who fell under his rule.

David had no idea that the three men had ever met, let alone been the close comrades they appeared to be. Young, dynamic, their bare arms and protruding muscles projected physical prowess, while their gazes reflected mental acumen. Both were necessary to excel in the wilds of the eastern taiga. They all looked away from the camera and into the distance, yet each in a different direction, as if their visions shared commonality, but not unity.

"When was the last time you saw your father?" Dzerzhinsky asked calmly.

David stared at the photo. He was not yet ready to look Dzerzhinsky in the eyes. "I haven't seen him since before the war."

"He was insistent that you come here, to this factory, wasn't he?"

"Yes. I wanted a different assignment. I wanted to serve closer to the front."

"I see," Dzerzhinsky said, putting his hand on David's. "David, I have some news for you, and this is part of the reason I called you urgently, in secret here tonight."

David swallowed hard. Moisture rose unbidden in his eyes. Somehow, he knew what was coming next.

"Your father passed away last week. Very few know. Only those who were close to him."

Tears rolled gently down David's cheeks. He knew his father had not been well, that he had slowed considerably in the past year. Bitter last letters they had exchanged regarding his assignment assailed him now with pangs of remorse. David resented him for being a figure who loomed so large over his life. He blamed him for the loss of his mother. Despite everything, though, David still wanted desperately to make him proud. He wanted to be worthy of the name "Zaslavsky."

"Don't fret, David. I was told your father went peacefully. He went to sleep, and that was that. He didn't wake up," Dzerzhinsky offered. A few moments passed, a silent memorial to the death. He squeezed David's hand. "You feel alone. You feel like you have been left with nothing, stuck here in the wilds of Siberia. I understand."

David nodded, staring at the photograph of the three men in their youth, admiring his father in this moment more than he perhaps ever had.

"But I also want you to realize that you are not alone," Dzerzhinsky continued. "You are here because of your father. Until the end, he was looking out for your well-being more than you know. He sent you here not because he was afraid of what was going on at the front. On the contrary, your father embraced this type of environment, where chaos reigns. Indeed, he sought it. He did so because he believed that out of chaos the opportunity for order, for something new and better, starkly presents itself. Think of the Revolution, materializing as it did out of the consequential tragedies of the Great War. Do you believe that Lenin would have prevailed if not for the collapse of the Russian military on the front, or if the Tsarist commanders had not demonstrated total and complete ineptitude against the Germans? Then, like now, the country cried out for leadership. What will happen if the Germans break through western Russia at Leningrad, Moscow, and Stalingrad? And even if they don't, will western Russia not be in such total disarray following this war that it will be begging for order, for a strong hand to steer it up from the ashes? Your father foresaw this months ago. He saw the same potential in this place, situated safely here in Siberia, beyond the Urals, where, absent Stalin's watchful gaze, something can be built to rival our finest cities in the West.[46]

"Your father, David, did not send you out here to keep you safe from the Germans. He sent you out here to fulfill his vision, a vision that I also share."

---

[46]   See endnote 13.b.

David wiped his eyes. He controlled his hitching breath, forcing an even rhythm. Once more his mind flashed back to the events of the day. He thought about the announcement he bravely made that very morning in front of his troupe, setting all of this in motion, and the unpleasant meeting with Koslov as a consequence. He thought of his belated realization about the potential of this city of industry itself; how if he only had the chance, he could take it to a place others had only dreamed— unlike Koslov, who had lost the will to lead it. And Natasha, that quiet, beautiful, and vulnerable creature, evidence for the existence of the ideal. She had ignited his initial inspiration for all that followed. With her by his side, the possibilities would be endless. If she were his, he would be able to conquer all before him. He could take his father's place out here in the frozen taiga, stepping into his inheritance. He would become even greater, more feared. But was becoming his father truly what he wanted? Was the risk, the trials that surely lay ahead... were they really worth claiming that legacy? Once again, David could not place his finger on what, exactly, was driving him.

"David. David...look at me." Dzerzhinsky lifted his withered fingers to David's face, touching him on the cheek. The feel of the old Commandant's hand against David's flesh emboldened him. Once again he felt special, chosen, ordained.

"By sending you here, David, your father was offering you an opportunity that only comes in the midst of chaos, in the midst of confusion. The eyes of the Kremlin are elsewhere. As they have been since the time of Peter the Great, they are fixated on Europe, forgetting that Russia is so much more than that which lays west of the Ural Mountains. It is the sum of the human experience itself. It is *us*. Not only the quantifiable, the scientific, as the West portends. It is also the spiritual—that vast region beyond the realm of the physical, largely unexplored, undiscovered, much like man's soul itself. And when the West and its rationality falters, when it no longer provides us the assurance and protection that we require, as we see happening now in Leningrad, in Stalingrad, in Moscow, it is the spiritual that will rise in its place to once again give us form and purpose.

"It is Siberia's moment. It is, David, *your* moment. But like Lenin you must seize it. Like the Bolsheviks you must want to rule. You must *want* power. You can save us. But you must trust me, you must trust the vision of your father. Most of all, you must trust yourself."

By invoking the Soviet Empire's current critical situation, Dzerzhinsky's carefully crafted words penetrated David's soul and fired his ambition. Visions from the dream he had earlier in his room bubbled up like a well overflowing with fresh, clear water. First, images of the beautiful expansive field, abundant in colors, welcoming and peaceful. Then mountains in the distant background sprang up, majestically providing a triumphant chorus to aspirations—so tempting, so inspirational!—that Dzherzhinsky had articulated. And lastly, the impassable river. In David's dream, he couldn't cross. He didn't dare step into those rapid currents rushing more violently than any he had ever seen. But oh, how he longed to reach the opposite side! How desperate he was to reach the other shore! Why? It was, of course, to reunite with her, that woman he beheld walking softly in the gentle sunshine. The woman who had been removed so suddenly from his life due to the ruthlessness of his father. Even to this day, loneliness burned throughout his entire being. Indeed, did not all the hardship, the pain, the sin he had experienced in the world begin at the moment of her death? Had he himself not become numb to the weeping he heard later on in life only after he had witnessed her lying on a bed, suffocating, her body having withered away by disease and sickness? Cries had rung out amongst the forests and fields of Siberia as his father worked his subordinates to death in the freezing snow. They pierced the deep silence of the taiga when swarms of mosquitoes and flesh-eating diseases devoured the human body in oppressive heat. But after *she* died, death and its agony ceased to affect him. After *she* left the earth, life itself lost its beauty.

David closed his eyes. Dzerzhinsky continued to talk, his thumb caressing David's face, wiping tears. The Commandant's hand moved and grasped David's forearm, as if trying to steady him, to lead him. In his self-imposed blackness, the image of the impassable river vanished. David found himself, through no other explanation than the force of his own will and desires, on the opposite bank standing next to his mother, flowing in white, alive once again. Tenderness and peace wreathed her face. To David, she had always been, and remained, the ideal, the perfect. He at last understood what was driving him. The temptation Dzerzhinsky offered rippled through his conscious. Presented with a chance to create a world where desertion, pain, indeed even want itself would never be felt again, he would not fail his mother, he would not fail Natasha, no matter the cost. He, the chosen one, would take power, build the bridge, and save them all.

"Do you trust me?" Dzerzhinsky asked. "Do you trust yourself?"

David met the old man's eyes squarely. "Yes. I'm ready. Tell me what I must do."

A smile crept across Dzerzhinsky's face. The flames in the room seemed to leap higher, engulfing the tight quarters, given free rein to burn, consume, ravage.

At the same moment, in a far-off village to the west, caught somewhere between the past and the future, as an unseen, but sentient Being spoke tempting words to a young soldier trapped in a cavernous prison cell, the following was heard floating through the still air…*"Again, the devil taketh him up into an exceeding high mountain, and sheweth him all the kingdoms of the world, and the glory of them; And saith unto him, All these things will I give thee, if thou wilt fall down and worship me."*

CHAPTER 14

The Being of temptation having departed, the discomforting threat it had made against Natasha loomed ominously in Arkady's mind. Leaning against the cell's wall, dejected and bewildered, his thoughts floated between the nightmarish present and longing memories of his last few moments with his wife...

Confusion intensified in the streets below. From where he sat on the edge of his and Natasha's bed, Arkady observed the senior enlisted leaders—outfitted in impeccable uniforms, rifles slung conspicuously over their shoulders, their voices rough, raw, and unforgiving—barking orders to the new soldiers piling out of their homes and onto the transports. Throughout the long halls of the dormitory-like dwellings, where Natasha and Arkady had lived since marrying, urgent knocking on the doors filled the air. One by one, each pound symbolized another stroke of the clock counting down to their appointed hour. Arkady imagined the doors opening- some widely, revealing faces penetrated by despair, while others only slightly, the inhabitants seeking to preserve a sense of stoic dignity. However, any noble efforts were eventually shattered, as muffled cries emanated from unseen beings. In his mind's eye Arkady had played out this scene too many times already. In every scenario the recruits, still sheltered and innocent to the sights that lay before them on the front, were seeing for the first time, in the hardened sergeants standing before them, violence in the flesh.

Arkady was dressed, his gear packed neatly in a tweed duffle laying on the floor at his feet. Natasha sat next to him. Both stared out the window framed along the side of their room. Sunshine poured through, but somehow its rays just missed them, instead capturing shadows from the chaos outside on the opposite wall. As the time approached for him to leave, Arkady had witnessed their shared dreams and ambitions fade from his wife's gaze. No longer, he felt, did Natasha's eyes reflect an endless horizon filled with joys and unexpected, but welcome, nuances, a horizon that would finally culminate in a life fully and beautifully lived. Her eyes had become hollow, reflecting dark and uncertain storms, the first gusts of which swirled in the pandemonium below and the cries outside their sheltered enclave.

The clatter of doors in the corridor continued: open, closed, open, closed. Arkady heard his neighbors next door speak and cry out in tones he recognized. His forced departure was near. He stirred, preparing to pick up his equipment and answer the inevitable knock.

Natasha flinched and placed her hand on his knee as if to hold him back just briefly, as if to claim a final moment of their time as hers and hers alone, before the state, the world, history itself instigated its cruel mockery of the simple, the plain, and the seemingly insignificant by devouring the peace they had fought so hard to achieve; as if Natasha intended to exercise authority, if just for a fleeting moment, over what she felt was rightly hers.

Arkady locked his hand over his wife's, but was unable to look Natasha directly in her eyes. He knew what he would see:

helplessness and vulnerability, two qualities that had not been indigenous to her being. Only as the hours counted down had he caught a glimpse of Natasha's fears. And for their sudden appearance, Arkady blamed himself. Could it be that, by giving all the passionate love he possessed to her, and she to him, he had inadvertently weakened his wife, contributed to the destruction of the unassuming bravery which he admired so much within her? At this critical hour, when Natasha needed her self-assurance the most, he, the one who had taken it from her, would now abandon and leave her. A cruel irony.

Twisting her palm upward, Natasha gripped his hand. Arkady could sense her uncertainty, her unspoken questions, wondering why her husband would not turn to her, wipe her tears, and kiss her one last time.

"You will come back to me, won't you?" she whispered.

Arkady looked down at their entwined fingers. He would not lie, nor give her any false hope. He could not cripple his wife any further.

The knock came. He threw her hand away and stood up, grabbing his bag.

"Vyshinsky! Arkady Vyshinsky!" the Sergeant yelled from out in the hall.

Arkady strode to the door. He paused, longing for one final look into Natasha's loving eyes, those penetrating eyes that first spoke to him in the market, and in which, to him at least, encompassed the answers to so many of life's secrets.

But he dared not turn. He could not let her see his anguish. He would not let her see his tears. He opened the door and stiffly walked out...

The cell was still black and impenetrable. Sitting on the cold, hard, and damp ground, Arkady felt vacant, emptied of life. He remained lost, stuck in this bizarre town somewhere between the past and the future, with little hope of salvation, despite the promise he made just hours ago to follow the Thrush from now on, no matter what. Yet Natasha dominated his thoughts. Because of him, she was in danger, her safety held hostage by the Being coercing him into some grand, complex scheme. In the face of this threat, Arkady regretted how his love had seemingly stripped her of power, leaving her vulnerable to all he intended to protect her from.

"I left you without saying goodbye," Arkady said out loud, the memories of his departure violently gnawing at his soul. With his head propped against the wall, he found himself staring up into the void, hoping against hope to see stars, wishing somehow they would appear above him. If he could catch a glimpse of the distant fiery orbs shining, blinking, as if they were in conversation with not just each other but him as well, he could read whatever he may, regardless of whether or not it was truth. That at least would give him comfort, false and pretend as it might be.

Arkady's lament echoed throughout the chamber. As it reached the other side of the prison, the movement he had heard just a few moments ago—when in a fit of rage, he threw himself against the stone walls—stirred again.

Temporarily setting aside the harsh memories, Arkady cried out, "Who are you?"

No reply. But Arkady thought he could hear breathing and, in between the gasps, moans.

Arkady strained to listen, trying his best to decipher what he could from the soft, sporadic sounds. This must be the person, Arkady reasoned, who had first held him when he awoke in the cell. Who, in a subtle way, attempted to warn him of the Being spinning perspectives and lessons from the

Holy Book. If this man, unlike Arkady, had refused to succumb to the temptations from that creature, if he had refused to be touched, healed, and soothed, then he had not eaten nor drunk anything. He would not have received the unholy communion that Arkady, in his weakened state, had eagerly accepted.

Arkady patted the ground around him, searching for his pack. Inside, perhaps there remained a few scraps of food he could offer his cellmate, crumbs that had collected at the bottom, as they often did, as a soldier hiked over steep terrain and stumbled over frozen protrusions in the ground.

Fumbling within his pack's main compartment, Arkady surprisingly uncovered one small piece of stale bread. It was all he had to give, but probably more than the man had eaten in days. His heavy soul lightened at even this tiny act of sacrifice, hoping to earn atonement and relief from the dark memories consuming him.

The scrap of bread clutched tightly in his fingers, Arkady pushed himself up and off the ground, using his other hand to steady his shaky legs. Never had he experienced a place so devoid of light and color. During the worst of the artillery barrages of Stalingrad, he had often fantasized about a place without any sound, a place with sturdy, protective walls that kept out the world and all of the pain and uncertainty it threw at him. But now, he would give anything to breathe in the crisp night air, to see the moon's light casting shadows upon the sparkling snow-covered taiga, to hear the Siberian wolves howling in the distant forests.

Braced against the wall, Arkady set out slowly, each step more careful than the last, his hand with the bread stretched out, as if attempting to coax an animal toward him, asking the beast to trust him merely because he possessed nourishment.

"Hello! I have food! Please, have some," Arkady offered, after walking five full steps. He heard a shuffle in front of him, closer than before. He stopped, his arm remaining outstretched, his hand shaking. He could barely see the bread in the utter blackness. Yet he felt a presence near him. Unlike the encounter with the Being, this presence was familiar, not from another realm. Someone living. A breathing human. As Arkady drew closer, he felt as if he were emerging from a dark vacuum, one in which he had temporarily been devoured, where he had forgotten himself, consumed by his regret and grief. He barely made out a hand before him, fingers reaching and tugging on the bread. Arkady let go. The sustenance safely delivered, he watched the scraggly limb retreat back into the darkness. Light crunching and a relieved sigh followed.

The hand reappeared, shaky, feeble. Arkady could only imagine what was opposite him behind the shadowed veneer: a face perhaps, poor, tragic, destitute. He was thankful for the opaqueness, grateful that he could not see what he was sure were hollow eyes, hair caked in dirt, teeth rotting out of swollen sockets. Arkady already had observed firsthand how humanity could take on debilitating and horrifying appearances. Death hid within everyone. From conception, burrowed deep within humanity, physical corruption gradually made its existence known. Year by year, event by event, painful tragedy by painful tragedy, it methodically emerged. A man's dignity was the primary element keeping the full effects of death's presence from overpowering and consuming all that he was. But in degrading, dehumanizing environments, where people were denied the very things that enhanced their value and worth, mortality showed through in vivid, morbid detail.

"I'm sorry. I have nothing left," Arkady replied. But the scabbed and filthy hand remained. Perhaps it wasn't asking for food. Perhaps it wasn't begging at all. Arkady remembered waking up earlier in the cell, cold, shaken. He remembered being held in a pair of strong arms, caressed by the hand now extended before him. Perhaps all this figure now asked for was touch, the recognition that despite everything, despite the surrounding horror and filth, that he too still possessed worth. In a place such as this, a prison cell devoid of humanity, soulless, caught in the in-between, maybe human contact was needed most.

Arkady stretched out his hand again, and the two met in the darkness. Their fingers wrapped together, becoming more intertwined the harder they gripped. Arkady felt as if there was a bond that tied them together, a comradery of those who wander. They were a species created by some god, created and then shunned, left to fend for themselves, to find a way across the river, to find a way home.

As their hold strengthened, Arkady's dreaded apparition appeared in the flesh just centimeters before him. A faint flicker of ambient light from the cell's door confirmed the grotesqueness of the squalid figure. But beneath the dirt, grime, and overgrown beard, a youthful face outlined in a worn and weary expression beheld him. Eye-level, each other's breath crystallized into tiny stars in the cold air. Arkady felt as if he had encountered his twin, a fellow traveler along a perfidious journey. Or worse, maybe they were like slaves passing each other along an ancient trading route, neither aware of where the other was headed, but certain of their ultimate, horrible fates. Time slowed. Stillness descended upon the cavernous walls, a stillness similar to what would suddenly plunge upon Stalingrad just before the Germans appeared in the sky, dropping—

BOOM!

The walls of the cell shook violently. Bricks crackled, shaking free from years of imprisonment plastered together in this haunted building. Arkady hit the ground, his arms reflexively covering his head.

BOOM! BOOM! BOOM!

Engines soared above. Munitions screamed down from the sky. He knew only seconds remained. In the blink of the eye the roof and walls would collapse completely, finishing off everything contained within them once and for all. Pulverized. Erased from existence.

BOOM! BOOM!

A blast of stones sprang from the wall which Arkady had been leaning mere moments before. Like from a detonating grenade, a spray of debris scattered across his body. The explosive force threw him onto his side. Rolling over, dazed, he blinked, wiping the soot and particles from his eyes.

"Stars, the moon..." he intoned, his head spinning, his ears ringing. Caught in a trance amidst a swirl of tormenting sounds and musings, he fought to regain focus and composure. But it was too late. The wound on his forehead broke open, oozing blood. Arkady slipped mechanically into a memory as if it were his natural state, a reminiscence echoing, in haunting parallels, the chaos encircling him now...

Grey buildings, smoldering in low flames. Steady plumes of smoke rising from ash piles reshaping the outlines of the city. Every so often movement could be detected within the hollow windows leading to darkness. But were these real people or ghosts, apparitions of the recently slain departing life, exiting the physical world to wander realms unknown even to the human imagination? Bursts of gunfire periodically rang out, explosions from the muzzles crackling, lighting the night sky in an array of brilliant, short flashes.

Arkady lay in a foxhole burrowed on the first floor of a building whose walls had been blown apart. His first night in Stalingrad. As he peered out of the gaping hole onto the mangled urban landscape stretching before him, he thought, has there ever been a place so devoid of the color of life? His surroundings represented in all their possibilities the very essence of depression. Was this what his mother, sick, dying, experienced in her mind prior to death, when the doctor proclaimed to Arkady in secret, "there is nothing left I can do," in somber tones? Was he now experiencing the heart of emptiness, that moment when man had cut himself off from God, forsaken, abandoned on earth, and left to his own devices?

"Therefore the Lord God sent him forth from the garden of Eden, to till the ground from whence he was taken. So he drove out the man; and he placed at the east of the garden of Eden Cherubims, and a flaming sword which turned every way, to keep the way of the tree of life."[47]

Then, like a falling star shooting down to earth, Arkady received a messenger of light into that world of darkness.

"I'm Sasha," the young soldier had said, as he crept stealthily into the crude refuge.

Arkady startled restlessly from his nightmares, turning his head toward the newcomer who just appeared without any semblance of warning, as his eyes, mind, and very being had been fixated on the sights surrounding him. The visons of this medieval milieu had convinced Arkady he would never again see the sun rise, feel the warmth of a cool summer breeze, nor hear the voice of his wife. Now this person lay beside him, having spilled into the fighting position unnoticed. The sound of an introduction, a simple and common name being proclaimed, pierced the horror of the fallen world in which Arkady dwelt.

---

[47]   Genesis 3:23-24 (King James)

"I'm Arkady," he replied.

Sasha smiled.

How does one smile in hell? How does one retain hope amongst the carnage, the blood, the violence surrounding oneself, seeping into one's soul, overtaking one's ideas of what define truth and reality, inch by inch, minute by minute?

The two young men spent the next three days crouched in that pit, harbored along the front lines strung loosely together—building by building—within the confines of the city, their reward for being the newest members of their unit. Their voices never rose above a whisper. Speaking in hushed tones only when necessary, they mainly communicated on levels that stretched beyond words. Pointing with fingers. Raising eyebrows. Their eyes growing wide in warning or narrowing with contemplation. Before knowing anything about each other, the soldiers established a trust centered upon a primitive extinct: survival. Like man's earliest days, when striving for existence, for life, had been his first priority. Absent any self-glorifying pretenses, the meaning behind the exercise of power was stripped down to its rawest and purest form. Even if the two had spoken different languages, they would have understood each other. Even if the two had spoken different languages...

"Damekhmare! Damekhmare!"

The foreign words rushed at him from across the cell. Arkady felt a sensation similar to his experience waking from his unconscious state after the ambush. It was as if his soul, hovering in tense limbo along the boundaries of death, was abruptly sucked back into the vacuous shell that was his body. The language was new to him, but even with his head pounding, even with blood dripping into his eyes, and with townspeople rushing in chaotic patterns beyond the cell's walls, he instinctively knew from whom these cries originated.

Arkady brushed the blood away and rolled to one side. A chasm in the decimated wall projected villagers rushing by, their shadows disrupting the moon's rays that otherwise would have poured through the crumbling cell. But in between the streams of light, Arkady saw his cellmate sprawled on the ground a few meters away, gyrating back and forth, back and forth, his hand reaching up to the sky. The image was nearly identical to the young soldier he had seen that fateful night at the ambush, the night when all his unit but he had been cut down. The night Sasha had sacrificed his own life for Arkady's.

Arkady crawled on his stomach as fast he could toward his suffering comrade, dodging exploding debris. His face oozed a thick layer of soot mixed with blood from his forehead. Smoke blinded him, as did the darkness from the night.

"Damekhmare! Damekhmare!" the man yelled out again, crisis lacing his voice.

Arkady finally reached him. With a heave he unearthed his cellmate from the remnants of large stones fallen from the collapsing ceiling. Much like Sasha had done for Arkady, he pulled the man close, almost laying on top of him, protecting him from the persistent blasts just meters away. Blood trickled from the man's mouth, his crushed chest revealing a labored moving up and down. Explosions reverberated through the air. Arkady knew he had very little time to escape before he himself ended up under a mound of rubble.

Suddenly, a faraway clock ticked loudly out of some nether region, as if it had been set in motion by the spirits of the land itself, and was now counting down not just to the end of the hour, but also to the final throes of this fortress town. Each incorporeal stroke seemed to sound a warning of imminent destruction. But Arkady could not draw himself away from this man. He could not leave him to die alone. This was a real, living being. A man abandoned, perhaps, by the very same dark forces which had led Arkady to this place.

The two men stared straight into each other's eyes. Arkady recognized in those eyes a familiar pain. The optimism so often found in a youthful face was gone. Only sorrow remained.

Arkady hung over the man, his heaving chest pulsating rhythmically with the man's own breathing. Two pairs of eyes locked yet again, their hands tangling in desperate grasps. The man's crippled frame steadied. His breathing slowed. And his stare indicated that lucidness had momentarily returned. One of the man's hands released Arkady's and slid down his own side.

For the first time, as he followed the man's tortured movement, Arkady noticed his comrade's clothes. He wore a thick jacket, and though faded and filthy, at one time it must have displayed brilliant colors, patterns interlocking in a sophisticated line-up of geometric shapes, the threads sewn in such a way as to create complex images in aggregate arrays of blues, reds, oranges, and purples. Also, now visible in the moonlight, lying next to him, was the dying man's satchel, similarly ornate and fantastic. These symbols and décor were not from the West. Like Sasha, this man was of a place diametrically opposite that of European Russia. Most likely he had arrived from the Caucasus Mountains further to the south, a land that contained within it myriad ethnic groups and lost languages. A land where Christianity and Islam were practiced side-by-side, and sometimes even in concert with the ancient pagan religions indigenous to the region. Like the Ural Mountains, these southern cousins represented civilizational divides. It was as if the earth herself had summoned these peaks in painful labor, seeking to force a truce between peoples that could never exist in a coherent and balanced peace. Arkady had never seen a man exhibiting these characteristics in the flesh. Only from drawings and photographs had he wondered at these people and the far-off places they inhabited.

The man's hand fumbled into the satchel and pulled from it a small, folded paper. With his other hand still gripping Arkady, the man drew him even closer to his dying body. As he strained, using what seemed the last of his strength, he placed the fragile object into Arkady's palm, forcefully folding the soldier's fingers around it. Like the non-verbal signals Sasha and he had developed, as clear and audible as a conversation between two people in a quiet room, Arkady believed this man was speaking to him similarly now:

"I have failed and for me all is lost. But perhaps through what I have given you, you may succeed where I have not."

Whatever this paper contained, it was a precious gift, imparted with urgency, as its former owner drew upon his last breaths.

Arkady heard the strokes from the clock intensify and with them so did the screams of the fleeing townspeople. The cries reminded him of the scene below his and Natasha's flat the morning he had to report for service in the war. And an explosion that howled from above, plunging into the earth right outside the cell, was the door slamming shut behind him as he departed, leaving Natasha crying, heartbroken, wondering if she would ever again lay eyes upon her husband.

He peered closer at the dying man's face. Such agony, such pain. But there was something new, something he had not observed in it up until now. It was hard to identify what it was. Hope? Perhaps. But what hope remained for a man whose body had been crushed, violently suffocating under the weight of his prison's collapsed walls? Maybe hope was part of it, but there was still something deeper in the man's expression, more profound, a concept that seemed to encapsulate so much more.

Arkady gripped the paper. And, with exaggerated gestures to ensure his dying comrade witnessed the action, he tucked the precious object inside his coat. Grateful contours outlined the man's eyes, as a weak but relieved smile crossed his face. He squeezed Arkady's hand hard once more and sighed, passing out of existence.

★

The next moments blurred in phantasmal bursts.

The ethereal clock struck midnight.

As the man from the south lay dead in Arkady's arms, the cell lit up, saturated by an angelic light.

A portal opened into thin air, and inside the portal sat the old men, still huddled around a flame, the Ural Mountains stretching into infinity behind.

They stared at Arkady, looks of amusement adorning their faces, as if they had been watching everything unfold.

Descending off the precipitous peaks in the distance, a flash of blue struck the sky like lightning.

Emerging from the flash, flying toward Arkady, seemingly in slow motion, was the Thrush.

Like thunder at last crackling through the sky following a splinter of lightning, the threatening voice of the Being of temptation boomed from the portal.

"*...you must promise me that when you are released from this place, when you are at last breathing the clean air of Siberia once again, marching east across its frozen landscapes, through its low valleys and* *dense forests, you must promise that the Thrush will be your guide. You must promise to follow it."*

The Thrush entered the cell, the portal closed, the old men disappeared, and the Being faded into oblivion once more.

Arkady and the Thrush. Together, alone.

★

The bombs persisted, as did the cries of the people. Fires raged outside the cell. The ground rumbled. Like waves rolling through the ocean, an earthquake split open the icy ground.

Arkady grabbed his pack, as well as his dead comrade's satchel. Preparing to make a dash to the outside, he paused momentarily. The satchel Arkady held in his hand was impersonal, and the note not ultimately meant for him. He needed to remember his friend's touch, the look on his tired, worn face. He needed an element that spoke of this man's soul. With no more time to consider, he tugged the thick, faded jacket—that coat of many colors from the south—off the man's body. Throwing everything over himself, he stumbled frantically through a jagged hole blown into the wall.

BOOM! BOOM! BOOM!

On his hands and knees he crawled, and then snow...his hands felt snow! The wetness soaked through his pants. He was, at long last, outside.

Arkady paused to get his bearings. The prison seemed set well away from the village center itself. Looking up, Arkady witnessed planes dipping in and out from the clouds in staggered formation, delivering what they carried into the heart of the fortress. He could see swirling flames encircling the ancient structures, consuming them in a torrent of red and orange, the smoke funneling their ashes into the heavens above.

The ground rumbled again. The Thrush flew directly toward Arkady's face, veering off along a crooked and rocky path, directly east, away from the town and further down into the vast Siberian plane Arkady had viewed from high in the Ural peaks so many nights ago.

Although now once again following the Thrush, Arkady did not flee in fear, nor did he turn around to behold the ultimate gasps of the Romanov's final outpost, its walls crumbling to the ground, its venerable center being consumed by an earth opening like a pair of unclenched jaws devouring the last remnants of one of the world's greatest empires. He didn't need to. He had heard the old philosophers, their musings on history. And now here, in the far reaches of Russia, where the spiritual could not be discerned from the physical, where time seemed to meld together, he had witnessed the ages fold one on top of the other, like currents lapping chaotically in the great river no one can cross. Staring each other in the face, the tragedies of man's ambitions became stark.

History, competing with itself, was about to end. How would it begin anew?

PART III

Early winter, 1942

CHAPTER 15

N atasha tossed and turned, twisting her covers around her shoulders like a lover's embrace, falling deeper into her dream...

"The raging tempest rushed whistling between the wheels of the carriages, about the scaffolding, and round the corner of the station. The carriages, posts, people, everything that was to be seen was covered with snow on one side, and was getting more and more thickly covered. For a moment there would come a lull in the storm, but then it would swoop down again with such onslaughts that it seemed impossible to stand against it. Meanwhile men ran to and fro, talking merrily together, their steps crackling on the platform as they continually opened and closed the big doors. The bent shadow of a man glided by at her feet, and she heard sounds of a hammer upon iron. "Hand over that telegram!" came an angry voice out of the stormy darkness on the other side. "This way! No. 28!" several different voices shouted again, and muffled figures ran by covered with snow. Two gentlemen with lighted cigarettes passed by her. She drew one more deep breath of the fresh air, and had just put her hand out of her muff to take hold of the door post and get back into the carriage, when another man in a military overcoat, quite close beside her, stepped between her and the flickering light of the lamp post. She looked round, and the same instant recognized Vronsky's face. Putting his hand to the peak of his cap, he bowed to her and asked, Was there

anything she wanted? Could he be of any service to her? She gazed rather a long while at him without answering, and, in spite of the shadow in which he was standing, she saw, or fancied she saw, both the expression of his face and his eyes. It was again that expression of reverential ecstasy which had so worked upon her the day before. More than once she had told herself during the past few days, and again only a few moments before, that Vronsky was for her only one of the hundreds of young men, forever exactly the same, that are met everywhere, that she would never allow herself to bestow a thought upon him. But now at the first instant of meeting him, she was seized by a feeling of joyful pride. She had no need to ask why he had come. She knew as certainly as if he had told her that he was here to be where she was.

"I didn't know you were going. What are you coming for?" she said, letting fall the hand with which she had grasped the door post. And irrepressible delight and eagerness shone in her face.

"What am I coming for?" he repeated, looking straight into her eyes. "You know that I have come to be where you are," he said; "I can't help it."

At that moment the wind, as it were, surmounting all obstacles, sent the snow flying from the carriage roofs, and clanked some sheet of iron it had torn off, while the hoarse whistle of the engine roared in front, plaintively and gloomily. All the awfulness of the storm seemed to her more splendid now. He had said what her soul longed to hear, though she feared it with her reason. She made no answer, and in her face he saw conflict."[48]

Natasha sat up in bed, her heart pounding, breathing heavy. Yet it wasn't a nightmare that had upset her sleep. On the contrary, it was the allure, the enticement of the alternate existence her dream presented, that sent discomforting waves through her soul. All of the women around her were still fast

---

[48]   Tolstoy, Leo. Anna Karenina, Part 1, Chapter 30.

asleep, and the moon shone brightly in the window beside her bunk. The sun was still hours away from rising.

"Vronsky's face..." she whispered to herself, the night's silence growing more deafening as her apprehension grew.

Rachel's library had continued to grow in the months since arriving at the factory; it was the source of much pride for her, and she meticulously cared for it, carefully chronicling each volume's condition, lending only to those she trusted the most. While Natasha had read previously Rachel's most recent acquisition, *Anna Karenina,* as in all of Tolstoy's masterpieces, the multi-dimensional characters seemed to change invariably upon subsequent examinations, oftentimes taking shapes and forms revealing the cloistered passions of the reader's own inner turmoils...including her own.

Natasha shook her head, maneuvered her body to the side of her bed, and jumped down. The cold floor, as it always did, made her grimace. She walked softly to the end of the hut, reaching the sinks located at the far corner.

Natasha twisted a faucet. The icy water dripped into the basin, and she lapped it into her palms and then up onto her face. Taking a deep breath, she considered herself in the mirror set in front of her. A dim light, hanging from a single cord, flickered, revealing evidence of mortality not usually exhibited in the contours of a young woman's face. Her skin was cracking from the persistent cold air. Heavy lines drew unnatural shapes between her cheeks and the edges of her mouth. Her once shining yellow hair now hung in limp, unhealthy strands down her deteriorating face. Natasha forced herself to smile, staring at her reflection and the disquieting crevices and dulling angles of her profile, testing to see if she could hold the expression. Her tiny muscles spasmed and quivered at the effort. Was she losing the ability even to give form to optimism, happiness, hope?

Her shoulders slumped and spirit sank. A single tear formed in her eye. But then the face from her dream, which appeared atop the body of Vronsky, materialized in her thoughts. Just a little, her mood lightened. Ever so slightly, the muscles around her lips twitched. A timid smile broke through. Natasha turned away from the mirror and started back down the dark passage toward her bunk.

Where was he? She had heard nothing of him in what seemed like an eternity. Reaching her bed, she climbed on the single step that allowed her to hoist herself upward, and huddled under her blankets once more. As sleep found her, she caught herself whispering into the night, "David, will you appear at tomorrow's formation?"

She drifted off.

★

"Lara!" the uniformed man taking roll call shouted.

"Here!"

"Natasha!"

"Here!"

It was the same as it had been over the past three weeks. Following the troupe's social, all had, depressingly, returned to normal.

Except for one notable fact: David had disappeared.

Since David had slipped out that night as the gathering wound down, as the cold wind swept discreetly from the open door, whipping through what remained of the couples waltzing intoxicatingly around the dance floor, not a soul in the troupe had seen nor heard directly from their leader.

In David's absence, Maximilian's presence had increased two-fold, and he had all but in official designation taken command of Natasha's troupe. Walking the factory, clipboard in hand, day in and day out, observing all that was happening from behind a pince-nez, he seemed to be everywhere at once. David's loyal Assistant was now more prevalent and visible then he had ever been, his demeanor serious and dour as usual. He was like the Commander of a Home Guard tasked with ensuring the well-being and safety of a settlement while a respected General was far away at war. Maximilian often spoke of David at the formations, relaying messages from him, sending greetings and congratulations on jobs well done or urging greater effort when not enough progress had been made. But David's whereabouts remained an enigma.

The three friends, meanwhile, continued as before. Lara remained pre-occupied with winning a position in the hospital. Rachel remained focused on building and improving her small library. And Natasha maintained a steady grace, assisting her friends where she could, assuring them and others that everything they knew now was only temporary, that they should always keep one eye on the future, on the day when they would no longer be in this place.

But despite her outward stoicism, David's sudden disappearance disturbed Natasha in unexpected ways. With David gone, the full emotional affects of their conversation that night at the social manifested in ways eerily similar to those she felt when Arkady left for the war. As much as she had fought against both, desertion and loss were her life's constant companions. David's absence scratched at these old wounds. She could feel her few remaining defenses, already weakened, crumbling. And as more days passed without any letters from her husband, Natasha's encouraging words to others about "looking toward the future" began to resonate abjectly within her own soul. She loved and felt deeply, following instincts and premonitions, not solely her reason. They were an aggregate of the moments in life she had already lived, the life she wanted to live, and the fears she harbored deep inside. Natasha related to David in unexpected ways, through shared experiences that touched her: his background, his own loss, his own sense of not belonging. As a result, his soul seemed to have melded with hers almost naturally, his presence filling a void that was deepening ever since Arkady left. And now David's absence had become not just noticeable, but distressing.

Thus, Natasha scrutinized his proxy Maximilian with increased suspicion. The way he moved stealthily amongst the troupe was like a bird of prey—keenly examining with watchful eyes everyone and everything, peering suspiciously and accusingly at those under his command. Moreover, his interest in Rachel seemed to have intensified, although his actions toward her—feigning interest one day, coldly shunning her the next—seemed odd and unnatural. His behavior invoked within Natasha memories of others she had encountered before. She recognized his mannerisms from days past, days that were among the most severe of her life.

Like many regions of western Russia in the early 1930's, famine had engulfed Natasha's village. Not able to retaliate against nature—against the droughts and pestilence—nor able to admit that any of the tragedies were brought about by their own conceit and misguided ambitions, the authorities struck out at the peasantry, accusing whole communities suffering from starvation and sickness of attempting to sabotage the Revolution by hoarding grain, poisoning crops, and resisting political directives.[49] Brigades of emissaries from local Party headquarters would arrive suddenly to procure unattainable quotas of goods. When the villagers were unable to give up what was expected of them, the accusations, arrests,

---

[49]   See endnote 15.a.

deportations, even executions would commence, before these Brigades moved on to the next village, repeating the demands, and handing down the inevitable punishments. [50]

Dressed in drab, plain uniforms and overcoats, the emissaries' eyes, when showing any emotion at all, projected abject cruelty. In Natasha's mind, Maximilian's gaze held a similar judgment. And also like Maximilian, these emissaries were young and tireless. Their arrogance regarding their political and economic assumptions, their sense of rightness, was evident in every word they spoke, and every action they took. They preached a truth they claimed was backed impenetrably by a scientific rendering of history.

"Who has the right to question any conclusion, any policy, when science is invoked?" Natasha could remember her father asking rhetorically, his eyebrows peaking in unison as he peered down at his daughter, imploring her, in his own provocative way, to question, to think for herself. "If numbers, the material, contain absolute truth, as the Party preaches, who cares about those concepts which are not quantifiable—the spirit, the soul, love? What is art, then, but just a collection of brush strokes or carvings, the sums of which culminate into nothing, really, but a drab, material view of existence? For to interpret a painting or sculpture any other way would reek of sentimentalism, an implicit admission that there is something beyond this world, perhaps in the heavens, to which man ultimately is accountable. And for men who believe they have found truth within themselves, this is unacceptable. Those things, and people who oppose them, must be done away with."

"Yes," Natasha thought, reflecting on her father's words as she watched Maximillian pace in front of the gathered troupe, listened to him spouting production statistics and future goals.

---

[50] Seen endnote 15.b.

"Father was so right." He had often railed in private against the pronouncements and actions spewing forth from these acolytes of the Revolution. Like the brilliant sculptor that he was, spirits beneath uncut wood and pre-chiseled stone spoke to him. If the spirits were worthy, good, he would labor day and night to free these souls from the natural prisons which held them captive. If they were not, if he sensed the souls crying out to him were rotten, deceitful, he would leave them entombed, cursed to remain in their scabrous dwellings until a lesser artist took their bait and released them. This insight extended to human beings, and his critique of these young partisans was ruthless.

"They should have never been unleashed on the world. They should have never been plucked from their obscurities!" he had bemoaned.

Pointing to the gleams in their eyes and jaggedly sharp words, to him they were not the rational, empirically based captains they perhaps imagined themselves to be, but rather converts to a newly formed religion, zealots who finally found a god after long and painful searches for personal meaning and fulfillment.

"Except," Natasha's father would proclaim, "these secular parishioners have found a god rooted in their own superiority, a god trapped in the confines of the real world, and thus barred from rising above all that is human, all that truly makes a deity remarkable. Their god is every bit as fallible and unforgiving as they are. Absent grace, the divinity they worship will inevitably assume brutal and grotesque shapes, wielding arbitrary and at times fatal judgment on the so-called sinful without mercy."

Still standing in formation, Natasha's thoughts led her eyes to refocus again on the present. Maximilian was about to take the stage. Like these crusading knights of the Communist Party she remembered from her village, he exuded an unabashed confidence. For now, at least, he seemed subdued. But Natasha instinctively feared that as soon as the time was right, Maximilian's true nature would be revealed. The urgency of the war had not chased him, nor creatures like him, away. They simply appeared in other places; their functions essentially remaining the same. If men like Maximilian had been sent to the front, to fight Germans, they would be useless. They had been trained to combat not an enemy that charged a bunker with machine guns, rifles, and grenades. Rather, they were conditioned to hunt special kinds of aggressors, aggressors that, just by their very normalcy, undermined the state. Men like Maximilian targeted the ordinary, the ones who wanted to be left alone, the ones who wished to be allowed to do the things, unmolested, they had been doing for centuries: farm, sell, raise a family, worship quietly in their own way. In short, the ones who were passive, the ones who had found God elsewhere, beyond the Party and its ideology.

As Maximilian walked discreetly behind the man calling roll, Natasha surreptitiously scanned the faces standing around her as she did every morning. There was Lara, standing one row over to the right and two rows up. Rachel…where was Rachel? Where was the mess of brown hair hanging from beneath her cap? The awkward stance, the shy reply to her name being called?

Natasha peeked over her shoulder. There she was, behind her, one row to the left. Their sights locked briefly. Yet today Rachel's usual smile did not reflect back at Natasha. There was something off about her gaze. Fear, maybe apprehension. Did Rachel know a piece of news from Maximilian that hadn't been shared with the rest of the Troupe?

The postings! Natasha's heartbeat accelerated. She turned her head again toward the front, staring without seeing the stage.

Was this the moment she would learn about her husband's fate? Was it her turn to feel tears running down her face, a weakness so severe in her legs that she wouldn't be able to stand?

The roll call finished, and Maximilian took center stage.

"Yes," Natasha thought. "He is about to make an announcement that will forever change my life."

Maximilian coldly scanned the crowd. The man has no empathy, Natasha concluded. David was kind, thoughtful; Maximilian mechanical.

"I bring important news this morning," he began. Relief loosened Natasha's tense shoulders. This was not how the announcement for the postings usually began. This was something else entirely.

"Commandant Koslov, commander of our sector, will be standing trial this morning. He has been accused, among other things, of sabotage and collusion with agents of the Third Reich."

A noticeable, sharp gasp swept throughout the troupe. Disobedient for once, the workers broke their rigid stances. They glanced at each other rather than Maximillian, wondering aloud what this could mean for the factory, for themselves. Natasha grabbed the opportunity to capture Rachel's attention again, yet failed. Rachel's expression remained stern, her face toward the front, as if she knew there was more yet to come.

"Order! Order!" Maximilian shouted, stomping one of his heavy boots on the wooden stage.

The troupe re-settled into familiar ranks.

"I know this comes as a shock," Maximillian said in quieter tones. "However, our troupe has nothing to fear. Comrade David, as you know, has been absent for quite some time. This is because he was the one who uncovered Commandant Koslov's scheme."

Ripples of hushed voices again rushed through the assembled crowd. Maximilian lifted his hand, signaling a final warning. The voices stopped. He began again, his indifferent gaze flickering over the assembled bodies.

"We have Comrade David to thank for the fact that no more damage was done than was already achieved. Commandant Koslov's trial will be later this morning. Comrade David will be in attendance, testifying, if asked. He wanted me to inform all of you of this in order to trample any rumors about his appearance in the courtroom." Maximilian paused. Natasha felt his eyes burrowing down upon her.

"I can assure you that we have nothing to fear," Maximillian continued. "As you all already know, we are very fortunate that Comrade David is our leader, and I'm confident that will become even more apparent in the very near future. That is all for now. Carry on the day as normal. Everything for the front! Everything for Victory! Dismissed!"

Maximilian stepped from the podium and marched off toward the factory. The troupe remained silent, watching David's Lieutenant depart as if nothing significant had happened, as if this were all normal. They slowly broke from their formation. Some followed behind Maximilian in single file, perhaps content that David himself was not the accused. Murmurs came from others walking in pairs, quietly discussing the ramifications about what had just been revealed.

Natasha remained rooted in place. Learning that David was somehow involved in this newest drama came as a shock. Her pulse raced. She only managed short gasps of breath. What was happening to her? Yes, she'd had apprehensions about his whereabouts. Her intermittent reflection on their conversation from weeks ago had nagged her subconscious, even invading her dreams. But... but, this was a man she had only talked to once, a man who was not Arkady. And even though Maximilian stated plainly that David, far from being the perpetrator, might very well be the story's hero, Natasha understood too well their existing environment. Laws and their objective applications, never a certainty in the Soviet system of justice, were even more liberally interpreted and applied during total war, especially beyond the reach of any judicial body here in Siberia. Personalities and their relationships mattered above all. And these relationships could change with the wind. Natasha knew none of the details surrounding Koslov's supposed treachery and trial, but she sensed David was playing a dangerous game. Who corroborated the accusations David made against Koslov, and was this person of a stature equal to the Commandant's? A misstep, a calculation in narrative gone awry, and David could be cast out, banished farther east. The wheels of the gulags, after all, had not ceased turning because of the war.

Lost in her thoughts, Natasha was startled by a light tapping on her shoulder. She jumped and spun around, discovering Rachel and Lara standing behind her. Natasha broke into a relieved smile, which immediately faded at the concern reflected in Rachel's face.

"I have more to add to all of this," Rachel said in a hushed tone. "But let's start walking toward the factory. We can talk along the way."

The three women stepped off toward the industrial center of the city. Small snowflakes began to fall straight in an uninhibited, direct trajectory to earth due to the lack of wind. Soft and unthreatening, their presence provided a surreal atmosphere to whatever details Rachel was about to reveal. Perhaps she knew more about David's role in this episode. The scene seemed perfect for a heroic tale, a story that would grow in legend, perhaps hoisting those involved to heights of mythical proportions. But it could just as easily be the setting for a tragedy, one whose characters would soon reflect the dead emptiness and silence amplified by the muffling flakes.

"I've been seeing Maximilian," Rachel offered shyly, her head down, gazing at the frozen ground. Natasha shot a wide-eyed look at Lara, who was flanking Rachel on the other side. Lara silently confirmed Natasha's suspicions with a knowing wink and a fleeting grin.

"There's so much going on in this camp, so much that those of us in the factory don't know. The Eastern Sector… Commandant Dzerzhinsky's sector…did you know that it controlled the airfield?" Rachel glanced at her friends. They shook their heads.

"Did you know that Commandants Dzerzhinsky and Koslov fought alongside each other in the Revolution?" They shook their heads again, and Natasha bet her face matched Lara's perplexed expression exactly. Indeed, there was a lot they did not know, personal histories and relationships they were unaware of, dimensions they were blind to.

"The two men have not spoken in years. Koslov, it seems, was at one time posted in a very high position in Moscow, in the Kremlin itself. And then for some reason, which Maximilian did not even know, he was sent here years before this place was anything like we know it now. Dzerzhinsky only arrived at the start of the war, with the specific task of constructing an airfield, which he did. But he had another task, one that was more secret and sensitive…to watch Koslov."

Rachel looked up at her friends, perhaps wishing to see the impact of the building political intrigue. Natasha motioned her to continue, clenching her teeth in apprehensive anticipation.

"Whatever Koslov did to be banished to the east must have been significant. No one in western Russia trusts him; but here he was, way out here, when the Germans invaded, a place well-protected from the fighting, and with an operation that suddenly became critical because of the war. The industrial capability this place already possessed to produce combat material was desperately needed by the authorities."

"So what happened? What did he do to end up on trial today?" Lara asked. Natasha remained silent, contemplating the implications of Rachel's tale, yet she was relieved to hear Lara ask the very same questions racing through her mind.

"Well," Rachel began, "Maximilian wasn't too detailed; I didn't want to pry too much. He, you know, can be guarded..." She paused. Natasha detected fear in her voice.

"Something happened after the social, perhaps that very night. I'm not sure. But somehow Commandant Dzerzhinsky had heard about what David had done for us, and he thought it was brave, unlike anything he had seen from other Troupe Leaders here in the Western Sector. And it seems that since David was new to the camp, perhaps Dzerzhinsky thought David might not be close to Koslov. Somehow over the ensuing days, Dzerzhinsky reached out to David and eventually was able to earn his trust, revealing to him that his purpose, in addition to operating the airfield, was to watch and report on Koslov. And, most importantly, Dzerzhinksy told David that, during his time in the outpost, he had indeed observed suspicious activity Koslov might be behind."

Lara wrinkled her brow and shared a concerned glance with Natasha. Of the three friends, Rachel was the one least likely to know secrets. She was the quiet one, shy and withdrawn, slow to speak to anyone new. The story Rachel recounted indeed held great significance. But just as important to Natasha was the fact that it was Rachel telling it. Rachel's eyes reflected an element of anxiety, yes, but there was also something else, something new.

"Anyway," Rachel continued, "David investigated for the next two weeks. Again, I don't know the details, but Maximilian was involved. Together they watched Koslov's quarters night after night at the request of Dzerzhinsky. They tracked his movements. It was difficult—Koslov has always been so secluded, you see? Maximilian said it was almost impossible to detect any sort of pattern in his actions, anything out of the usual that might signal treachery. They were about to give up a few days ago, but late one night Maximilian, under orders from David, was observing Koslov's headquarters. Long past midnight, the light in Koslov's office suddenly lit up. This had never happened before, so Maximilian immediately notified David."

Natasha detected an air of triumphalism from Rachel as she announced the actions of Maximilian. And to her surprise, Natasha too felt a similar pride in David's actions, as if everything she had believed about him was being confirmed.

"The two of them watched as Koslov left his building," Rachel said. "Maximilian said the Commandant seemed nervous; he walked fast, and kept looking back over his shoulder and around him as he departed his compound. They followed from a distance. Koslov headed directly toward the camp's outer-most edge, until he reached the newly constructed fencing. There he waited by himself, in the cold."

"How completely incredible!" exclaimed Lara. "Who was he waiting on?"

"Well," Rachel answered, lowering her voice even more, "it's well known that out here the locals have not been easily subdued. Ever since the Revolution numerous Russians and non-Russians alike have been resistant to any directives from Moscow. And with the Germans having invaded, some out here have seen yet another opportunity to cause problems for Comrade Stalin. Many, especially those from the Caucasus region, were of course relocated to Siberia to scatter any possible resistance. But many have continued to fight. And it appears Koslov, having been sent out here years ago, has been quietly supporting them!"

She paused and dramatically flung her hands out. Natasha noticed how Rachel's voice had grown more confident with each sentence, as if having this inside knowledge gave her a sense of authority and uniqueness she had never felt before.

"Then," Rachel resumed, "David and Maximilian watched Koslov greet two men who approached the outer fence. Koslov actually allowed them into the camp through a broken section. This was the proof they had been waiting for. David ordered Maximilian to hurry and notify Commandant Dzerzhinsky immediately. Returning about thirty minutes later, Maximilian arrived not only with Commandant Dzerzhinsky himself, but also with enough men to arrest Koslov and his conspirators. But by then, David had already confronted Koslov and the two men, holding them both at gunpoint! Can you believe it? David knew he had to act quickly, no matter what danger awaited, in order to prevent Koslov from being able to deny anything that happened."

"And the two men?" Lara asked, "Who were they?"

"As expected, they were from the north Caucasus Mountains, probably Chechens, but there's a hundred different nationalities in those regions. They could have been from any of them. Koslov was apparently furnishing sensitive information to them, providing times for passing convoys and trains that could be raided for supplies—sharing anything that could support their efforts to cause trouble for the war effort out here."

The three women had reached the factory door, the last of their troupe to arrive. Steam billowed from the stacks above them, the heavy machinery roared inside. The quiet of the snow which had engulfed their slow walk was completely overtaken by the grinding of Soviet industrialization. And Natasha found herself equally overwhelmed, indeed knocked speechless, by David's valor.

Rachel stood in front of her two friends, beaming. Throughout the relaying of the incident, Rachel had seemed to transform from a shy bookworm into Maximillian's messenger.

"All of this is quite extraordinary," Lara finally spoke, breaking the strange wonderment that had settled amongst the women. "So the trial is going on right now, this morning?"

"It should be starting in about one hour, in the newly constructed Grand Auditorium building near the city's administrative center," Rachel answered. "I'll see if there is anything more I can find out later this evening, once it is over."

The three women nodded and opened the door in silence. It was time to go to work. Time to stand on the factory floor once again, waiting impatiently for the clock to strike noon for lunch.

★

Natasha worked robotically at her position along the assembly line. Her hands moved, her eyes focused on the pieces she was assigned to inspect and polish. But her mind was elsewhere, in another world altogether. In her thoughts she was Anna Karenina boarding the carriage, just like in her dream. And as she was about to depart, David, playing the role of Vronsky, had unexpectedly joined her. Her hand slipped from the carriage door post. Her lips softened and quivered. She stared back at him in the grip of a sensual glow as his hand lightly touched hers...

Behind her, she heard a voice suddenly say, "Go to him."

Natasha jumped. Indeed, there was someone close beside her, touching her hand. But it was not Vronsky. It was Rachel, her formerly subdued gaze now lit with the fire Natasha noticed earlier, a low flame, not yet completely mature, but burning intensely with purpose nonetheless. Rachel's eyes unnerved Natasha, in a way not dissimilar from Maximilian's gaze.

"Go to him," again Rachel said, this time more forcefully.

Natasha's heart sped up. It pulsated against her breast. Did Rachel really mean...go to David now? Her cheeks grew hot. Despite her own misgivings about what her presence at Koslov's trial might mean for her, and for Arkady, David's prolonged absence and their unspoken connection dominated her emotions, obliterating any semblance of her usual rational logic. She glanced up at the clock. In fifteen minutes the trial would begin. In fifteen minutes David could be ordained a great man, or be ruined, dragged out of the courtroom for unlawfully charging a hero of the Revolution with treachery, falling victim to the whims of the harsh political climate of war-torn Siberia. Either way, she could not allow this young man—who had suffered so much already, who had known so much of the pain she herself had known in life—to be alone. She had let Arkady go without demanding an answer from him as to why he could not promise his return. She would not, nay could not, let someone else, another person whom she felt a spiritual and kindred semblance to, face this peril alone. She did not know what she could do, but she felt the need to be present, to witness and help David bear his fate, unlike she had been able to do, tragically, with Arkady.

Wordlessly she beseeched Rachel for guidance. Eyebrows raised, Rachel crossed her arms at her waist and tilted her head at the exit in unspoken command, exhibiting more authority than Natasha had ever expected a woman of her demeanor to possess. Natasha nodded submissively and undid her work apron, handing it to Rachel. She turned and fled outdoors, stepping into a blinding storm rather than the light snow of just an hour ago.

"Don't go," she heard her father say across the wind.

She shook her head, his warning voice countered by the one she had heard in her previous night's dream...

"What am I coming for?" he repeated, looking straight into her eyes. *"You know that I have come to be where you are,"* he said; *"I can't help it."*

At that moment the wind, as it were, surmounting all obstacles, sent the snow flying from the carriage roofs, and clanked some sheet of iron it had torn off, while the hoarse whistle of the engine roared in front, plaintively and gloomily. All the awfulness of the storm seemed to her more splendid now.

CHAPTER 16

Awake!
Awake!
Awake!

Arkady stirred uneasily on the ground, freezing. It was his first rest after having fled the inferno the evening before. Having walked all that night and the following day, trying to keep up with the Thrush, he collapsed under the first secluded crop of low vegetation and rocks he had found as soon as the sun set. Natural camouflage and protection became more and more sparse the further east he made his way across the vast plain.

"Who are you?" he asked the Voice, still in a waking trance.

This time it answered, but spoke cryptically. Words full of passion, they were from another place, from years passed, but timeless and universal.[51]

"If I do not [return], my dear Sarah, never forget how much I love you, nor that, when my last breath escapes me on the battle-field, it will whisper your name...But, O Sarah, if the dead can come back to this earth, and flit unseen around those they loved, I shall always be near you in the garish day, and the darkest night amidst your happiest

---

[51]   See endnote 16.a.

scenes and gloomiest hours always, always, and, if the soft breeze fans your cheek, it shall be my breath; or the cool air cools your throbbing temples, it shall be my spirit passing by."

This declaration of unyielding love even into the afterlife was followed by an equally moving expression of the same nature.

"My darling if this should ever reach you it will be a sure sign that I am gone under and what will become of you and the chicks I do not know but there is one above that will see to you and not let you starve. You have been the best of wives and I loved you deeply, how much you will never know."

"These are passions that speak to me," Arkady cried, "but in words that I was unable to articulate to Natasha, who deserved to hear them. Why is my soul so empty? Who are you?"

Silence.

Arkady drifted fitfully back to sleep. Even having escaped the inferno of the Romanov's last outpost, the tortuous mysteries would not end, it seemed.

★

The Thrush fluttered in and out of the falling snowflakes. The way Arkady had followed since he fled the doomed town four nights ago was populated with rare, intermittent forests, and ice-cold streams, but was mostly characterized by flat, barren plain stretching out to infinity on all sides. The Ural Mountains themselves had receded into the west behind him long ago, their peaks no longer visible. He encountered neither human nor animal. The unending landscape reminded Arkady of the black hole he had sensed that first night away from

239

Stalingrad in the grove, when the Thrush appeared, when Sasha handed him the image of Christ on the cross. And though he loathed to do so, Arkady followed the winged enigma. Of course, he could turn whichever way he wanted, whenever he wanted. His life was not predestined, it was not directed from on high by the whims of either man or spirit.

"*The choice is yours,*" he recalled the soothing, but unidentified Voice on the slopes of the Ural Mountains proclaim. That Voice that seemed always to be with him, appearing inexplicably in the twilight of sleep or unconscious fever, urging him to awake. From whom it originated remained, in a journey of vast mystery, the most mysterious question of all.

Choices had consequences. Each time he had chosen an alternate way from where the Thrush pointed, disaster had struck, and he came no closer to finding his wife. So Arkady's choice was to continue following the bird, to trust that it would take him to Natasha. All that mattered was she and him reuniting. From there, he hoped he would be able to weather whatever design the old men had lying in wait—the "third temptation", as the sinister Being in his jail had described it.

Besides, as he trudged through the emptiness reflecting on all that had occurred, he believed he had already witnessed what happened when one resisted, when one did not succumb to the help offered by the spirits of this land. Death ensued, as he witnessed in his cellmate, an option he had ruled out long ago.

Since fleeing the burning town, Arkady's thoughts had been consumed by this poor wretch from the Caucasus. In prison, in the brief moment they were able to see and touch each other, a bond forged. Arkady was even now wearing the man's heavy coat. Studying the material covering his arms, the faded but still brilliant patterns jumped out at him in the moon's stark light. This man had somehow defied everything Arkady had given into. He had subtly warned Arkady of the Being's presence, as if his cellmate understood the subversive nature of its words, how it would all lead, in the end, to threats against someone he cherished. He himself must have been tempted. But instead of succumbing to the food, drink, and the enticing touch of hands springing from the darkness offering healing, the man resisted. Beaten, bruised, filthy, he died of his own volition, spurning the invitation for release from captivity on unholy terms. Arkady recalled the perplexing expression on the man's face when he handed Arkady the fading, folded paper. It was one of sadness, but also something more complex. It was the same look awash in Sasha's eyes in the grove, the inexplicable smile on his comrade's face.

"Reconciliation," Arkady said aloud, at last stumbling upon the word for which he had been searching since that night long ago with Sasha.

In the end, Sasha and the man from the Caucasus were both reconciled to their lives, experiences, and their fate. Their guise was one of peace and resigned satisfaction, content to claim victory, even as death approached, knowing they had fulfilled whatever duty they had been put on earth to fulfill. Neither man's end, surely, was how he imagined it would be. But Sasha had made his case concerning the soul, and the critical need to protect it at any cost. And as for the man in the jail, he had defied the Being of temptation, refused to relent, choosing death instead. Perhaps his sacrifice gave him the surety he needed to die, access to the bridge required to cross the river, reuniting with whatever lay on the far shore.

The bridge…

Sasha's crucifix, still tucked safely in Arkady's inner coat pocket, came to mind. Christ also chose death, as did Sasha, as did the soldiers they served with in Stalingrad, those soldiers he had cursed, mocked, and despised in his heart for remaining loyal to a cause that appeared to be of no immediate use to themselves. Shame and embarrassment rose within him at his belated understanding of sacrifice. He had questioned constantly its utility in a world that had viciously taken his mother, and then his wife, from him. What did he owe anyone?

The folded paper...

Arkady had not yet examined what his cellmate had handed him. In the man's earnest expression, Arkady had sensed the final element of reconciliation, a final act that made his sacrifice worthwhile. Most likely it was a letter, one entrusted to Arkady to deliver. But to whom? He had no idea. He had slipped it into a compartment in his pack, protecting it from the elements as he fled the collapsing village and trudged through the wilderness, determined not to lose it, as he had lost his wife's final note to him.

Letters, declarations of love...

His heart sank, remembering again Natasha's beautiful writings. All his wife's letters encapsulated an otherworldly love. Her words carefully crafted, to him they possessed an innate ability to transmit over hundreds of kilometers a stratum of intimacy usually achieved only through a look between eyes, or the smell and touch of another's skin. They relayed her characteristically passionate longing for life. Arkady's shame deepened. His words in return had been so empty, guarded, always trying to keep her at arm's distance. They had not embodied how he truly felt about her.

Why?

Arkady remembered the Sergeant knocking furiously on his and Natasha's door so many months ago. He was convinced he would never see her again. So how could he, and other men, write to their wives in good conscience, words dripping with affection, promising they would soon be together? And if one did return, would things be the same? Would he have not suffered irreparable wounds, tragedies and horrors that no one should desire to share with the one they love? War—its burden was immense, and dark. Once exposed to its images, the visions never truly disintegrated. They remained seared in memory, haunting one in the night, even appearing in the furthest corners of wherever home may be. Or in latent far-off sounds, a creature taking shape in the distance, creeping closer and closer until it devoured the mind, the soul.

True, but…

Why keep these feelings locked away, allowing them to burrow into his soul, when there was someone willing to share this pain? To not embrace this gift, this sacrifice, was such a superficial treatment of commitment, an aberrant conception of love that disrespected its very essence, as well as his wife herself.

Arkady halted in his tracks, standing stock still as the snow wafted around him.

There was a darker aspect to his callousness.

The words spoken by Mikhail Bakunin that night in the Ural Mountains floated in the breeze, haunting, taunting:

"He has no love for life, as he currently understands it, or as he has experienced it. A bitterness exudes from him that derives from the hardship of losing those you love, one after another, and finding no reprieve from the emotional anguish burrowing into one's being as a result. He believes that to live is to suffer. This is the only truth he recognizes. And aren't those who believe only in regret, sorrow, and pain, are they not the most susceptible to causes such as ours?"

And his own words, spoken to himself, during moments of suffering, despair, a mantra he had derived in the horrors of Stalingrad to excuse the cruelty he felt towards life:

There is no god. There is nothing. Only pain.

A shiver crept down his spine at the truth laid bare. His soulless letters had nothing to do with protecting Natasha. His empty words were not some noble attempt to keep her safe. They were selfish, an effort to isolate himself from any further pain by pushing away the one person who desired to show him what it meant to be embraced, the one person who wished to teach him that life was not solely about suffering. He instinctively knew his wife could bear these, and other burdens with him. After all, his spirit had been drawn to Natasha for a reason. She alone was the person he could have written letters to, expressing his deepest and most complex feelings. She was the one human he could have relied upon to talk about the mysteries of death openly and honestly, the one woman who could have truly made him whole. Instead, he considered only himself and his pain. Allowing his bitterness to swell, he had pushed her away, even if deep down his longing for Natasha remained.

And that is how the old men found him.

They knew him, better than he knew himself. These sages, each with their own consciousness interwoven and intertwined with the lapping currents of regret, swirling in the Bardo, tapped into the part of Arkady's soul left vacant by his rejection of Natasha. As his wife, that empty place was rightfully Natasha's to inhabit, to soothe, comfort, and fill with a genuine and lasting peace. Taking her place, the old philosophers had used Arkady's pain and bitterness to ensnare him, and then used Natasha, and all that she potentially offered, as bait.

How utterly stupid and selfish! In rejecting the most consequential aspects of his wife, he had isolated her, his callousness resulting now in his own perilous predicament.

A torrential avalanche of guilt and fear cascaded into Arkady. He fell to his knees from the weight of this revelation and began crying, prostrating himself into the snowy earth, his arms wrapped around his head.

A wolf howled from far away. It was the first animate sound Arkady had heard in days. Still on his knees, he looked up from between his arms. A short distance away and shrouded in mist, a massive, dark shadow stood unmoving, seemingly unnerved by the emptiness surrounding it. Arkady picked himself up and started toward it.

As Arkady cautiously crept forward, the outlines of an old cathedral, standing resolutely in front of him, became clearer. Not quite in ruins but verging on collapse, three onion-like domes, clustered narrowly together, shot up from the nave toward the heavens. Collectively they represented the Father, the Son, and the Holy Spirit. Their colorful contours had long since turned a sullen grey, and their roofs showed signs of weariness and fatigue. Arkady stepped closer. The church was constructed of wood, like so many other structures he had seen while deep in Siberia. Without care and attendance, it would not last long. Reaching its ancient walls, he stretched out his scarred and freezing hands, touching its sides, feeling, as best he could, the hand-hewn panels that formed its base.

Silence.

With one hand still on the church, he traced its edges, walking away from the top of the nave, toward the entrance, inevitably located at the bottom of the cruciformed arrangement. Upon reaching the end of the long wall, he peered around the corner. The entrance to the cathedral was closed shut. Carefully he approached it, but before pressing down on the door's rusted lever, he halted and glanced around, even squinted up at the sky.

"The Thrush—disappeared without a trace," Arkady muttered, considering the implications. Could it be this holy site refused the presence of a creature in communion with the wandering dead, a creature in concert to harm the living with baneful impressions, ill feelings, and temptations left over from pernicious lives still existing in the Bardo? He remembered his ordeal in the mountains many weeks ago, the morning after his encounter with the old philosophers, when he had attempted to find his own way without the Thrush. In that struggle he had come upon a cave, a cathedral of sorts, but one empty of the divine, leaving him to question and contemplate on his own the mysteries of his journey thus far. The Thrush again having left, would these same questions now come full circle inside this consecrated and sacred dwelling? He decided to find out.

The latch clicked as Arkady's finger clamped down. He nudged the door open the requisite few centimeters and slipped inside. Darkness pervaded, save for three small candles at the far end illuminating what appeared to be an icon. He sniffed the human-induced smells of incense, that mixture of holy vine, lilac, lavender, night flower, and rose, transporting him back many years to when he would accompany his mother to mass. He took comfort not only in the aroma arising from the flames, but also in the sweet memories the thick smoke carried along with it. He stepped through the narthex and into the circular nave itself, absent any chairs or carpets.

"Hello," he said warily.

His voice echoed off the stone floors. There was no reply. He stepped over to the icon for a closer look. The image of a thin man covered in animal skins, standing in a flowing river, centered the painting. To his right stood another man, haloed, bowing his head as the man dressed in the skins poured water onto his head. A bird hovered above them all. A snow-white bird, not dark like the Thrush Arkady had been following. It was a dove, symbolic of the Holy Ghost, one of enlightened and spiritual purity. The icon depicted the baptism of Christ by John. But like many icons, the central image was not the only scene portrayed. Around the figures of John the Baptist and the Savior were other stories. There was the crucifixion itself, in small detail far off in the distance. There was also a cliff where two small figures stood looking across a ravine at a walled medieval city. Angelic beings with wings stood ready in another corner, staring at the two men on the cliff. Arkady peered more closely.

"The third temptation!" he exclaimed.

It was a common scene, its repetitious appearance in paintings a reminder of just how critical this moment was for the One tasked with saving the world. Indeed, the picture portrayed Christ and the Devil, the latter proclaiming to the former that if he, the Devil, were worshipped, all Christ saw before Him—as symbolized by the walled city—would be His. The angels hovered in position with baited breath, ready to assist the Son of God if he collapsed, if He was unable to overcome his human desires, if He decided to forego death and not fulfill His purpose, which was to hang on that cross in the distance, defying all mortal logic by rejecting earthly power in the name of something much grander.

Mortal logic, the measurable, the seen...

...a linear worldview that defined victory only by what could be changed, transformed, conquered on earth. Arkady had learned there was so much more beyond that which he could feel, smell, hear, or see. There was that empty space, the vulnerability that all humans shared. Without love as its occupant, it was so easy for this emptiness—this Siberia of the human soul—to be attacked, bombarded, occupied by lesser, sinister forces, such as the Germans had done in Russia, and the phantom philosophers had done within Arkady.

...and death—that passage to an unknown state which Arkady first became intimately familiar with as a child. Its haunting prospect hung like a shadow over everything he encountered. He could not comprehend it, an inevitable end rendering everything meaningless. History's greatest leaders, philosophers, scientists—none had managed to conquer it. Except one, perhaps. His image surrounded Arkady now in various forms, and had been with him, tucked away in Arkady's coat, since he first crossed the Ural Mountains. His was the life that underwent the same temptations all men undergo. But He never relented, even in the face of the painful destiny that awaited Him, symbolized by the crosses pictured in the distance in the icon. By sacrificing Himself for others, the ultimate act of love, was Christ not, somehow, offering to fill that empty void if He was not rejected, as Arkady had rejected Natasha's spiritual presence? But to what end? What was the utility of this sacrifice? Comfort? Was Arkady simply easing toward an inevitable and painful death of his own, tossed around indiscriminately by powerful forces of history? Not exactly a rousing call to embrace faith in Christ.

Arkady let slip his pack from his back. It tumbled like some heavy burden released to the ground. He removed one of the tiny candles from its holder and steadied it in his hand. Cupping the flame from the front to prevent it from being extinguished, he spun carefully around to gaze at the iconostasis. As a child, he had never dared approach this barrier. His mother had once reverently described its purpose: to separate those in the nave from the sanctuary in the apse hidden behind it. There, it was believed, the very spirit of God the Father dwelt when believers congregated to worship Him. Arkady had not entered a cathedral in many years, but the sense of awe at the sight of this structure still resonated deep within his being.

Stretching from an elevated platform, this bejeweled and ornately crafted gold-plated wall was overlaid with ancient, painted scenes and faces. Most were unrecognizable, the pigment peeled and scratched from years of neglect. But others were still visible. In the center of the wall a gate was carved out through which only the Priests attending the slouching cathedral were allowed to pass. On the gate's immediate right was Christ depicted in the second coming, His body elevated by clouds, being carried down to the Mount of Olives outside of Jerusalem. And to its immediate left was Mary, the mother of Christ, tears dripping from her eyes and down her face—for all eternity mourning the death of her Son. Directly above the door was another image of Christ, now enthroned in heaven. In this scene all prophecies had come to pass; the immaculate paradise long promised had arisen in perfect balance, reuniting heaven and earth into one kingdom ruled by a faultless King, a King who had suffered for rejecting earthly power, but who ultimately emerged victorious in the heavens as the righteous and just Ruler of all. Martyrs—those killed in the name of Christ—flanked Him in celestial scenes, their heads bowed, their bodies crooked and broken from years of hardship and persecution. But like Arkady, his pack on the ground, his back relieved, their burdens had been lifted now that they were reunited with Christ. Was this, then, the ultimate purpose of the sacrifice? Unity with Christ in heaven, the devils of the earth and all of their worthless pursuits of power, banished? Is this how victory against the forces of history is at last realized, death conquered, eternal life attained?

Arkady considered opening the gilded door, searching for the diaconicon, the room adjacent to the sanctuary where the priests would prepare for mass. This could mean food, water, a warmer place to spend the night, yes. But what else was contained in this forbidden place, the holy-of-holies where only the ordained could tread?

Just as Arkady put his hand to the ancient structure to push it open, a cold breeze swept in from behind him. The two candles in front of the Icon of the Baptism swayed but remained lit; the one Arkady held extinguished, its light disintegrating into the nether regions. Arkady turned, and heard a door swing shut, along with padded footsteps crossing the nave. Arkady struggled to see who had entered the church, but he couldn't make out anyone—or anything—through the darkness.

"Hello?" Arkady said again. He heard breathing, he felt life, but still could see nothing.

The footsteps re-started, this time walking away from the lighted icon toward the opposite wall. Whomever was out there knew to stay in the shadows. Arkady felt like prey, a hunter circling around him. He squinted in that direction. Still nothing. He considered walking toward the icon, lunging toward the candles and seizing one to at last shine light on all these secrets. He was so tired of darkness.

"Do not move," a female voice said out of the black.

"Who are you? Why don't you let me see you?" Arkady demanded.

No reply, yet Arkady sensed the woman staring at him.

"Your jacket," the woman at last answered. "Where did you get it? And don't lie and tell me it's yours. You're not from the Caucasus."

Stunned, Arkady instinctively glanced at his sleeves and the material hanging loosely around his body. Of all the things she could have noticed about him—his uniform, his haggard appearance—this is what stood out to her? He fingered the rough, heavy wool, its colors more vibrant now even in the low candlelight. This woman, cloaked in the darkness, confident enough to ask straightforward questions, possessed the advantage. Given his state and condition, he had very little choice but to comply and answer her.

"It was given to me…" he paused, and added, "…by a friend."

"What was your friend's name?" Her question pierced the darkness with the speed and intensity of a bullet finding its mark.

Arkady was stumped. He hadn't lied. Their bond was the closest thing to friendship he knew. But it would appear to this stranger that he had, considering he had not learned his cellmate's name.

"I don't know. He died in my arms before I had the chance to ask him."

Click.

Arkady instantly recognized the sound of a rifle hammer cocked back into position. Next would be the trigger pulled, followed by an explosion from the barrel. A shot fired.

His stomach clenched but he remained firm, unflinching. He did not recoil, nor collapse on the ground and beg for deliverance. The candles burned brighter in the background, the tears of the Virgin on the iconostasis reflecting off the glow. Her sorrow seemed to magnify with every action elevated, every fear released. Was it then, after all, the death of her Son she was mourning? Or was it the sins of man, the same sins Christ assumed unto Himself, those horrors afflicting Him, causing the sun to hide while He hung on the cross, turning the world impenetrably black, like the darkness which Arkady could not see through?

"I don't believe you!" the woman cried, her formerly steady voice shaking with anger and confusion. She strode out of the shadows, a rifle pointed directly at him. Small in stature, almost delicate, she was bundled from head to toe in rags. Like Arkady's coat, they were stained with faded colors, probably from surviving the grey, harsh weather of Siberia. She shoved back deep black hair flowing from beneath her cap, and Arkady caught a glimpse of fierce, uncompromising eyes dominating an unlined face.

"I can prove it!" Arkady said, his eyes widening. He had seen this look before. Something deeply personal had wormed its way into the woman's soul. Something had taken hold of her. Whatever happened next, her actions would be hers, but they would belong to something—or someone—else.

"Please! Let me show you! I have a letter from him...over there!" Fully recognizing the severity of his situation, Arkady darted back to retrieve his pack and the letter contained within.

He heard the trigger pulled. The shot fired. A fiery bullet pierced his leg. He collapsed, crying out. The church started spinning, yet he crawled forward on the wooden floor. His purpose remained...get to his pack, show the young woman the letter.

It was his only chance.

His fingers dug futilely into the stone. His breathing became hoarse, gasping for life. A trail of blood followed him along the hallowed ground. The paintings which had been still just moments ago, now lit up in animating motions before his eyes. The Virgin's tears flowed more freely than ever. Christ enthroned in heaven turned his face toward the dying Russian soldier below Him; the Martyrs, however, remained fixated on their Savior's regality, his scepter, his crown. They could seemingly bear no more death.

Arkady reached his pack. He thrust his hand into the compartment and fumbled inside. At last he wrapped his fingers around that scrap of paper. He yanked it out and threw it toward his assailant watching from a safe distance, her rifle still held to her shoulder, ready to fire off the shot that would end his life.

Over the clamor of his plangent heart he heard a thundering Voice radiating from behind the iconostasis, that holy-of-holies, the sanctuary that only the special few could inhabit. It was not the voice of the Being of temptation in the cell, nor the noise of convoluted debate that emanated from the old philosophers. This one was indecipherable, but at the same time it seemed all at once to say everything. As its piercing sound rippled in waves throughout the church, the gold on the holy gate shone brighter, the peeling and faded paint from the coarsened paintings on the walls and ceilings were vigorously renewed, revealing in all their sparkling splendor esoteric symbols and prayers. To Arkady the booming Voice was louder and more powerful than anything he had ever experienced. Yet, in some related, lesser form, he had heard it before. It conjured within his soul the same sensation he experienced while in the presence of Natasha, a feeling of belonging, one of completeness that in the deepest recesses of his heart he knew he could never be without. It delivered a sense of wholeness akin to a mighty waterfall quenching a deep and lasting yearning for what was real and true.

The tones of the Voice echoed and bounced throughout the nave, circling like a storm around the ancient beams. Arkady watched in awe as the Angels depicted in the icon came to life. As one, they turned their attention from Christ and the Devil on the cliff, as if acting on command. Descending from the ancient wooden panel, their spirits moved together through the candles, assuming full stature and form when they touched the ground. And as they alighted in front of Arkady, in unison they each drew from a hidden sheath a bright and flaming sword turned every way, their wings spreading wide around Arkady, sheltering him from any further harm.

Arkady's vision blurred, and the cut on his forehead—that deep wound that would never heal—once again spurt blood. Through his daze Arkady watched the woman drop her rifle, with no indication that she saw nor heard any of the fantastic and surreal phenomena circling around them both. She retrieved the note and opened it. Her eyes narrowed, like she just had been stabbed with a poisonous blade. Falling to her knees, crying, suddenly she appeared more alone than anyone else in the world.

Arkady's eyes drifted closed to the tender notes of the woman softly chanting:

> The hills of Georgia are covered by the night;
> Ahead Aragva runs through stone,
> My feeling's sad and light; my sorrow is bright;
> My sorrow is full of you alone,
>
> Of you, of only you... My everlasting gloom
> Meets neither troubles nor resistance.
> Again inflames and loves my poor heart, for whom
> Without love, 'tis no existence. [52]

Floating in a state of semi-consciousness, reeling from the pain and loss of blood flowing from his body, Arkady acutely absorbed the woman's emotional outpouring. As her grief floated through the air and into his flickering consciousness, the bitterness and guilt burning throughout his being revealed in full their source. Letters, notes, poems and declarations of love—these were all foreign to him. He had never fully confronted his passion for Natasha, nor the semblance of

---

[52]   *The Hills of Georgia*, by Alexander Pushkin, 1829

completion and peace she could offer him. He had never allowed to infect his soul the dimension of love that inspired men to write prose of longing, or suffer death on another's behalf, as the soldiers at Stalingrad had done for their country. As Sasha had done for him, or Christ for all mankind. And neither had he experienced the passion compelling this woman to fire a shot in an act of vengeance for another.

CHAPTER 17

"Don't go..."

Natasha hurried out the factory door into the snowstorm, brushing off the warning of her father. But his haunting voice persisted, echoing in her ears, as if his spirit was not content to allow his daughter to be swept away by the weakening of her will.

"What is it that you seek?" he implored her. "In every act of free will exercised, what desire is man, truly trying to fulfill?"

Hesitating at the crossroad leading toward the center of the city, Natasha sensed a drumbeat of destiny driving her. The voice of her father in the back of her mind caused doubts and uneasiness to gnaw at her soul. To leave the factory floor without permission and witness the trial, to alleviate all of the burrowing passions that had worn her down mentally, physically, and spiritually, Natasha had succumbed to forces more powerful than she had ever known: loneliness, sorrow, anguish. In the absence of Arkady's loving warmth, pronounced by the cold, matter-of-factness of his sporadic communication, her defense of their life commitment had indeed started to fade. The dream where she was Anna Karenina, and David was Vronsky, had not been a one-time occurrence, but reappeared over the course of many nights, chasing her, haunting her, speaking directly to the despair slowly overtaking her. Her spirit begged for color, for the strength to lift the contours of her mouth into the form of a smile, to once again be beautiful and worthy in the eyes of someone who needed her.

The physical world of Natasha's current existence was small and confining. It consisted of a narrow corridor, one that stretched from where she slept at night, to where she assembled for formation in the morning, to the cafeteria where she ate, and to the wing of the factory where she worked. On her way back to her barracks in the evening, she had never turned left— always straight, always returning to the familiar thoughts and dreams of another life that existed far away, in another time.

This morning, however, she veered left instead, heading directly into a section of the factory town, and into a corner of her soul, she had never stepped. Leaving behind the places she knew so well, ahead lay undiscovered realms. In the distance these kingdoms appeared bright, welcoming, but Natasha knew mirages, especially in a desert such as Siberia, were many. These seemingly majestic skylines of opportunity could, in reality, be badlands, jagged peaks of earth that look so enticing and protecting from afar, but upon arrival were infertile, shifting mounds of sand.

Although focused assiduously on making her way to the trial, as Natasha moved from one sector of the city to the other the subtle evidence of immense activity caught her eye. Strewn around the area were ponderous logs, monochromatic steel beams, fencing, cinder blocks, and other material stacked high for construction. Next to these piles, carefully positioned for eventual use, were mechanical contraptions that could dig, hoist, pull, and forcibly push civilization into existence.

"Lenin once proclaimed, 'Communism is Soviet Power plus electrification of the whole country'," another of her father's warnings whispered in her ear. "These machines are intended not just to build for the sake of building. They are instruments of revolution, time machines ushering in a new age. They are present in order to turn mere mirages into reality."

Natasha's mission remained singular. Nothing that she saw was of consequence enough to distract her. Bypassing everything without a second glance, the desires of her heart, her spirit, paid little heed to the fleeting whims of man's quest for modernity. Her soul's need for fulfillment, even in this age and under these harsh circumstances, drove everything.

Rounding a corner, Natasha found herself on what appeared to be a broad street. Here at last, something of consequence captured her attention. Not too far off was a crowd. The horde of people congregated around the tallest, most imposing building on this cluttered street. It was the Grand Auditorium-the newest architectural wonder in the ever-expanding industrial landscape. Unlike the older buildings made of wood, it was concrete, rising five stories into the air with wide stairs ascending into a lavish, but serious entrance. A steel Hammer & Sickle was placed prominently above the heavy, cathedral-like copper doors. Adorning it, carved into the building itself, was a stone wreath. Newly installed windows on the ground floor were elegantly draped by white lace curtains inside. Natasha slowed her step and approached the building cautiously. She would have to push her way through the crowd of people, all of whom, she was sure, were there to bear witness to the trial, too.

Natasha walked gingerly up the first few steps, approaching the edge of the crowd. Although one of the imposing doors gaped open, someone stood before it, blocking the entrance, picking who could enter. Determinedly, Natasha made her way forward, uttering polite excuses and platitudes for what even she would generally consider rude behavior. She leveraged her delicate frame, unassuming expression, and breathless apologies to push through the bodies to the top of the stairs, at last finding herself face to face with Maximilian. As always, he stood guard, ensuring no person, action, or event would interfere with the carefully crafted plans of those whom he served.

The two locked gazes. The mob encircling Natasha faded into the background. Maximilian showed no emotion, his usual calculating stare instead conveying to Natasha an offer: Entrance in exchange for what? The moment of consequence arrived; she faced a decision.

Natasha bowed her head and stared unseeing at her feet. Should she turn around, return to the factory and all that was familiar, forgetting the impulsive decision to attend the trial? A firm, reassuring hand suddenly touched her shoulder. Surprised, Natasha followed the line of the hand up a uniform-sleeved arm over a muscular shoulder and met Maximillian's eyes. This time, instead of his usual dourness, she sensed a hint of compassion, as if he empathized with her uncertainty. Natasha's vivid dream again raced through her mind; at the same time, she felt both the warmth and vulnerabilities David had revealed to her that evening at the social, Vronsky to her Anna.

"What am I coming for? …You know that I have come to be where you are, …I can't help it."

Maximilian's grip on Natasha's shoulder tightened, and as he drew her near him, Natasha imagined David's face instead of Maximillian's, directing her under his arm, and into the open lobby behind. She did not resist. Capitulating to the invitation, she allowed herself to be led, and in she ducked.

Once inside, Natasha felt like she had entered another realm, much like her experience when she entered the train station so many months ago. She stared in wonder at not just the craftsmanship on display before her, but the sheer audacity of what was being conveyed to all who stood beneath its arches. Similar to the depot, this was a palace. Red carpet graced the floor, while portraits of Marx, Lenin, and Stalin hung triumphantly above three ornately carved wooden doors leading toward what must be the main theater. Stately staircases, meanwhile, ascended the far sides of both ends, their smooth white and grey marble set precisely under intricately woven, multi-colored runners—a nod, surely, to the region's indigenous peoples and their legacy of woven carpets.

Natasha barely had time to catch her breath before she heard voices on the other side of the three wooden doors, and a gavel being swung violently onto a table, calling all present to order. Maximilian had shut the door to the outside—apparently whoever was in, was in—and walked silently away without another gesture toward Natasha. Belatedly realizing she was all alone in this monumental but cold foyer, Natasha stepped to the furthest door on the left. Like someone returning late to a show after it had already started, she eased it open, wincing at each slight creak, anticipating anyone who might be standing on the other side. Unnoticed, Natasha slipped through the narrow gap and surveyed her foreign surroundings.

On the other side, there was indeed standing room only in the large, half-oval spectator hall spreading out before her. The stage up front, carved from what appeared to be local timber, was as ornately decorated as the majestic entryway. Admiring it, Natasha heard her father's voice again, as if he seized yet another opportunity to further press his case.

"The stage is a beautiful spectacle," he began, his soothing tones rippling through her conscious. "It has been chiseled from the minds and hands of serious artists who know their craft and applied it expertly. Through it you see the heights of man's abilities when, unopposed and without interference from the authorities, he is allowed to burrow deep within his soul, relying on talents and hidden passions that could only be defined as divinely inspired."

Natasha peered at the intricate carvings, seeking the artistic manifestation of such passions.

"For that reason this stage is a work of art," the ghostly voice sighed, "not to be truly understood by any who do not believe in those spiritual forces summoned to create it."

Absorbing all that her father said as she stood watching, observing from the rear of the voluminous room, she jerked when the gavel came down swiftly again. Forgetting momentarily the beauty of the stage, she noted two men and one woman in military uniforms seated together in a straight line atop it, centered on a heightened platform. Directly below them was a lone, solitary, unadorned chair. Still empty, she realized it was meant for the accused himself: Commandant Koslov. Perched from lofty heights, the judges were positioned in such a way as to be peering down upon both Koslov as soon he was marched out, as well as the gathered audience, who would be able to witness their mouths form every question, every word of judgment, witness every expression creeping across their faces.

"Sometimes, in even these serene environments, events force ironies in the most obvious way, at least to those with no vested interest in their outcome," Natasha's father continued, reorienting his observations as his daughter shifted hers. "For all appearances, these judges are assembled, facing the crowd, to hear arguments, both for and against the accused, and to deliver a verdict free of passion or prejudice. But, my dear, look closer! The stage—its original purpose to transport the audience to realms of the pretend, surreal, or fantastical—counters, to all who have eyes to see, the purpose of this trial itself. Unseen by those who decided to have the proceeding in this venue, blinded as they were by their desire to have as much visibility and communal participation as possible, the stage, unwittingly, becomes the fourth, silent judge! One that, just by its very existence, renders a devastating judgment on the nature of this spectacle, before it even takes place: a fantastic sham, a surreal joke of the highest but most deplorable order, where we, the willing participants, so consumed by our own self-regard, neglect to see the organizers as the puppet-masters they truly are, and ourselves as the unwitting stooges in this tragic charade."

In these moments her father had never seemed so real, so passionate as he did now. Up until now, she had tried to disregard his voice as just merely her own conscience, shadows of memories that would, every so often, worm their way into her mind. But this was different. This place, this land, these proceedings, were so far away from what she had ever defined as real. She decided to ask the question which she had yearned to ask for so many years.

"Father, why did you return suddenly from Moscow in 1937? Why did you abandon the work into which you had so passionately poured your soul? What was it that made you come home, depressed, causing you to hole away in your room for weeks at a time, only to die a year later, in abject despair?"

As she asked this question, she grew dizzy. The stage blurred, all but disappearing. The judges remained, but seemed to shift in space and time, their faces growing longer, older, although the uniforms remained essentially the same. The crowd around her expanded, as did the auditorium, opening up into a wide, grey-paneled room. The empty chair multiplied several times over, and suddenly sitting upon them were two men in a spotlight, while situated around them were fourteen, faceless others. Natasha recognized the two under the lights from the newspaper photos she had stared at as a youth: Lev Kamenev, and Grigory Zinoviev.[53] Like Koslov, they were Revolutionaries, both colleagues of Lenin, the "old" Bolsheviks, founders of the Soviet Union and members of the original Politburo54 that first met in 1917 to oversee the consolidation of power of the new Communist state. Later, after Lenin's passing, these two men had formed a ruling triumvirate with Stalin. As Stalin consolidated power over the ensuing decade, their political situation became more and more tenuous, until they were finally accused and convicted of collaboration with foreign agents and sabotage, not unlike Koslov now.

"Why show this to me, Father?" Natasha asked. "Did you witness this?"

"It is for me to show you what really happened, to give you eyes to clearly see the origin of that which is occurring in your city as we speak, deep within Siberia. I have seen the parentage of the trial in which Koslov now finds himself. I have seen history. And it will repeat itself today. I already know Comrade Koslov will be led, handcuffed, out from behind the curtains. I know he will be placed in the center of the stage in that plain, wooden chair, and the troika of judges, as required now by NKVD Order No. 00447,[54] will hear arguments from a single prosecutor, a prosecutor most likely shaped from the same mold as those young, idealistic zealots who rode into our village while I was away in Moscow, casting judgment from atop their horses, intoxicated by newly found power and visions of leading

---

[53] Seen endnote 17.a.

[54] Order establishing tribunals intended to simplify trials. See endnote 17.c.

a paradise on earth. I already know that following the charges read against Koslov, the prosecutor will make an impassioned, but previously rehearsed speech, laying out in harsh terms why the accused is among the worst form of creature to ever walk the earth, shaming and humiliating him, proposing not just political excommunication, but, ultimately, death.

"At the same time, the virtues of the ideas of the prevailing political winds will be extolled. These ideas will be presented as absolute and unchanging truths. There will never be the faintest, humblest suggestion that these notions, as fashionable as they are now, could change as history changes, as ideas inevitably do."

Natasha's father paused. As if on cue, from the center of the courtroom in Moscow, as the two disgraced Revolutionaries in the spotlight bowed their heads in shame, a fanatical, accusatory voice extolled the judges concerning their fates:

"Shoot these rabid dogs. Death to this gang who hide their ferocious teeth, their eagle claws, from the people! Down with that vulture Trotsky, from whose mouth a bloody venom drips, putrefying the great ideals of Marxism!... Down with these abject animals! Let's put an end once and for all to these miserable hybrids of foxes and pigs, these stinking corpses! Let's exterminate the mad dogs of capitalism, who want to tear to pieces the flower of our new Soviet nation! Let's push the bestial hatred they bear our leaders back down their own throats!"[55]

"When all this is done," her father began again, as the accusatory voice faded into the background. "When the so-called evidence is presented, the dots connected, the witnesses brought forward to corroborate, and the final speeches made, I know that, to the shock and bewilderment of those watching

---

[55]   From the concluding speech by Andrey Yanuaryevich Vyshinsky, State Prosecutor at the Moscow Trials of 1936-38 (aka "The Moscow Show Trials").

from afar, Comrade Koslov will relent and confess. Upon hearing his confession, we will all wonder why Koslov refuses to make a spirited case for his innocence. We will ask ourselves why, having spent decades leading hardened soldiers, with his experience razing and building empires in the harshest terrain known to man, will the Commandant not mount a rousing defense, demand cross-examination. Why confess to crimes he most certainly did not commit?"

Here Natasha's father paused again, as if catching his breath, a breath that seemed to be increasingly difficult to take the longer he went on. Her eyes remained fixated on the illusory courtroom spread out before her, some figures moving in and out of the scene like shadows, others, like the defendants, the judges, and the prosecutor, all remaining sharply in focus. However, at times their faces would change, the defendants every so often taking on the form of Koslov, the judges sometimes taking on the faces of the judges in Natasha's town.

"When I heard Zinoviev and Kamenev confess," her father continued, "I wondered these same questions. Were they, in fact, guilty? Had they corroborated with foreign influences, seeking to undermine that which they had shed so much blood and sweat to help build? I thought this to be unlikely as I left the courtroom following their conviction. Throughout the next two years, more and more trials exactly like theirs played out. On a similar fantastical stage these proceedings were replicated over and over again. And in similarly severe although less consequential cases throughout the whole of the Soviet Union, they also multiplied. Soon my feelings were confirmed. The innocent were being convicted for crimes they would have never committed. Lives uprooted, families destroyed, they were sentenced to hard labor, some even death. But why, I continued to ask myself, were the accused always implicating themselves? This was the most baffling question to comprehend. I searched deep within myself, searching for clues in everything I had ever believed, or thought I had believed. After all, if these men, men who had built so much could be toppled by so little, was I not also at risk? Could I also not be ensnared, forced to admit guilt, by a version of events I had never voluntarily participated in? As I pondered answers, I stumbled upon ancient truths about the nature of man, many of which were reinforced by an examination of my own faith, a faith that all my life had seemed so distant, so mundane. I was reminded that man is a spiritual creature, one fallen from grace. And being in a fallen state, out of alignment with his Creator, he never ceases his search for redemption, the path to a higher state of existence. Metaphorically speaking, he never ceases to search for a bridge across the river, to reach the opposite shore where his god awaits him, to make him whole again.

"When everything I witnessed was put in that context, all became clearer. I came to believe that the accused—Zinoviev, Kamenev, and now Koslov, as well as the faceless others— remained true believers in the faith and vision they had fought for their entire life. In the end, they could not renounce what they had been so integral to creating. In the end, they perhaps truly believed they were guilty, that they had sinned against the god they themselves had created. These acolytes, in their imprisoned intellects, never dreamed of a victory possible beyond this world. They believed until the end that their salvation—that bridge across the river to a higher plain of existence—rested with the State, the Party. So, they relented and confessed, wanting nothing more than to be remembered as heroic beings, perhaps flawed, but loyal forever to the cause, their faith. In doing so, salvation would be theirs."

Natasha noticed her father's voice fading, as if, since arriving in Siberia, when it first became most animated and real, he was concluding what he had set out to do.

"Upon realizing all of this, my precious and beautiful daughter, I became sickened by the spectacles, ashamed to have been counted among those who had cheered them on. As time wore away, as I reflected more and more on what was happening, I lost all interest in what I had been sent to Moscow to do—to build, sculpt, glorify through the underground stations, the Soviet cause, a false and destructive faith. I eventually lost all inspiration. Perhaps if just one person in those courtrooms had raised an objection to the proceedings, shown some small act of kindness to the defendant, my hope would have been partially restored. But there was no one who would speak up, not even the accused themselves. Indeed, even the newspapers of the West—those pillars of the liberal press that were free to observe, write, and speak truth—fell prey to the lies that were occurring in these trials![56] My work on the metros reflected my shifting attitude; I had left my occupation, so to speak, before I was even eventually let go and sent home. Returning to you and your mother, to a land already ravaged by famine and persecution, I succumbed to my despairs, and died."

At that, her father's voice ceased. His final breath, as it floated away, seemed to land on her forehead, a last kiss goodbye. During these brief moments she had been unable to discern the spiritual from the physical; time seemed to meld together, the ages folding one on top of the other. The image of the distant Moscow courtroom waved like ripples in a river, currents lapping chaotically against the present age. The temporal disturbance made her dizzy. She heaved, and found herself once again fully in Siberia, the beautiful stage in front

---

[56]   See endnote 17.d.

of her, the prosecutor towering over Koslov, one arm raised high, fist clenched for all the audience to see. The whole trial had occurred in tandem with the one she had just witnessed, in another place, another time. Its conduit still in place, its effects continuing to disfigure events through the ages.

Natasha watched the prosecutor sit down, triumph obvious on his face. As her father had predicted, Koslov had confessed. It was the final act in the play. The swift pronunciation of guilt neatly tied up the loose ends.

Koslov—slouching, broken—slumped in the small wooden chair facing the crowd. He appeared as if he had no strength to lift himself from his seat, straighten his uniform, to raise his chin proudly into the air as he marched himself to the gallows. On the contrary, upon hearing the panel of judges from on high proclaim his fate to be immediate death, the old man swayed as if he were being spun violently around in an invisible storm. His fat frame tipped over and off the chair as he fainted in embarrassing disgrace, plopping onto the stage floor and sending a dull thud throughout the hall.

Gasps raced through the auditorium. But a few moments later, slithering through the vacant spaces under the rows, between the feet, and rising into the empty void above the audience, came a singular, isolated laugh—a shrill, demonic taunt arising from a faceless source, reaching octaves that seemed to burn forth from another dimension. Upon hearing it, Natasha's stomach twisted into a queasy knot. Was this what her father had felt as he pondered what he had seen in Moscow? Nausea, combined with despair and disgust, crept over her. Surely, Natasha thought, that crude and cowardly laugh would elicit overwhelming condemnation from those in the audience? Is that not the utterly human reaction to have? But just as she had feared, and as her father had all but foretold, one act of inhumanity begets another, and then another, and then another. The chain of events that started with the trial itself had climaxed with the whole auditorium filled with loud jeers and condemnations, as if each man and woman present were in competition with the next to demonstrate how much they despised Koslov and everything he had been accused of representing.

At the reaction of the assembled crowd, Natasha grew more sickened. She put her hand over her mouth, starting to slowly back-out of the auditorium. She could take no more, her hopes and expectations for something better once again dashed. Her father had been right. Trying to shield her, and then warn her through his own experiences, she now felt what he felt, repulsed by what repulsed him.

But as she was leaving, the laughter abruptly ceased. Instead of taunts, arising from the crowd Natasha heard, "Shhh!", "Be quiet!", and "Look what he's doing."

Already partially through the doorway, Natasha turned sideways, hoisting herself on her toes, some inner compulsion driving her to glimpse what was happening now, to see who "he" was. Peering as best she could over and between the tops of heads, she gasped as she watched David kneel down on the stage next to Koslov and help the old man to his feet. David must have been sitting toward the front this whole time!

The crowd hushed, their faces full of admiration as David walked the old man off the stage, the ex-Commandant's future out of sight, and forever out of mind. As they exited, the audience rose as one, granting thunderous cheers to this young man who had shown benevolence and mercy to the enemy.

Natasha shook her head in amazement. Just a moment ago she was convinced, as her father had been when witnessing such trials, she had entered a realm in which she did not belong, a land where it was accepted to trample on a man already condemned to death, where dignity was a luxury only afforded the powerful. But David's actions demonstrated there was indeed hope, that there existed one person willing to challenge the most savage instincts of man, even in an environment where savagery was most prone to reward. David's gentle, magnanimous act reassured her. Here was the symbol of hope her father had desperately wanted to see in his own experience, that ray of goodness letting him know that the whole world had not spiraled into cruel insanity. Regardless of what crimes Koslov had committed, David's instincts, so like hers, would not allow suffering. He risked scorn himself, risked the very reputation he so recently and bravely earned.

Natasha beamed. She remembered her father's laments. Without David and his actions, she too would have succumbed, finally, to despair. Her faith restored, she departed in peace.

"He will not return as leader of our troupe," she thought to herself as she crossed the vacant lobby. "Another path has been laid before him, as it should be. He is honest, true. He is the one who should rightfully take Koslov's place. I may never see him again."

At that possibility her spirit, surprisingly, lightened, as if a torment she had been unable to temper was suddenly removed. David's future beckoned in a different direction than hers. Yet having met him, spoken with him, and seen more than once the kindness that seemed to permeate everything he did, she felt a familiar sense of calm return after having been missing for a very long time. If all of these unexpected events could come to pass, could not her husband also return to her, safe, unharmed? Could she not, after all, heal the wounds Arkady would inevitably have upon his eventual arrival? Could the two of them not create the life of love and happiness together she so dreamed of?

The snowfall had ceased; weak sunshine broke through the leaden clouds. A gentle breeze blew at her back, pushing Natasha toward her factory, in the direction of the life she had so briefly left behind. Approaching familiar domains, she saw Lara and Rachel waving to her from afar, as if they stood on a distant shore. The three women soon clasped hands and together walked, laughing, smiling, happy to have each other. Koslov: gone. David, their Troupe Leader: ascendant. Life in Siberia was about to change, and the three were confident of the future that awaited them.

★

Much like the rest of the crowd, it shocked David to see Commandant Koslov spin out of his chair and collapse onto the floor. As the gasps morphed into laughter, David too broke into a smile. His rage still simmered. Hatred toward Koslov still percolating in his heart, the satisfaction of seeing his now-disgraced enemy broken and submissive was as fulfilling a feeling as he had ever experienced.

Seated directly next to David, however, not seen by the majority of those assembled in the hall, was a man. Old, small, and physically frail, he was, to David's liking, easily overshadowed by David's taller, stronger build and considerably more handsome youthful features. Just as every play has its antagonist, protagonist, and a compelling narrative that distills into an inevitable, climactic clash, so too does it have its Director, the one who plots carefully the story's arc, the characters' roles, bringing each into perfect alignment throughout the course of events. The result is a conclusion satisfying to not just the audience, but, perhaps more importantely, the Director himself. In today's performance, Commandant Dzerzhinsky fulfilled that role of Director, murmuring in David's ear at key points in the trial, capturing the judges' attention to ensure they noticed the new heir to Koslov's power sitting by his side.

When Commandant Koslov's sentence was proclaimed, Dzerzhinsky's running commentary analyzed the scene with an objective restraint nurtured through decades of experience maneuvering campaigns, both military and political, in perilous environments. David respected that Dzerzhinsky's eyes were trained to recognize opportunities that all else missed. His elder's finely honed instincts to leverage these opportunities to his advantage was what had kept him astute, feared, and alive. David soaked up his new mentor's advice like a sponge.

As Koslov fell to the ground, David drew a breath, fully intending to join the crowd in taunting Koslov. But as he was about to let out his own shrill boff, Commandant Dzerzhinsky discreetly grabbed David by the elbow and whispered in his ear. The idea conveyed did not and likely never would have occurred to David, yet he immediately realized the wisdom of Dzerzhinsky's advice and regained his composure.

Stiffening his back, he rose to his feet, and with a confident and noble gait, ascended the stage. Already the hero, he had nothing left to prove. The plot to the sequel was his to develop; the arc of the new story, his to create. He would allow no one else—especially this unruly mob—the opportunity to determine how this next saga would play out. Here, as designed by Dzerzhinsky, was an opportunity to write the first chapter on his own terms. David would lead, not follow. He had already established himself in so many ways: the one who provided hope to those he led, the one who courageously defended the camp from saboteurs. Now, in the next story, he would become the graceful and wise leader, the one who could be counted on to act decisively, but also with benevolence, even to those condemned for the worst transgressions.

David recalled the morning he had been ordered to report to Koslov. He had left the Commandant's building humiliated, unholy seeds of retribution planted in his soul. Looking up to the towering stacks protruding from the factory, he had watched as its machines spewed forth ash and smoke into the clear, crisp skies. The potential David had realized in those moments would be realized in this next act in front of this large gathering; the glorious results would forever banish the shadow of his father from his name. The paradise he would oversee would bridge the chasm between him and his mother, the symbol of divine perfection. What he would build would deliver to him peace, power, eternal life.

As David approached Koslov, the ex-Commandant regained consciousness and stirred. Ignoring the old man's obvious delirium, David whispered in his ear, "Take my hand, you worthless fool. I'm here to lead you to the noose."

Koslov's face turned deathly white, but he grabbed David's arm. His fate sealed, there was no more struggle left within him. His story had ended.

David escorted him off the stage to roaring applause.

CHAPTER 18

A man hurried down a winding passage. His stare fixated adhesively on an elusive object somewhere in the blackness ahead. Inordinately tall, his height prevented him from moving as quickly as he liked, especially in the dark, as dangling debris protruded obtusely from sagging ceilings; rocks and ruined concrete jutted up from the ground without pattern. Every few meters a low glow emanating from a candle lit the path. The man wore a dull, wool jacket, and leather boots which grew stiffer by the day. They were cracking from prolonged exposure to sub-zero temperatures that had afflicted him and his companions ever since they had arrived at this deserted and ruined village months ago.

At the end of the passage, the man turned the corner leading into an adjacent tunnel. There he immediately confronted a locked hatch where a faint light seeped through the ill-fitting and rickety doorway's frame. He knocked three times, paused, and then once more. He heard shuffling on the other side, followed by two latches sliding back. The entry opened, and he pushed his way in.

"How is she?" he asked the attendant standing on the other side, his voice laced with the same concern his steps had exuded.

"She's in shock; been mumbling Pushkin to herself, over and over again, since the patrol found her."

"And where was that? What alerted us to her?"

"The watch heard gunshots," the attendant answered, lowering his eyes.

"And...?"

"They found her in the Cathedral."

The tall man shook his head; he frowned, but more out of sorrow than anger.

The attendant drew closer and whispered, "You knew she wouldn't stay away, no matter what orders you gave. When the patrol arrived, they said candles were lit in the nave. It looked like she had been caring for it for a while."

He nodded. The attendant was right. It was impossible to keep her away. But his position required him to try. Everything, now, was his responsibility—the woman's safety, the attendant's safety, the watch that had reacted to the sound of gunfire, the patrol sent to investigate, the people working in the crude, makeshift infirmary surrounding him. This realization sat like an oppressive burden on his shoulders. He had not been outside in weeks, had not seen the sun nor the stars in ages, it seemed. He never asked for this duty. With each passing day his weariness grew and became that much more difficult to conceal.

"So, besides being in shock, she's not hurt otherwise?" he asked.

"No. There are no physical injuries. But she was holding this." The attendant handed him a worn and folded paper.

Taking hold of it, the man carefully separated the fragile edges, opening it along the sharp creases. Looking at what it beheld, his eyes widened.

"Oh my..."

"It seems she was right after all, from a certain perspective," the attendant stated.

"And the person who gave this to her? What happened to him, or her?"

"We have him isolated, in a separate location, being guarded. Follow me."

The two men walked out of the main ward through a small, short hallway. At the end was another room; a single guard sat at a table outside its entrance.

"Here he is," the attendant said, walking under a low overhang. He pointed at a young man lying, unconscious, on a small bed near a corner, his clothes hanging nearby. His bearded face had been wiped clean. Covered with blankets, his chest moved up and down in easy rhythm.

The man asking questions, expressing concern, burdened by all that was happening, seemingly in command of everything, stepped up to the edge of the bed for a closer look.

"The reports were that the gunshot wound was to his leg," he said to the attendant.

"Yes. Oksana's work, I'm afraid."

"Do you think he attacked her?"

"Unlikely. I think he startled her. And you saw what she had in her hand when we found her."

"Yes, yes," the apparent commander replied. This was a truly puzzling case.

Analyzing the young man's features, he pointed. "Look at that gash on his forehead." he said, astonished.

"It's what concerned us the most when he was brought in. Nearly killed him, not the gunshot wound. He lost so much blood. Before you arrived, we had just stopped the bleeding. We'll bandage it permanently in a moment."

"What do you think caused it?" the commander continued, still staring hard at the young man's forehead.

"Unclear, but have a look at his clothes."

The two men stepped over to the chair positioned at the end of the bed. Draped over its back were a pair of torn, wool trousers. A tattered grey shirt, sleeves ripped, but military patches and insignia still intact, lay spread out on the table next to the chair.

"He's a soldier from the front," the commander observed. "How he got this far east...I don't understand. But these wounds...he's been through hell." Could his small band of refugees possibly endure any more mysteries? Had they not suffered enough already?

"That's not all," the attendant said. "Look at this."

In the corner hung a well-worn, shapeless coat. But it was thick and intact, a mis-match to the tattered uniform. Despite the fading luster of its previously brilliant colors, it still appeared capable of fulfilling its core function: warmth, protection from the elements.

The commander had seen the coat before. A missing piece of the mystery filled in.

"It's starting to come together for me," he said, half to himself. "I bet the soldier wandered into the cathedral looking for shelter. From the looks of his wounds he needed it. Oksana returned to attend the altar, to keep the candles lit, waiting, as always, for *him* to return. But instead, she saw this soldier, wearing *his* coat."

"But why did Oksana shoot this man?" asked the attendant. "You think she would have been elated hearing something—anything—about *him*."

"Unless he gave her news she wasn't expecting." He sighed, crossing his arms before continuing. "There's still a lot to learn. And until one of them is well enough to talk, we won't know anything for certain. Keep them apart. Don't let either one out of your sight."

"Of course."

"Did the patrol seal the Cathedral when they left?"

"I believe they shuttered it, removed the candles, and locked the doors."

"Good. No one else goes above ground or outside the compound. Only the scheduled patrols. Keep me posted. I'll be in my quarters."

★

The commander left the infirmary and headed back the way he had come, pensive. The rays from the rising sun pushed through cracks in the ceiling, lighting up the passage. As he strode down the crooked path, he extinguished the candles, one by one. Everything was in short supply. Nothing could be wasted.

At the opposite end of the passage he faced two doors. The one directly in front of him led to the areas where his comrades lived; clusters of old stone and brick houses that, from the outside, appeared deserted, but from the inside were connected together by a combination of underground passages leading to cellars and other small, cavernous carve-outs. However, not all the areas were connected. Sometimes going above ground was required in order to retrieve food and other supplies from storage areas, but special paths had been designated to reach these. They had been meticulously camouflaged and were restricted to dedicated personnel who knew where to go and the precautionary procedures to take.

The other door, at the top of a short, crude set of stairs carved from stones and shaped by small wood beams, was one of the few in the compound that led directly outside.

Approaching the two options, the commander hesitated. Peering at the door at the top of the stairs, he saw sunlight creeping through small crevices. A burning temptation ignited within him to break his own order forbidding exit to the outside. He was so tired, so heavily laden with impossible responsibilities. Perhaps if he could just set his eyes on the sun, the forest, the snow, for a few minutes, smell the fresh air as a light breeze carried the fragrance of pine past his nose, he could alleviate this burden, at least temporarily. But then he thought twice. He had a duty to keep his promise, especially in the face of what he had just seen. This incident—whatever inspired it—was evidence that his friend and fellow refugee from the Caucasus, indeed, *his* commander, might be alive. Suffering perhaps, but still trying, in some far-off place, to bring to an end to whatever or whomever was hunting them. The commander intended to keep this promise, even if it killed him.

Tap, tap, tap.

The faint sound came from outside the door at the top of the stairs. A wayward branch from an overgrown tree being tossed about by the morning wind? Another soldier, perhaps the companion of the one now lying in the infirmary?

Tap, tap, tap.

Too sharp to be a man, yet not random enough to be the scraping of a twig.

Tap, tap, tap.

The sun called out. The breeze and aroma of the forest beckoned him. Against his better instincts he decided to investigate. The tapping provided a good excuse to go outside. Slowly he made his way up the staircase, careful not to make a sound.

The tapping ceased.

Reaching the top, he pressed his ear against the door, listening for any sign of life. No breathing, no movement. Nothing, yet he could sense the sun rising, warming the frozen earth. In his mind's eye he could see dazzling lights reflecting golden rays on the snowy ground, heightening the scent of the trees, their tops swaying against the clear, crisp sky. The commander unlocked the rusty padlock, letting it fall to the ground. Slowly he opened the door and peeked his head around the corner.

Still nothing.

He gingerly placed one foot outside. Wind caressed his face, and he reveled in this inexplicable mystery brushing past his skin. As he stepped fully into the fresh air, he squinted, his eyes having grown accustomed to the darkness. They could barely handle the light, the red glow on the horizon shining brilliantly along the Siberian taiga. He drew a deep breath, absorbing the natural elements surrounding him into his nostrils, and further into his soul. As he had hoped, his spirits instantly improved.

The sun climbed higher, and as its beams stretched they illuminated the landscape and the distant Cathedral. It was at least a kilometer away, but set against the vast emptiness extending out from the cluster of ruins that made up the village, the three domes became easily visible. Upon seeing them thrust majestically toward the heavens, still standing despite their age and condition, upright and uncompromising, the commander's feelings remained mixed. When they had first arrived, the refugees, especially those who were Christian, saw it and cried. In their eyes it represented a haven from the tragedies that had befallen them; a symbol of hope, inviting and promising. But the Cathedral instead became the scene of their first devastating encounter, the confrontation that drove them underground, forcing them to scavenge for food, supplies, anything that would keep them alive. After that, the old church sat vacant, an apparition standing, haunted-like, in the mist. No one dared return, until now.

Sighing, he whispered partly to himself, partly to his missing commander. "She kept saying that is where you would return to her, Denisov. After you left us all, she never wavered in that belief."

He took a deep breath.

"I'm sorry. This is my fault. I promised you I would look after everyone, but she became lost in the crowd. She was the one I should have been watching the closest."

His relief from being outside subsided, a superficial and temporary bandage that he knew could only last as long as the dawn itself. Once more the full weight of his responsibilities bore down on his soul. He never understood why Denisov had left when they needed him most. Nor could he ever understand how a man so devoted could abandon all of them, including his wife, Oksana.

The snow was now fully bathed in light. The sun had ascended to a point where the commander was no longer comfortable being outside. It was time to return. During the day is when they all slept; at night another party would have to be organized to search for food and supplies. He would join them.

Tap, tap, tap.

This time the distinctive noise came from behind. He whipped around. On the soil in front of the door, tapping as if asking to be let in, perched a bird. Not just any bird—a Siberian Thrush. The bird's dark blue body caught the sun's rays and gleamed against the snow. The commander stood still. His breathing slowed. It spread its wings, and bolts of white lightning appeared beneath. As the Thrush flew up to a nearby branch hanging low over the doorway, the man's eyes tracked it as it landed and settled facing him.

The two stared at one another.

"You've returned," the commander said. Out of all the mysteries he had experienced so far today, the bird's reappearance, after so many months, was the most troublesome. Its presence seemed to indicate that the young Russian's arrival, and the altercation with Oksana, was not just chance.

The Thrush cocked its head and flew off, away from the commander, away from the Cathedral, and into the ruins of the village.

The commander watched it float away. His uneasiness returned now in full. His breathing intensified, his heart raced. Suddenly the twisting passages and underground dwellings he had just stepped out from seemed like shelters from a coming storm, rather than tombs. He turned quickly around, his height causing him to stoop as he ducked back into the camouflaged entrance.

Forcefully he shut the door, surprising even himself with the strength he used to slam it closed. Safely inside again, he stepped back, staring at the barricaded gateway.

"Such a small creature," he thought ironically, searching for the padlock laying on the ground. Finding it in the darkness, he clicked it back into place. Only then did his nerves begin to calm.

CHAPTER 19

Shoulders back, Natasha stood in formation. The morning was crisp, cool but not cold, as if spring somehow stood still all around her. Birds chirped, a fragrance hung in the air that reminded her of flowers blooming. What respite in the middle of a long winter!

Since Koslov's trial a month ago, changes had come hard and fast. David officially became Assistant Commandant to Dzerzhinsky, who himself now commanded everything, while Maximilian formally took over duties as Troupe Leader.

Rachel took her place at the very front of the formation, below the stage and facing the troupe, as if watching over them. Reflecting her growing influence and authority, she had assumed this position every morning for the past three weeks. The shy girl Natasha had befriended on the train now possessed confidence, poise. Maximilian had taken her under his wing, and diffidence had all but been cast out of her, an unholy Being exorcised from the astute confidence that now enveloped Rachel's entire demeanor.

Lara was excused from the daily morning formation as her wish was finally realized. Two weeks ago, she had been transferred to the hospital ward. She would receive the training she had always dreamed of. But despite her new responsibilities, she had not forgotten her friends. Although rarely, a now-revived

283

Lara, her spirit and beauty no longer wilting, met Rachel and Natasha for lunch whenever she could. Together they would exchange stories, rumors, laughs, just as they always had. But then Lara would return to the hospital, and Rachel, who had been transferred into a clerical job, would return to her desk at a building within the camp's administrative center.

Only Natasha remained in the factory, standing at the same post where she had always been, inspecting, assessing, and critiquing various contraptions of metal and steel as they emerged across the assembly line. At the end of the day, as the sun drifted down past the hills in the distance, she would walk slowly back to her living quarters, alone.

Natasha sighed as the morning sun poured down on her. She wanted to embrace its rays, allow them to soak into her soul, lift her up. To make her happy. In all this time, there was still no word from Arkady. As the war waged on, as reports continued to trickle in regarding military advances here and setbacks there, the lives of her friends had not stood still, as hers had. If only a letter would arrive from her husband! If only she could read words assuring her that not only was he safe but that he still loved her! Perhaps the promise of an uninterrupted life in the not-so-distant future would inspire her. Natasha's hope could reignite. She might escape this unending time loop in which she found herself suspended, transcend this vacant realm of emotions that mirrored in spiritual form the relentless emptiness of Siberia.

The roll call was nearly complete. By this time, usually Natasha would have made eye contact with Rachel. The two often met briefly after the formation before heading off to their respective duties. She stared at her friend, smiling, trying to catch her attention. But a stern and serious Rachel looked past her this morning. Natasha's gaze remained fixed on her friend as a sense of foreboding crept through her. Something was terribly wrong. Sudden changes in patterns, with no visible explanation, were rarely happenstance. Like aquatic disturbances in a calm sea, the aberrations begin somewhere. Soft ripples have their source in disruptions far away, while waves, the type that can crash suddenly down upon unsuspecting vessels, are linked to closer, more severe, origins. Regardless of distance, however, something always changes, some direction is always altered. Rachel's refusal to look at Natasha represented an aberration close to its source. Natasha braced for a wave, but she had no anchor on which to hold.

Roll call ended, and almost as if on cue, Rachel walked away, her head down, arms and hands hanging loosely at her sides. She still had yet to look at Natasha. Would she ever again?

The stage was empty. All was quiet, but the troupe had not been dismissed. There was more to come. The spring air that just moments ago had invigorated Natasha, now carried a sharp chill. Maximilian appeared stage left, walking slowly up the stairs, a stack of papers in his hand.

The postings.

Natasha's heart sank. Rachel's refusal to make eye contact, even acknowledge her presence with a sympathetic smile, now became clear.

"Comrades," Maximilian began, his voice stern, emotionless, "The names of those who gave the ultimate sacrifice for our Soviet motherland and Comrade Stalin are in my hands. My condolences to all of you who have suffered a loss. The lists will be posted here on the stage momentarily. If a name of a relative or loved one is on this list, you may have the day for yourself."

Maximilian signaled with his arm to an assistant, who promptly joined him on the stage and nailed the lists to four support beams at the rear of the small platform. With a final thud, the assistant surveyed his work, nodded at the Troupe Leader, and hustled off the stage.

"Everything for the front! Everything for victory! Dismissed!" Maximilian yelled. Walking confidently down the stairs he headed toward the factory, its stacks spewing forth grey smoke into the clear morning, as always.

The troupe broke ranks. Those who had reason to worry immediately crowded around the small staircase struggling to alight the stage and learn the fate of those they loved. It was not long before a spectrum of human emotion filled the vacant courtyard. Unseen as these forces were, they were more real and consequential than the concrete upon which the workers stood. Prayers for the dead, as well as for the living, rose with tears up into the heavens. Would they reach ears capable of hearing, acting? And if so, what would be the response? A swift intervention, ending not only the war, but all of man's injustices against himself? Or, more likely, silence?

Natasha remained where she was, standing completely alone. Rachel had not approached from behind to comfort her. Her friend would not be there to wrap a blanket around her, to hold her through the night, as Natasha had done for her so long ago. In her time of need, Natasha had been forsaken. She could not face what was written on those sheets of paper.

She bowed her head, and walked, as if in a trance, back to her bunk, falling asleep amidst a torrent of abandonment and emotional betrayal, seeking escape into her favorite dream.

The rain did not last long, and by the time Vronsky arrived, his shaft-horse trotting at full speed, and dragging the trace-horses galloping through the mud, with their reins hanging loose, the sun had peeped out again, the roofs of the summer villas and the old lime-trees in the gardens on both sides of the principal streets sparkled with wet brilliance, and from the twigs came a pleasant drip and from the roofs rushing streams of water. He thought no more of the shower spoiling the racecourse, but was rejoicing now that—thanks to the rain—he would be sure to find her at home and alone, as he knew that Alexey Alexandrovitch, who had lately returned from a foreign watering-place, had not moved from Petersburg.

Hoping to find her alone, Vronsky alighted, as he always did, to avoid attracting attention, before crossing the bridge, and walked to the house. He did not go up the steps to the street door, but went into the court.

'Has your master come?' he asked a gardener.

'No, sir. The mistress is at home. But will you please go to the front door; there are servants there,' the gardener answered. 'They'll open the door.'

'No, I'll go in from the garden.'

And feeling satisfied that she was alone, and wanting to take her by surprise, since he had not promised to be there to-day, and she would certainly not expect him to come before the races, he walked, holding his sword and stepping cautiously over the sandy path, bordered with flowers, to the terrace that looked out upon the garden. Vronsky forgot now all that he had thought on the way of the hardships and difficulties of their position. He thought of nothing but that he would see her directly, not in imagination, but living, all of her, as she was in reality.[57]

Natasha stirred, half awake, half still asleep. Dreamy impressions replete with characters and events, both real and fictional, clouded her thoughts and memories. What was true? What had she imagined?

Darkness pervaded the barracks. The only sound was the gentle, subdued roll of the factory's machines in the distance.

---

[57] Tolstoy, Leo. <u>Anna Karenina</u>, Part II, Chapter 22.

She blinked open her eyes and sat up in her bunk, looking around at all her companions fast asleep in their beds. Reality came rushing back, as did the old familiar melancholy. Just weeks ago, after the trial, life had seemed so hopeful, so bright. But now, the possibilities life seemed to offer were drowning in despondency. She felt as if she had traveled back in time to before she had met Arkady in the village market, ignored and disused.

But maybe there was still hope.

Maybe there was still a chance she had misread Rachel's actions.

Natasha crept silently out of bed. She donned her clothes, heavy jacket, and boots. Fleeing the hut, she raced down the path leading to the courtyard, her mind in another dimension, her eyes fixed firmly ahead.

She pulled up short, astonished how easily her feet had unconsciously led to the stage, only a short distance in front of her. Low floodlights placed sporadically around the plaza made the lists of the deceased nailed to its beams barely visible in the shadows.

Roughly standing in the same place she stood every morning, where she was left all alone earlier that day, Natasha stared ahead, her heart pounding. Drawing a deep breath, she climbed the steps and approached the far-left corner. Her finger traced along the faceless names.

On paper, they were only ink, she thought.

The list on the first beam…nothing.

These dead matter not to me.

The list on the second beam… nothing.

But names, much like bodies—do they not possess souls, created and formed as spiritual inflection points denoting passages to the metaphysical realm?

The list on the third beam…

Her finger stiffened, halted, as if having run full speed into an unmovable wall.

Beating heart.

Weakening knees.

The world swirling around her.

Stars in infinite, adorned chaos.

Natasha's knees wobbled and loosened, tears swelling in her eyes. Never before had she felt like this. It was if all the emptiness embodied in the vast, undefinable space of Siberia had suddenly rushed into her soul, that part previously occupied solely by the love, devotion, and passion reserved for her husband, Arkady, now declared dead, killed in action.

She prepared to hit the hard floor, to crash against the wood amidst a torrent of confusion, bewilderment, a planet spinning hopelessly into a black void. But as she sunk lower toward the unyielding platform, two arms suddenly caught her from behind, reaching out seemingly from the beyond, as if Vronsky himself had jumped from the pages of Tolstoy, appearing unexpectedly in the outer reaches of space. Tenderly, these arms eased her onto the stage, drawing her torso against a strong chest.

Shaking, Natasha grabbed onto those arms, wrapping them close around her. It had been so long since she had felt any support, any strength from someone other than herself. What little remained of her spirit and will after all these months had collapsed along with her body. She had nothing left to offer anyone, least of all herself.

Turning her face to her unexpected savior, she saw, of course, David; his gentle smile, his kind but reassuring strength, slowly caressing her broken soul, soothing her wounds.

Grasping his hands, as if clambering onto a ship sent to rescue her from a tidal wave, Natasha cried as never before, her face safely buried within his warm embrace. He rested his cheek on top of her head, the tiny pull of whiskers against her scalp hauntingly familiar, wonderfully comforting. Gently nudging her to stand with him, she did not resist. Together they stood up, his arms the strength her legs needed to support her now frail state.

As they descended the platform, arms intermingled, steps in sync one with the other, Maximilian appeared out of the darkness, a warm blanket in hand. Natasha's mind flashed back to their last meeting, outside the trial, the Assistant Troupe Leader's dour eyes suddenly softening as the two stared at each other. This was the look she now saw as he handed David the blanket, who in turn wrapped it around her shoulders, shielding her from any further exposure to the harsh surroundings.

David and Natasha, joined arm in arm, walked away from the courtyard, toward the center of the town. The factory belched steam and flames around them in the crisp night, and Maximillian disappeared again into the background, into the darkness from where he had emerged.

EPILOGUE

"Awake!"
"Awake!"
"Awake!"

"Who are you? I asked you before, and there was always silence. Are you an apparition perhaps, like the old philosophers, caught circling in your own vanity, searching always for living vessels who might carry your ideas into a world you no longer inhabit, so that you may live forever? Are you an ancient sovereign, a builder of empires and enslaver of men, whose portrait hangs solemnly among other relics of the past, dead, but waiting, thirsting for an animating life to emerge in order to lead your armies against the forces of modernity? Or are you a tempter, a Being in the darkness offering healing, nourishment, but only for a price—follow that unholy spirit, the Thrush, or else suffer the loss of those I love?"

"Whom do ye say that I am?[58]"

"I say you are none of those. I say you are that man whose image I hold in my breast pocket, the one depicted in the Cathedral, a so-called savior who cannot save the innocent from the tragedies and horrors of war, a worthless ally against

---

[58] Matthew 16:15 (adapted slightly from the King James)

those who wish to do harm to my wife. You refused the crown of earth that was offered to you. You chose to die. You turned your back on all those men whom the powers of the world aligned themselves against, simple men who needed you. What good are you, hanging dead on a cross?"

"*Yet still you talk to me. Still you carry me with you in your coat. Still you contemplate me in terms of your love for your wife, and the sacrifices made by the soldiers you considered weak and powerless. Why?*"

"Because you keep appearing. You will not leave me alone. And the peace I seek remains elusive. You, more than the demons I have encountered here, beyond the Urals, in Siberia, in the deepest recesses of my soul, are an enigma! What is it that you want from me?"

"*Behold, I stand at the door, and knock: if any man hear my voice, and open the door, I will come in to him, and will sup with him, and he with me.[59]*"

So I command you again, Arkady, awake!"

And Arkady awoke.

TO BE CONTINUED.

---

[59]   Revelation 3:20 (King James)

ENDNOTES

1.a. Following the German invasion of western Russia in June 1941, the Communist Party of the Soviet Union (CPSU) created the State Defense Committee (Russian: Государственный комитет обороны, ГКО, romanized: Gosudarstvennyj komitet oborony, "GKO") (See Endnote 7.a. below for additional information concerning the GKO) with the intent of centralizing procedures for evacuating Soviet citizens living close to the Eastern Front. One of the GKO's first tasks was identifying cities along major train routes, and evacuating workers from those cities to designated centers deep within eastern Russia. Within three months, the GKO had 128 centers identified and operating.

Beginning in August 1941, mass evacuation of heavy industry and factories deemed critical to war production was also undertaken, with the GKO officially overseeing the relocation of more than 1,500 plants of military importance into similar eastern regions. (Notably, this number only reflects large facilities. When all factories, to include even simple workshops, are considered, as many as 50,000 may have been transported east). Factories were, literally, dismantled in place and carried by train into the Ural Mountains, Central Asia, and Siberia, before being again reconstructed. These regions offered safety to inhabitants and evacuated workers due to their isolated locations. Beyond the reach of enemy troops, tanks, artillery, and even airstrikes, they also offered Soviet industries an abundance of natural resources to continuously supply the recently moved factories and plants.

This map (and accompanying summary) provides a depiction of the general movement of industry from west to east at the beginning of the war: https://www.themaparchive.com/dispersion-of-soviet-industry-194142.html

5.a. Reference to the Soviet famine of 1932–1934 and its aftermath. This man-made famine, considered by some to be genocide, particularly as it pertained to Ukraine (aka the "Holodomor") and Kazakhstan, also killed millions of people in regions as diverse as the Northern Caucasus, the Southern Urals, and the Volga Region. The exact number of deaths are commonly disputed due to a lack of accurate records, but estimates range from 3.3 million (low end) to over 10 million when birth defects and still-born deaths directly related to the famine are taken into account. Major contributing factors to the famine included the forced collectivization of agriculture as a part of the Soviet first five-year plan, and forced grain procurement, compounded by a shrinking labor force and droughts. While some historians view the famine as a targeted campaign against Ukrainians and Kazakhs specifically (hence the accusation of ethnic genocide), others emphasize the class dynamics that were in play during this period. Historically, wealthier peasants who owned land were known as "Kulaks", and were portrayed as class enemies by the Bolsheviks due to the Kulaks' interest in private land ownership. Upon consolidating power, Stalin ordered the Kulaks "to be liquidated as a class." This culminated in a campaign of terror and political repression throughout the agrarian regions of the USSR, which included mass executions. With their deaths, the experience and knowledge to successfully farm land disappeared.

6.a. Reference to the Red Army purges of October 1940–February 1942, which followed the "Great Purge" of 1937-39. These purges, which were initiated by NKVD Head Lavrenty Beria and directed specifically at the military, targeted high ranking officials for supposedly anti-Soviet activities, to include sabotage and spying, and against those field commanders who lost early battles when the Germans invaded in 1941, essentially using them as scapegoats for battlefield defeats. It is generally believed that these purges severely crippled Red Army combat effectiveness and strategic acumen for the first part of the war between the Soviet Union and Germany given that many of the Soviet Union's most seasoned officers, to include General Dmitry Pavlov, commander of the western front forces, were arrested and executed.

7.a. The State Defense Council/Committee (aka the GKO) was a supranational emergency body established by Stalin on June 30, 1941. Its purpose, based upon the model of Lenin's Defense Council utilized during the Russian Civil War, was to consolidate all wartime decision-making within a single unit with the aim to streamline processes and procedures involving domestic and military affairs. With Stalin as its Chairman, it was also comprised of Vyacheslav Molotov (Deputy Chairman), Kliment Voroshilov, Georgy Malenkov, and Lavrenti Beria, while also including any number of subject-matter experts depending on the issues being debated and discussed during a specific session. The results of the GKO were mixed. Although it did indeed enable quick rendering of decisions regarding strategic importance, it met sporadically and was prone to act without regard to any agenda, but rather in accordance with what was important to Stalin at any specific time. Additionally, most of the existing bodies through which it implemented and exercised power had been evacuated to Siberia at the time of its creation. Hence, the physical distance between the GKO headquarters in Moscow and its subordinate offices hampered effectiveness.

10.a. A reference to the 1717 Central Asian expedition of Alexander Bekovich-Cherkassky. Generally considered the first Russian military expedition into Central Asia, it was intended to subdue the Khanate of Khiva and by extension bring his and other dominions in Siberia under Russian patronage. The campaign ended in disaster as the entire expeditionary force was slaughtered.

11.a. **Ой, то не вечер**, aka "The Cossack's Parable" (Казачья Притча), or "Stepan Razin's Dream" (Сон Степана Разина). The ballad was first published by composer Alexandra Zheleznova-Armfelt (1866–1933) in her collection *Songs of the Ural Cossacks* following time spent in the Ural District during 1896–1897. The subject of the ballad, Stepan Timofeyevich Razin (1630–1671), known as Stenka Razin, was a Cossack leader who led an uprising against the nobility and Tsarist bureaucracy in southern Russia in 1670-1671.

11.b. The administrative center of the Jewish Autonomous Oblast, which was established in 1931 with the objective of answering, with regards the Soviet Union's Jewish population, the "National Question", as first articulated by Joseph Stalin (later the first People's Commissar of Nationalities of the Soviet Union) in 1913. Using the slogan "To the Jewish Homeland!", the Soviet Union sought to encourage Jewish workers to move to Birobidzhan. The slogan and experiment initially proved successful in attracting Jews not just from the Soviet Union, but also from other parts of Europe, South America, and North America. However, the idea eventually collapsed due to multiple factors. Among these were the fact that the Jewish populations moving to Birobidzhan had few, if any, cultural connections to the land, and espoused competing ideas of how to best to construct a "Jewish Homeland", all while facing profound hardship in settling and developing the severely isolated region.

13.a. David is dreaming of himself as Stepan Razin from the song played at the social in Chapter 11: "The Cossack's Parable" (Казачья Притча), or "Stepan Razin's Dream" (Сон Степана Разина). The subject of the ballad, Stepan Timofeyevich Razin (1630–1671), known as Stenka Razin, was a Cossack leader who led an uprising against the nobility and Tsarist bureaucracy in southern Russia in 1670-1671.

13.b. Dzherzhinsky is outlining a strategy for eastern Russia to take advantage of western Russia's destruction following the war, and rival the western cities for political and economic control of the Soviet Union. Given the destruction of western Russia, as well as the large amount of industry that moved east, this calculation was not far-fetched, as outlined here in this 1948 declassified CIA memo regarding the industrial growth of eastern Russia in the post-war years: https://www.cia.gov/library/readingroom/docs/CIA-RDP78-01617A000200010001-4.pdf

15.a. Referencing again the Soviet famine of 1932–1934.

15.b. During the Soviet famine of 1932-1934, the Soviet government set and demanded the fulfillment of quotas from villages on foodstuffs, particularly grain. In order to enforce and collect on these quotas, villages were divided into a number of subdivisions, to which a special "Brigade" was attached. The Brigades were tasked with monitoring and collecting the grain quotas. The Brigades themselves varied in size and composition, but were usually comprised of a variety of local party officials and representatives led by an official who was *not* local to the region, as well as so-called "activists", who could include teachers, students, clerks, and even ex-convicts. In many cases, the composition and ferocity of the Brigades reflected the conditions of the environment in which they operated— the poorer the conditions and the less grain produced, the larger and more severe the Brigades became. Importantly, the Brigades contained within them a series of "specialists" whose responsibilities and expertise consisted of finding hidden grain storage areas. The tactics utilized by these Brigades, especially their specialists, in uncovering hidden storage spaces consisted of simple searches, to destroying whole houses by tearing down walls. All-night interrogations, beatings, deportations, and executions were common enforcement and punishment techniques for any peasant found to have hidden grain.

16.a. The first excerpt is from a letter composed by Major Sullivan Ballou, USA written to his wife two weeks before he was killed at the First Battle of Bull Run in the American Civil War on 29 July 1861. The second excerpt is from a letter written by Private Albert Ford, British Royal Army, written to his wife shortly before he was killed in the First World War on 26 October 1917.

17.a. Natasha's father is showing his daughter an excerpt from the "Trial of Sixteen", the first of the three trials that would later become known as The Moscow Show Trials of

1936-1938. The Moscow Trials were held at the direction of Joseph Stalin against so-called Trotskyists and members of the Right Opposition. The Case of the Trotskyite-Zinovievite Terrorist Center (Zinoviev-Kamenev Trial, aka "Trial of the Sixteen," 1936) was the first, followed by the Case of the Anti-Soviet Trotskyist Center (Pyatakov-Radek Trial, 1937), and the Case of the Anti-Soviet "Bloc of Rights and Trotskyites" (Bukharin-Rykov Trial, aka "Trial of the Twenty-One," 1938). The defendants in all of these trials were Party leaders and top officials accused of conspiring with the Western powers to assassinate Stalin, and subvert the Soviet Union politically and economically by restoring capitalism.

Specifically with regards the trial in question here—that of Lev Kamenev and Grigory Zinoviev (aka "The Trial of the Sixteen")—it was held from August 19 to August 24, 1936 in Moscow. The main charge was that the defendants formed an organization with the express purpose of killing Joseph Stalin and other members of the Soviet government. The defendants, of whom Kamenev and Zinoviev were the most prominent and well known, were tried by the Military Collegium of the Supreme Court of the USSR. The Prosecutor General was Andrei Vyshinsky, who is quoted directly later on in Chapter 17. All the defendants were sentenced to death, shot in the cellars of Lubyanka Prison by NKVD Chief Executioner Vasily Blokhin.

17.b. The highest decision-making body in the Soviet Union.

17.c. Formally named "About Repression of Former Kulaks, Criminals, and other Anti-Soviet Elements", the order was issued in July 1937 during what is now called the "Great Purge". It set about creating "Troikas" operated by the People's Commissariat for Internal Affairs (aka "NKVD", the precursor to the KGB) at various regional levels with the intent to simplify and speed-up investigations, trials, and sentencings, many of which resulted in death sentences. The Troikas themselves consisted of three individuals acting as both judge and jury. The defendant was rarely, if ever, afforded a defense, and in most cases the proceeding was for show, the outcome having already been determined.

17.d. There are many examples of the American and European Press reporting at face value, with very few inquiries made, what they had been allowed to observe by the Soviet Government, not just during the show trials of 1936-1938, but at multiple other instances over the course of Soviet development. The most famous example, perhaps, of media dereliction comes from this quote from *The New Republic* on September 2, 1936, reporting on the trial referenced by Natasha's father in which Kamenev and Zinoviev were convicted:

"Some commentators, writing at a long distance from the scene, profess doubt that the executed men (Zinoviev and Kamenev) were guilty. It is suggested that they may have participated in a piece of stage play for the sake of friends or members of their families, held by the Soviet government as hostages and to be set free in exchange for this sacrifice. We see no reason to accept any of these laboured hypotheses, or to take the trial in other than its face value. Foreign correspondents present at the trial pointed out that the stories of these sixteen defendants, covering a series of complicated happenings over nearly five years, corroborated each other to an extent that would be quite impossible if they were not substantially true. The defendants gave no evidence of having been coached, parroting confessions painfully memorized in advance, or of being under any sort of duress."